What they have said about the
SHORT STORIES
of Daniel Hoyt Daniels

I loved your stories -- they are delightful, especially the surprise endings. They are even better than O Henry and Maupaussant. I read all thirty of them in two days; I couldn't stop myself.
> -- Maria Atansov, Hilton Head, SC

Well done.
> — Jack Harris, Sarasota, FL

Poignant; touched my heart.
> -- Suzanne Brailey, Gloucester, MA

Extremely creative.
> -- Evelyn Harris, Lincoln, MA

Your tongue in cheek is indeed producing chuckles here. A great job.
> -- Capt. Giles Kelly, USNR, Ret, Washington, DC

Your stories delight me. Your characters are so funny.
> -- Suzy Wolf, Beaufort, SC

We liked your stories.
> -- Ed Wendell, Orange, VA

They all simply flow so beautifully.
> — Nancy Parten, Monroe, NY

As though he were in the room, telling the story.
> — Anne Harris, Sarasota, FL

We loved "Happy Thanksgiving" greatly. We were both very moved. You are a really great writer; I mean that. I shall Xerox it and send it to my children. This story is marvelous.
> -- Frances Huxley, Playwright, Concord, MA

What they have said about the
SHORT STORIES
of Daniel Hoyt Daniels

I liked the prose style – easy to read, and the plots evolved smoothly. The use of words was carefully chosen and concise. The variety made each one stand out by itself. I especially enjoyed reading Baked Alaska, You Took the Words, My Brother-in-Law Is a Jerk, and A Few More Days. Each touched me in a different way. Marie in A Few More Days is a wonderful character. On finishing each of these stories, I had a warm feeling.

Your bitterness in the war stories did not surprise me. The tragic ending of each of them made me think and feel the pain of the protagonists. They were extremely well written.
> -- The Hon. Irving Tragen, former US Ambassador Panama,
La Jolla, CA

Quite a few chuckles. You write very well and get the reader's attention right away, and your endings are wonderful. You are also able to write from a woman's point of view, like in "A New Start." "The Rabbit" is great! Reminds me of my time in South Carolina when I volunteered in a school there. I really enjoyed reading these stories.
> -- Ingrid Lander, Longmont, CO

Interesting.
> -- Buzz Richards, Falmouth, MA

Your book is delightful. We especially liked "Happy Thanksgiving" and "John Harvard Fantoma." "Bastille Day" has everything: nostalgia, youth, politics, sex, humor, and history.
> -- Miriam Mauzerall, Dobbs Ferry, NY

My guests liked it too.
> -- Tinica Mather, Silver Spring, MD

I like your style.
> -- Nancy Myers, Beaufort, SC

I am savoring your stories   I chuckle to myself every time I think of "My Brother-in-Law is a Jerk." Thank you so much. I have ordered some copies through Amazon for Christmas presents.
> -- Coleman Nee, Yarmouthport, MA

What they have said about the
SHORT STORIES
of Daniel Hoyt Daniels

We read your stories with pleasure; we especially liked "Turkey in the Straw,."
-- Henry and Lois Ross, Nokesville, VA

It is as though O Henry himself were with us again. Daniels is a master storyteller. Delightful.
-- Ethard Van Stee, Novelist, Beaufort, SC

Made me laugh aloud. You write beautifully. Very clever endings.
-- Mimi Rankin, Vienna, VA

A wonderful collection of stories. You are a wonderful writer. "The Live Oak" is my favorite; it made me cry. Also "Hypocrisy" and "Bastille Day." "You Took the Words" was lots of fun.
-- Nancy Shaw, Summerfield, FL, formerly Beaufort,SC

We like your stories. You are a natural writer. We took turns reading them at La Posada Inn..
-- John Snyder, Laredo, TX

I'm enjoying one at a time.
-- Judy Osborne, Boston, MA

Enjoying your book of stories. Appealing style. I like the fact that each can be enjoyed in a short time. Just right when there's a minute or two when one wants to be productive.
-- John Trask, Beaufort, SC

Très bonne humour. Amusing and philosophical at the same time.
-- Michele Wernert-Piper, New York, NY

You are a gifted writer.
-- Mr. and M rs. Francis Williamson, Beaufort, SC

Entertaining and thought-provoking; you are a word-master; sounds so real and true; a treasure.
-- Peg Flanagan, Beaufort, SC

SHORT STORIES
and a novella
FOR ALL
YOUNG
OR
OLD
by

DANIEL HOYT DANIELS

author of

"BAKED ALASKA
AND OTHER
SHORT SHORT STORIES"

with
Whimsy, Humor, and Tongue-in-Cheek

Tradepaper edition ISBN 9781582188751

First DSI Printing September 2021
Published by Digital Scanning Inc. Scituate, MA 02066

Preface

I love bringing humor into people's lives, and most of my stories do little more than that, although a few do go further and touch upon various human attributes and foibles, such as devotion, determination, stupidity, naiveté, greed, and hypocrisy.

Most of the stories in this collection were previously published in the first eight books of the "BAKED ALASKA" series. Some of the stories in those publications might be considered too risque, or not suitable, or of little interest to young people, so I have left them out of this volume. The stories here were not written for any particular age group or target audience; I hope they will interest and amuse readers of all ages.

The stories are not in any special order, but are presented more or less in the order in which they were written.

Stories can be a significant part of people's lives whether read aloud or read for themselves. Stories can help explore the world about one, sometimes close at hand and very specific (EAU DE COLOGNE), sometimes vast and intangible (WHERE DID WE COME FROM?). I bring tears to my own eyes when I read STORY TELLING, but feel better for having shed them.

If you read to your children, some of them may memorize a favorite story after hearing it three or four times, and correct you if you "inadvertently" misplace or omit a word or two. They love to learn to read by sitting in your lap and following with their eyes the words as you pronounce them. After a while a parent or grandparent will feel the thrill of having his child read back to him.

Whether you are the adult or the child, enjoy as many of such story-moments as you can. If you have no children, read and enjoy them anyway, if you haven't already done so, or even if you have. The writer is always interested in readers' views.

Finally, once again I want to thank Digital Scanning Inc. and Mr. Brian Shillue for their splendid work in the publication of this book and other works of mine. Any errors are of course my own. Comments on these pieces, or requests for reproduction or other use of them, will be welcomed by the author.

Winter		Summer
Daniel Hoyt Daniels	or	Daniel Hoyt Daniels
Unit 47		PO Box 42
2724-B 61st Street		Spencertown, NY 12165
Galveston, TX 77551		
		danielhdaniels@yahoo.com

Foreword

Daniel Hoyt Daniels – what can one say about a friend of a lifetime – the person everyone would want in a lifeboat?

I'll tell you: Dan is the best story-teller and word-smith I have ever known, and now he has put together a special collection of selected short stories for young and old of all ages. Stories we can read to our children and grandchildren, stories they can share with friends.

Let this collection, ranging from "BAKED ALASKA" to "THE BEAUTY OF THIS WORLD," enliven our spirits as we read, dream, and enjoy our progress regardless of where we may find ourselves on our journey through life.

Most of Dan's stories are very funny or hilarious little anecdotes; some are sad, some perhaps even uplifting. Some may hold a lesson to be found within, sometimes clear, sometimes slightly veiled. Many have a surprise ending that may surprise you. All worth reading!

I hope that you, the reader, will enjoy reading them == and re-reading them -- as much as I do.

They are meant for sharing, and make an ideal and thoughtful gift for your grandfather or for your grandchild, and, of course, for you.

Molly Bennett Aitken
Athol, MA

August 2021

Short Stories for All

Page

Page

Short Stories for All

Breakfast at Tiffany's Anyone?

I went into McDonald's Restaurant in Union Station, Washington, D.C. at 9:15 one Monday morning. I ordered a small cheeseburger.

I was told, "We don't serve lunch until 10:30."

"Sorry, I thought you were open."

"We are open. But we are only serving breakfast."

"Well, may I have a small cheeseburger for breakfast?"

"No. I told you we don't serve lunch until 10:30."

"I don't want lunch. I just wanted... "

"You said you wanted a cheeseburger."

"But not for lunch. I wanted a cheeseburger for breakfast."

"You'll have to come back after 10:30."

"What are all these other people doing here?"

"They're having breakfast."

1

"Well, I would like to have breakfast too."

"What would you like?"

"Well... I thought a small cheeseburger... but you seem to be saying that cheeseburgers are like... uh... you know... and that I should wait until the time is right."

"Yeah. So, what do you want?"

"What do you have that's... uh.... sort of like a small cheeseburger?"

"You can have an Egg McMuffin or a bagel."

"Oh! That's exactly what I want! I've always wanted an Egg McMuffin.! ... By the way, what's an Egg McMuffin?"

"An Egg McMuffin is a muffin and an egg."

"It sounds delicious."

"Would you like anything else on it?"

"Well, if it isn't too much trouble... uh... could you add a bit of hamburger and some cheese?"

THE END

Eau de Cologne

My cousin Barry was four months older than I was, but I was smarter than he was. At least I didn't believe all the unbelievable things and hooey our parents and other adults told us, or things they read to us from nursery rhymes and fairy tales, when we trusted them and were too young to know any better.

Barry believed almost everything he heard, and *absolutely* everything he read, when we were old enough to read. He believed the story of *Jack and the Beanstalk.* He got some beans from his family's pantry and planted them outside his window. He watered them every other day, and weeded all around them once a week whether they needed it or not. He cared for them devotedly, convinced that they would grow to a stalk that would let him climb "way up there" to some other land in the sky that was so far away you couldn't see it. Crazy.

Before that he even believed there was a cow somewhere that had jumped over the moon, and for several months he kept pestering his mother to take him to the zoo or the farm or wherever this remarkable animal was, so he could see it himself. Crazy kid. His mother and my mother thought he was "cute."

3

I thought it was an abomination although I didn't know what that word meant. It was abominable, abhorrent, ignominious, and gross, that they would feed him that stuff and let him believe all that hooey, because it amused them to see what ridiculous things they could make him believe, not just Santa Claus and Sugar Plumb Fairy Tales either.

Another example: he believed "What little girls were made of," and "What little boys were made of." Barry would lick his little sister's arm and tell everyone that she didn't taste like "sugar and spice," and that maybe they had made a mistake and that she was a boy because she tasted more like puppy-dog tails, especially if it had been a while since her last bath or diaper change. Crazy things like that.

I hated this junk the grownups fed us -- all that hooey. I wanted to know what was real. I wanted to know facts. I remember one day when I was a little older, maybe six or seven: I was sitting next to Mom as she was driving our old 1935 Chevy with the stick shift on the floor. I noticed that every now and then she would push the stick forward or pull it back down. I wanted her to let me pull it back down at the right moment, but she said no, I couldn't do it. I then asked her how she knew when to pull it back down, and her answer was, "When it's shaking up and spitting around."

I have told that story to other adults in subsequent years, and the ladies would usually say something like, "Oh, isn't that a cute way to put it! How sweet. I know exactly what she meant." Men were more likely to say to just ignore it as meaningless.

I did not feel that Mom's answer was satisfactory: I wanted her to explain gear ratios and how it was necessary to allow the engine to keep operating in a relatively constant RPM range even though the car was traveling at varying speeds down the road or up the hill. I wanted facts.

My mother even told us that thunder came from wagons and chariots -- whatever chariots are -- rolling across the sky, up above the clouds where you couldn't see them. That, I knew, was hooey, even when I was three and a half years old, but Barry believed it, and he was almost four.

I wanted to believe what my mother and other adults told us, and read to us. I really did. If there was ever any question or doubt in my mind about the truth of something, I would try to give them the benefit of that doubt. Take the case of the "Eau de Cologne." Mom had a little bottle of stuff with a fancy green and silver label with "4711" written big across it. Underneath the 4711 numbers it said "Eau de Cologne." /1 Mom was opening the bottle and getting ready to put some of it on her cheeks and under her ears.

"What does 'Eau de Cologne' mean, Mommie?" I asked.

"It just means 'Cologne'," she said simply.

"Well, what does 'Cologne' mean then?"

"It means -- it just means 'toilet water'," she said quite clearly. Those were her words. I couldn't believe it.

5

"But Mommie! *Toilet water?* You're not going to put
<u>toilet</u> water on your face, are you? Yuck!"

Crazy adults.

THE END

/1 Just last year I met a German tourist from Cologne and
could not resist telling him I was writing a story about
"4711," -- siebenundviersigelf -- a popular cologne my
mother liked back in the 1930's. I was delighted to hear
him respond in 2016 that 4711 was still going strong.

Where Did We Come From?

Dad?

Yes, what?

Dad, I've been thinking.

All right.

No, seriously, Dad. I've been thinking.

That's fine. That's good. It's good to think sometimes.
It can be good for you.

Well, I've been thinking and I've got a couple of
questions.

All right, shoot.

Dad, where did we come from?

We came from Cleveland. You know that -- you were in
the car the whole way. Our old Chevvy.

I don't mean how we got to Nashville. I meant where
did people come from, like people living here on the earth.

7

Most of them came just like you came. Your mother went to the hospital to have a baby, and as luck would have it, you were what came out.

Dad, you just don't understand what I am trying to say. Where did PEOPLE -- people on this earth -- come from in the first place? The Bible tells you -- at least it's what they say in Sunday School -- that it all started six thousand years ago, in October of 4004 BC, when God created Adam and Eden. I mean Adam and Eve.

Yes, I think there are quite a lot of people who believe that that is true. I've wondered about that too, but maybe we are not supposed to take it too literally.

Well, I'm having trouble taking it any way at all. If Adam and Eve were the first two people on earth, how was Cain able to go over the hill, after he killed Abel, and find a woman to marry so he could start populating the earth?

Like I started to say, I don't think you can take it all literally.   It's like poetry and beautiful bedtime stories: it might not be exactly true. Perhaps it's what some people would call symbolic. Peter Pan is a nice story, even if you don't believe it all, like the part about his flying out the window. One kid I knew a long time ago -- Peter Arnheim his name was -- tried it once and broke his arm. I also think it would take more than five days to make a mountain, and probably a good bit more than just six thousand years to make a whole continent, or even a piece of land as big as Montana, or all those oil deposits in Oklahoma and Texas. So I don't believe you have to take all that literally.

8

Yeah. That's what the geologists and the atheists say too. The scientists say that the earth is around four billion years old, and that most living things, including people, evolved from the same simple primitive organisms over a long, slow process, taking hundreds of millions of years.

Yes. The earth and the solar system are miracles of nature.

But Dad, it's not just the earth and the solar system. Our galaxy has millions of stars in it, and it's enormous. I have read that it takes light almost 100,000 YEARS just to go from one side of the galaxy to the other, and light travels 186,000 miles per second. It's that big. And besides, with the Hubble telescope and all, we can now see and even analyze thousands and millions of other galaxies that are so far away it takes over ten billion years just for their light to reach us, and they are all made of the same 92 elements we are made of..

All right, so what is all this leading up to?

Well, Dad, it seems that by the Law of Averages there must be lots of other solar systems with planets that could support life, just because of their sheer numbers. So, if a portion of them have life, some of them could have intelligent life far more advanced than ours. And maybe, a long long time ago, they could have dropped off a few of their undesirables here on Earth, people or animals that were evil and that they wanted to get rid of.

You see, that brings up my second question. Do you believe in the Devil? And where did all the evil and sin on Earth come from? And what is the point of it all? What is the purpose of life anyway?

Hold on! You said you had a couple of questions. That makes at least three or four.

All right, so maybe I said a couple. I meant SOME. So, do you believe in the Devil?

In the first place, believing IN something is not quite the same as believing in the EXISTENCE of something. I believe Fascism exists, but I don't believe IN it as a good political or social system. Your little brother can be devilish sometimes, but I wouldn't say he IS the Devil or that he has ever seen the Devil or talked to him. Maybe nobody has. Maybe the Devil is more of an idea than anything real.

But Dad, one bite of an apple doesn't seen quite enough to explain all the evil that has spread all over the Earth. Maybe it's possible that there was a society of mostly good people on a distant galaxy that were so far advanced that they no longer had wars, and had no hate or violence, but still had a few evil people among them. Maybe the good people took the evil people off in some super-fast UFO's and dumped them on the earth to get rid of them. They didn't just kill them outright because they did not believe in killing of any sort, even killing of bad people. So maybe that's how evil got into the world, and it wasn't just the work of the Devil. It could have been in the genes of early people from another galaxy, and they could have been the first ones to populate the Earth. But the question I would most like to answer is WHY are we here, and what is the purpose of life? I mean, even if mankind with all its evil did originate from extraterrestrial sources, why was life already out there, and how did it get there in the first place? It just moves the question further back in time.

You have packed a lot of ideas into a few words. Now, just what is your question again?

My question, Dad, is simply: where did we come from and why are we here?

I don't know. Go ask your mother.

THE END

The Duel

I'm getting a little older than I used to be, and my memory is no longer perfect. Very good still, but no longer perfect. I may even have occasional little lapses of memory, especially when I get mad. That's very rare, of course, but sometimes even rare things do happen. I'll give you an example of what I mean:

It had been a busy week, and by Friday afternoon I was tired. It was almost Thanksgiving already, and Christmas would be on top of us before you knew it. For many years I've been the manager of the Hallmark Stationery Shop downtown at the mall, and although that doesn't sound like much, it's more work than you would think.

One of the things I always try to do on Friday is to check my calendar for Monday, to see if there is anything I need to get done or get ready for by Monday, which means do it today, because so many things are closed over the weekend. I like to "be prepared," for what's coming, as the Boy Scouts used to say. Do we still have Boy Scouts? I haven't heard them mentioned in the news for a long time, not even in reports of bullying or recent sex offenses. Maybe they are getting more courteous and kind and reverent, and less brave, or getting better at keeping their peccadilloes and escapades hushed up.

There were a lot of things on my office calendar, but nothing much of immediate importance, fortunately. Then I

13

remembered to check my little personal calendar that I keep folded inside my wallet, even though I don't use it very much, and almost never for business.

Imagine my surprise when I saw there, in sort of a scribble, not my usual neat printing: "Duel, Monday, 6:30 a.m. behind old quarry." I had no recollection whatsoever of having written that, and had to wonder whether someone or something were trying to play tricks on me. However, even though the handwriting was sloppy and obviously hurried, I did recognize that it was probably my own. When could I have written it? I don't often use that little second calendar book; it's just a tiny fold of paper really. I sometimes go for a week or two without opening it.

I had to ask my chief clerk, Stan Bullock, who also serves as our driver and sometimes a loader, and consequently is in a good position to keep track of what is going on, to tell me what he knew about this duel thing. Well, the stupid fellow said he didn't know anything about it. I couldn't tell whether he was lying and trying to cover something up, or whether he really didn't know anything. Then I tried Janice, our cashier, who also does most of the bookkeeping, but the dumb woman said she didn't know anything either. Well, if Bullock were lying, Janice would lie too, because I know they are usually in cahoots with each other, and probably had something illicit going on between them on the side, even though that sort of thing was supposed to be strictly forbidden by company policy.

Maybe there were some interesting activities taking place over at the fairgrounds that didn't have to involve me particularly, perhaps a demonstration of fencing or something. No, that would be unlikely at that hour. Oh, if only I could remember what I was thinking when I wrote those little words! Maybe they could be filming a movie with dueling in it, which would be fun to watch, and maybe they were looking for extras, you know, seconds. Or maybe I did something myself and made somebody mad. I do that occasionally, I suppose. But if my honor is at stake, I can't let that be impugned or traduced.

I had seen duels in the movies, when I was a kid, with swashbuckling heroes like Errol Flynn and Douglas Fairbanks Jr. battling it out in Sherwood Forest, or on the Shores of Tripoli, with swords and sabers -- I am not sure which, or what the difference is, for that matter. I know sometimes you hear about people dueling with pistols, but dueling always seemed more suggestive of swordplay to me. Pistols seems like cheating, like just shooting it out at high noon. I would never want to do that. If Burr and Hamilton had fought with rapiers instead of pistols, Aaron could have stuck Alex in the gizzard and be remembered in the history books as a former vice president who was merely defending his honor against some undocumented immigrant who should have been sent back where he came from. A pistol should be kept in your home where you can use it to shoot intruders who may be intruding with malice aforethought and intent to do you harm, or even poking around where they have no business poking around.

* * * * *

So there didn't seem much choice for me but to go on out to the old quarry, the area we always used to call the "dueling grounds" for reasons no one remembers. Maybe that's the very place where Aaron Burr shot Alexander Hamilton for all I know. But my note also said "duel." I had no idea of what I might have gotten myself into, but I would find out. So I dressed in my customary country gentleman's attire, loose shirt, brown knickerbockers, and corduroy hunting cap that I had bought in Brussels. I looked almost like a sportsman out for a skeet shoot. I wonder, do they ever use shotguns for duels? At thirty paces or so, you would be sitting ducks, so to speak, and it would all be over in a hurry. Well, I hoped I wouldn't have to shoot some poor jerk with a shotgun, but that did seem unlikely. I was letting my imagination run amok. I should think more positive thoughts.

Well, it wasn't too far to the field behind the old quarry, and I arrived there at 6:18 according to my reliable old dollar Ingersoll, which I try to adjust every evening, with the seven o'clock news, if I can remember to do it. I have never been late for a duel in my life, and I wasn't going to be late for this one, my first one, if duel it was to be. As soon as I arrived there, I knew right away that they weren't making movies or getting ready for a county fair, for there was just one other car there, parked at an angle as though it might want to make a quick getaway, like the cops always do. I parked a polite distance away from him, a hundred feet or so. I looked his way for a couple of minutes, and then he slowly opened his door and got out and sort of stood there, looking at me. So I got out too, and sort of stood there, looking at him.

After a couple minutes of silence, I said, very politely, "Excuse me, Sir -- do you happen to know anything about a duel or something that was supposed to be going on here at six-thirty this morning?"

16

"Sorry, I can't hear you," he shouted, somewhat more loudly than necessary, I thought. Then he started walking toward me, and when he got a little closer, he said, "Excuse me, Sir -- do you know anything about a duel or something that is supposed to be going on here this morning about now?"

"You took the words right out of my mouth," was what I might have said in other circumstances, looking for a laugh, but I wasn't sure it was a laughing matter this morning, whatever "it" might be. And so, with my genteel country gentleman's accent, I gently replied, "I was just wondering the same thing, and hoping you might clarify something for me. May I ask why you came here at this hour, Sir?" I must admit I was surprised at his response. It looked as though the stupid fellow had come all the way out here without knowing why he was doing it.

Then he explained: "I have to apologize, Sir. My memory isn't quite as sharp as it used to be when I was younger, so I keep a little calendar right in the glove compartment of my car." He paused, seeming to want a response from me.

"That's sometimes a good idea -- it can keep you from forgetting things," I offered.

"Yes, but . . ." he continued in ever-friendlier tones . . ."I forgot what it was that I was supposed to remember."

Now he was really beginning to sound like a jerk, so I said, "And what was it that you were supposed to remember?"

"That's just the problem; there were only a couple of words on my date calendar for Monday. It said, 'Duel, 6:30 Monday behind the quarry.' Even though I am pretty sure it was my own handwriting, I have no idea what it meant. I thought perhaps they were going to make a movie with fencing in it, you know, with Errol Flynn and Douglas Fairbanks Jr. -- that kind of fencing, not border fencing or wall fencing -- Ha ha," he laughed feebly at his own weak humor. "I used to like swashbuckling movies with fencing and stuff when I was a kid."

"Errol Flynn and those guys are dead and gone, my friend. It must be something else. Maybe you have had a bone to pick or gotten into an argument with someone and shot your mouth off and made him mad, to make him want to come out here and have a duel with you. What did you plan to use as weapons, sling shots?"

"I . . . I don't remember everything anymore. I think maybe I did get into an argument with someone, but I don't remember what it was about. I only get mad rarely, but sometimes even rare things do happen, you know."

"Well, I'll tell you what, Buddy. You go on back home and forget about it for the rest of the day, and I'll stay here a little while, and if someone turns up looking for a duel with you, I'll get my shotgun out of the trunk of my car and tell him that you were a good guy and didn't mean anything by it. I'll tell him to go on back home. Okay?"

"Well, sure . . . that's fine."

"That's your car over there," I said in my most serious tone of voice.

"I know which is my car -- I'm not that dumb."

"Are you sure?" I said to the old fart, as he got into his car and drove away, but I don't think he heard me.

* * * * *

It wasn't until Wednesday evening that I remembered who the SOB was. It must have been that bastard who flipped me the finger last week when I honked at him for making an illegal left turn into Seventh Street. Yes, that's who it was. I remember now -- he screamed some nasty words about how they should have built a wall to keep people like me out of the country. I guess I called him an SOB because my ancestors on the Hispanic side of my family have been living in California for over two hundred years, since long before that guy was born, and even before California was part of the United States.

Yes, that was it. That must have been the guy, but I am older than I used to be, and don't remember everything. But I do remember him, now anyway. I guess at that moment I must have written the note about meeting at the dueling place, for there it was, in my own handwriting. I am sure it was my own handwriting.

What a jerk he was, to go to all of this . . . and a duel . . . Imagine! But I had to defend my honor, didn't I? I should have blown his head off back there with my shotgun. And now, dammit, I've lost my chance, just because I was a little forgetful. Shit.

THE END

19

Without My Glasses

I can't see too well without my glasses, you know. One of my wife's duties is always to watch where I might put my glasses down, whenever I take them off to go swimming or take a shower or go to bed. Things like that. So she can find them when I need them.

We had been living in a nice house with a picket fence in the suburbs for about twelve years when a pretty young widow lady moved in next door. A sweet little thing, if I do say so myself. Even a tender morsel wouldn't be an exaggeration. My wife and I tried to act like friendly neighbors toward her. At least I did. No ulterior motives, of course. She would come over occasionally for a drink or a barbecue with some other local friends, and soon we were on a first name basis. Her name was Bianca, which is Italian for Blanche.

So, one evening when my wife was out for her Planned Parenthood meeting, the doorbell rang, and there was this Bianca standing on the porch. Not really unusual; she had rung our doorbell before, although never when my wife was away. But we have always been hospitable, so I asked her in for a drink. No harm in that.

Well, to make a short story short, it turned out that a drink wasn't all she wanted. She wanted company. as well.

21

Preferably masculine company. She insisted I sit by her on the couch, which was all right by me. Then a whiff of her delicate Chanel perfume wafted over me. I felt the touch of her hand on my forearm. I felt the ineffable sensuality of her half-closed eyelids and the inviting beauty of her half-opened lips. And I felt for a moment that I was no longer in control of my actions or my destiny.

Then, distracted as I was, somehow I must have dropped my glasses, just as her tender breath caressed the lobe of my right ear. "Kiss me, my Handsome Hunk," she said.

How could I refuse? She had me where she wanted me.

But oh, the sweetness of those lips! I hadn't tasted anything like that since I had my first chocolate-caramel upside-down cake at the Chevy Chase Hot Shoppe when I was a freshman in high school. I... was... in... Heaven.

Then something happened.

The front door burst open and there was my wife, frozen in horror at the panorama she was beholding. "What do you think you are doing there kissing Bianca?" she stammered.

"Bianca... ? I thought it was you I was kissing, Honey. You know I can't see too well without my glasses."

THE END

The Yellow School Bus

A while ago our local newspaper invited its readers to submit a 250-word story sharing favorite memories of riding "the yellow school bus." I sent in my own school bus story. It was published August 7, 2009. And it's the truth.

I kissed a girl in the back of the school bus.

"So what?" you say.

Well, in those days things were different: I was an Army brat, an eight-year-old third-grader, living on a small isolated post up north. Our school bus was an Army mini-van that took about a dozen of us kids to the elementary school six miles away.

Sally and I liked to sit in the back. She was the most gorgeous creature on two pigtails you ever saw, and her braces gave her the most sparkling smile imaginable. Even before I knew what love was, I was in love with Sally, and one morning when I could no longer resist the temptation I gave her a little kiss as a mark of my deep affection and admiration.

A fraction of a second of ecstasy, but a big mistake.

You see, public kissing in those days Before the War was tolerated at about the same level as frontal nudity on

23

Broadway this afternoon. Our Holier-than-Thou driver, one Sergeant Fournier (pronounced: Four-knee-her), must have spotted me in his rear-view mirror; he pulled over, stopped the bus, and gave me a round and most embarrassing chewing-out in front of my friends and schoolmates.

And, as if that weren't enough, he (without due authority, I might say) suspended me from riding on the bus for a month, which meant my father had to drive me to school, which meant my father was then ten or fifteen minutes late for work, which meant that the General was not at all pleased with my father, and my father was not at all pleased with me,. And he let me know that too.

Isn't that enough? Well, it's not the end of the story.

As luck (bad luck, that is) would have it, I fell ill a few months later with an affliction known as "rheumatic fever," the effects of which lingered for some years before gradually tapering off. One of its effects was that I became the laughing stock among the annual summer gathering of my cousins, who had the bright idea of associating my illness with my affection for Sally. They described my problem as "romantic fever," asserting that it stemmed from my unrequited love.

"He met Sally and got romantic fever," was the taunt, which sounds pretty funny and even laughable now, but then cut deeply into the heart of an eight-year-old.

Dear Sally, you would be eighty-one now, and I don't know where, or if, you are living today, but, in spite of what I suffered from knowing you, the memory of our one kiss, my first ever, and my best ever, was worth it all.

THE END

Stormy Night

Maybe I could have been a comedian. But I don't think I was cut out to be a Shakespearean actor. I was only nine at the time of this story, although I was big for my age and already in the fifth grade.

I'm older now, much older, but not as smart. I think that that must have been my peak, and that my smarts have been going downhill ever since. But at that time I was the top kid in my math class. So, with infallible pedagogical logic, they picked me for a big part in the school play coming up that spring.

The title of the play was "The Little Hams Do Hamlet." (Good Grief!) The parts and the scenes were all cut up and passed around so no kid had to say too much. I got given a bunch of weird lines beginning with "To be or not to be... " which I was told to memorize. It was called a soliloquy and was about this guy Hamlet, who was mad. I mean, really mad -- mad enough at his mother-f . . ing stepfather to want to kill him, but couldn't make up his mind to do it.

But I am not good at memorizing stuff, and I told my teacher I didn't think I could go through with it. It wasn't like math, which was something you did because it was logical and where you didn't have to just memorize things. She insisted I COULD do it, and said I HAD to, for our reputation and honor -- words like that -- reputation and honor, of Jones Elementary School, J-E-S, "jeese." (We

27

kids called going to school "going to Jesus," but of course we never let our parents or teachers know that.)

Anyway, I worked on it for a couple of days, and it wasn't so hard to learn as I had feared. I got so I could say it straight through in the shower in the morning. But even so, I was afraid. How do you know that something you can do in the morning in the shower at home is something you can do in the evening at the school auditorium with all the other kids looking at you, and all their parents looking at you, and all the teachers looking at you, and Mrs. Abernathy from the school cafeteria there looking at you, and even the principal -- Mister Grunt was his name -- there looking at you?

And fear seized me, and I was sure I would forget my lines, and I even threw up at the breakfast table just thinking about it, although I had gone through the whole thing without a mistake in the shower a few minutes before. That was on a Monday, and the show was to be the next Friday night at seven o'clock. Eat an early supper, we were told. But what if I threw up my early supper right there on the stage? In front of all those people? And what are you supposed to do if you forget your lines? Vanish into thin air?

Tuesday afternoon I stayed after school to tell my teacher I couldn't do it. By now I was a walking wreck; I had the fear jitters and the fear shakes so bad I had to go to the bathroom about once an hour, and every day it was getting worse. Just waiting to tell her made my palms sweat and brought stomach acid to the back of my throat.

"You'll be fine," she said, "you're smart."

"No I'm not!" I said. "I'm dumb, I'm dumb, I'm dumb!"
What I meant was I'm scared, I'm scared, I'm scared.

She said, let me hear you try some of it now, so I did. I
started right off, "To be or not to be, that is the question -- "
and it wasn't really hard at all, with her there, with her en-
couraging smile. I just went right through it, like in the
shower. Maybe I could do it after all!

But that evening, at home, I kept hearing the words as I
was trying to eat supper. It was as though the words were
coming up and meeting the food in my mouth trying to go
down, and neither of them getting through. And it continued more or less like that right up until Friday. I could
hardly eat or sleep or do anything but worry about whether
I might forget my lines up there on that stage. I was really
scared. I could say them all right when I didn't HAVE to --
as long as I wasn't eating at the same time. But how did I
know I could do it when I DID have to? Up there in front
of all those people? The truth is I was terrified. And you
don't have to tell anybody this, but I even wet myself.
Thursday night, thinking about it, the night before the show
was to go on.

Friday was the nightmare of nightmares. I staggered
blindly through the day like a zombie, saying to be or not to
be and all that to myself over and over again, but still possessed by the fear that I wouldn't be able to do it that
evening, and that people would laugh. Not laugh WITH
me, but laugh AT me.

As you can imagine, I couldn't eat any supper, not right
before we were to go on stage. As the time for my entrance

29

approached, my palms went into a sweat again, my temples throbbed, and my knees shook, even though my teacher was there behind me, watching, saying softly, encouragingly, "You can do it; you can do it." She always makes me feel good and, you know, I began to believe her.

When my time came and I was alone on the stage, with 180 pairs of attentive ears cupped in my direction, I felt my throat relax and my knees strengthen. I lifted up my chin and took on a pensive, Shakespearean look as I had been told to do. I had overcome my fear.

I opened my mouth to let the words pour freely forth, and out they came:

"It was a dark and normy stite...:

THE END

Epilogue.

I stopped, lost, not knowing what I had said or where I was. There was pin-drop silence. Then, after about ten seconds, the hall went into thunderous laughter and applause. It was -- as they said when the Titanic went down -- it was a night to remember.

And that is why I say that, if I had chosen to follow the theatre as a career, it would have been as a comedian. The ability to make people laugh is an uncommon gift.

Turkey in the Straw

Our golden retriever, Gwendolyn, is the sweetest, the gentlest, and most loving creature on four legs -- or even two legs -- that you ever saw. Like collies, golden retrievers are justly known for their tolerance and friendly nature, and make ideal pets and companions, especially in families with children and babies where the tolerance and good nature of most pets might be pushed to the limit.

Gwendolyn's life was people. Specifically, our family. In spite of her breeding as a bird-dog, Gwendolyn never showed any interest whatsoever in the feathered species, and not much interest in other dogs either, for that matter. It was people she loved, played with,
lived with, wanted to be with.

So you can imagine my astonishment when, one Saturday afternoon, after wandering off from our country home for a couple of hours, Gwendolyn returned with her body all wiggly with smiles and excitement, her tail swishing about like an airplane propeller, and with a freshly killed 17-pound turkey in her mouth. Not a wild one, but a domesticated variety. I wouldn't have thought she could get her mouth around it, let along carry it. But here she was, as proud as a General of the Army Who Had Just Returned from Battle. She dropped the bird at my feet and sat, smiling at me, awaiting a pat on the head and a commendatory "Good Dog."

31

What to do? I couldn't breathe life back into the bird and make it flutter away. I didn't even know where it had come from. It certainly looked like a strong, healthy young bird, still warm, not something I would want to just throw away in the garbage, so I gathered up this mass of dead-weight meat and feathers and jammed it into the freezer. My wife would soon be back from her ladies' club meeting in the city; maybe she would know what to do. She is smarter than I am and always good in minor crises.

So I just sat down to read the Saturday paper which I hadn't seen all morning.

When my wife did come home and I told her what had happened, she went straight to the heart of the matter and said we had to find out who the turkey belonged to and make amends.

So we spent two days of discrete inquiries all over our corner of the county, talking in the abstract to gas stations, convenience stores, feed and grain operations -- places like that -- asking in general terms for information about who around here might be raising chickens and turkeys. It was through the farmers' market that we identified a number of remote possibilities, but only one that was close enough to be even reasonably likely, a little farm just a mile away from our house, but on the other side of the woods, which made it about five miles by road. Volmer was their name. John Volmer. It seems they raised mostly chickens but also had a few turkeys, sort of as pets. But we still didn't know what to do, and after a couple more days of worrying and fretting, we still had not made a decision and could not agree on how to face the unattractive prospect of telling them. Maybe we could somehow work up to it slowly, I thought.

32

Then a strange thing happened, and we read a "Dear Abby" letter in the newspaper about an almost identical case of someone's dog stealing a neighbor's chicken and bringing it home. Abby's advice was to do something nice for the offended neighbors, like taking them out to dinner or something like that. But she had no explicit advice as to how, or whether, to confess and take responsibility for the dastardly deed.

"That's what we'll do," my wife said. "I'll send them a card telling them we are inviting a few friends in for dinner from around the neighborhood and would like to have them join us."

"Good idea," I replied. "Soften them up some and make them feel a little beholden to us before we drop the bomb about Gwendolyn in their chicken-coop... or turkey-coop, or whatever it is." So we did it -- sent out a nice note asking them over for the following Sunday afternoon.

Mrs. Volmer promptly telephoned to accept and to trade a few "do-you-know-so-and-so's" with my wife.

"She really sounds very nice," said my wife. "Maybe we should have tried to make friends with them when we first came here, three years ago."

"Well," I said, "there's plenty of time. We can still do it." The next day Mr. Volmer called to thank us once more for the invitation and repeat their pleasure in accepting in i. I was the one who answered the phone this time.

"It sounds delightful," he said. "We are looking forward to meeting you. And we'd like to bring something, maybe a bottle of wine... What're we having?"

"Well, since it's this close to Thanksgiving, I thought we'd have... uh... turkey."

ORIGINAL ENDING

Epilogue

Two or three months later, after we had seen the Volmers a few times and sort of gotten to know them, I decided, with my wife's help, that we should bite the bullet and clear the remains of our guilty consciences. When I had a chance one day I said to John, "There's something I need to tell you."

But let me back up a minute. Even before that famous dinner party, my wife and I disagreed on what we ought to do about the bird and what we ought to say to the Volmers.

She wanted to tell them everything right away and I thought we should hold off and think about it, at least for a while. And I felt we might as well cook the turkey for our dinner as it was certainly perfectly good, but she thought that was gross and wanted to chuck it and go buy another turkey or, better still, a ham instead, to get the taste of turkey out of our mouths, as she put it. So we went round and round, getting more and more nervous and upset with ourselves and with each other.

She said it wouldn't be right to feed them their own turkey. "It would be almost cannibalistic."

"You want to waste that beautiful bird?" I insisted. "Probably specially bred for taste by people who know turkeys. The Volmers must be experts and might appreciate its fresh country flavor. They should know what's good."

And as for telling them about Gwendolyn's part in this, I felt that there wasn't anything to be gained by doing that. It wouldn't bring their pet back; and we could make all the amends we wanted and ease our consciences by contributing to the Red Cross or maybe the Audubon Society in their name, or perhaps making a donation to the garden club that Mrs. Volmer belonged to and loved. Anonymously, I thought, would be best.

Finally we compromised.

She agreed we would serve the turkey for dinner so as not to waste a good bird and because we might not have been able to find such a fine one at the market anyway.

And I agreed that in due course we would make our confession to the Volmer's, as long as we didn't have to do it right away. Work up to it slowly, was my idea. I would let out the grim facts of the case gradually, sympathizing at first, then confessing, and finally contritely apologizing. Of course, I wouldn't connect the loss of Volmer's turkey with the turkey we had eaten for dinner that Sunday. No need to go that far; that would be too much. Unnecessary and perhaps... upsetting.

35

They could guess if they wanted to, but we didn't have to spell it out for them and throw it in their faces. And my wife began to accept that view too. I can't speak for Gwendolyn. She was definitely in the dog house. As you can imagine, neither of us was speaking to her.

So, as I was saying... When I saw John again sometime later, I took a deep breath and started in. It wasn't going to be easy. "There is something I need to tell you."

"Yes? What is that?"

"We were sorry to hear about your loss."

"Loss...? What loss?"

"About your pet turkey. Someone said you lost one of your pet turkeys, and..."

He interrupted me to say, "Oh, you mean the one that fell in the well last year and drowned? Yes, that was a sad day for us."

"Well no," I said. "Didn't you lose another turkey a couple of months ago?"

"No," he replied, "the one that drowned in the well was the only one we ever lost."

THE END

My Brother-in-Law is a Jerk

My brother-in-law, Jimmy McIver, is a real jerk. I've never liked the guy much; he always seems to be putting on airs or trying to get something for nothing, and he's not even my brother-in-law actually. He is the husband of my wife's sister, whatever that makes him to me, but unfortunately he lives in our neighborhood, just down the street. So we get to see them from time to time, or rather, HAVE to see them, at family get-togethers, barbecues, etc. But I always feel that he is trying to put me down because he has a better job than I do, or because he has three kids and I only have one, or because he went to Harvard and I went to Slippery Rock. Things like that.

Anyway, getting on with the story: I was home one Saturday morning, reading the paper after a late breakfast, and vaguely pondering whether I had time to cut the lawn before the football game began, when the doorbell rang. Saturday doorbells usually mean Jehovah's Witnesses or Heart Fund drive I thought, as I went to the door. But no, it was neither. Rather it was just a young man, very clean-cut looking, perhaps in his late teens, wearing a wide smile and an open-collar shirt.

"Excuse me for bothering you, Sir," he said politely. "I am working my way through college and I have something you might be interested in."

Now, I don't usually welcome traveling salesmen, nor do I buy from wandering street vendors, but the young man seemed sincere, and I wasn't pressed for time, so I said, "Very well, let's see what you have."

With that he opened his briefcase and took out a some-what oversize paperback book sealed in a clear plastic wrapping. The title read, "The Question Book -- What Are Your Questions?" Underneath the title, printed in large let-ters that you could easily read through the plastic wrapping, were several enticing suggestions as to what might be dis-covered in the interior:

"WHAT ARE THE DOW JONES AVERAGES GOING TO DO?

"WHO WILL WIN THE WIMBLETON TENNIS NEXT YEAR?

"HOW HIGH ARE GASOLINE PRICES GOING TO GO?

"HOW CAN YOU MAKE LOVE LAST?

"AND MANY MORE VALUABLE QUESTIONS"

"Let's open it up and have a look," I said.

"Oh, I'm sorry, Sir, I can't do that unless you buy it. Company regulations."

That should have been my clue, but the innocence of the shining face of that young fellow, and the natural interest I had in knowing what the Dow Jones and gas prices were going to do, overtook what should have been my better judgement, and I asked, "All right, how much is it?"

"Eighty-nine dollars, Sir," he said. "I have only a few left."

That should have been another clue; $89 is lot for a paperback, I thought. But the idea of predicting the Dow Jones had really piqued my curiosity, and that alone would have been worth more than any eighty-nine dollars. And furthermore I have to admit that some of the other come-ons cited on the cover did attract my interest. "Eighty-nine dollars?" I said. "That's a lot for a paperback."

"Oh," said the lad, "there are many other questions inside that I think you will find instructive." So I said okay, went and got my wallet; I just happened to have enough to give him the $89. I took the book and peeled off the plastic wrap, as he and his smiling face turned and started to go.

Well, I could see right away that the book was a bunch of garbage. Things like: What are the Dow Jones Averages going to do? ANSWER: They are going to go up and down. And: Who will win the Wimbleton? ANSWER: A fine tennis player. And: How high are gas prices going to go? ANSWER: As high as some people are willing to pay. And -- get this: How can you make love last? ANSWER: Do other things first.

39

I felt like poking him in the nose and accusing him of being what he was, a con artist, but that wouldn't have done any good. I'd been had. I tempered my tongue and corked up my fury, merely saying, "Hey, is this some kind of a scam or something?" as he was heading off across the lawn.

"Oh, no Sir," he said as he looked back over his shoulder. "I'm sure you can learn a lot from that book."

I was already learning. Learning that I had been taken. Conned. But thinking fast and biting my lip, I said, "Wait a minute."

What I was thinking was that if my wife found out about this book of trash that I had paid eighty-nine dollars for, as she surely would, and the story got back to her sister's husband, that McIver son-of-a-bitch I was talking about, I would be a laughing-stock, and he would never let me live it down. So I calmly said to the young man, "I've got a suggestion for you. There's a fellow down the street, in the yellow house on the corner, named James McIver, who I know would just love to have a copy of your book. You should go see him."

"Oh, I've been there, Sir. He's the one who recommended I come see you."

THE END

Thumbs Up

"It's a boy!" the doctor said. Or the nurse, or the midwife, or somebody there in the hospital. It's what they always say when there is a new arrival, isn't it? Or anyway, about half the time. At least that's what someone always says in the books you read, although in this particular case I was too young to know just who it was that announced the good news. You see, the boy in question was I. So I don't remember the conversation too well, but it probably went something like this:

"Is he healthy?" my mother must have asked. The usual question.

"Yes, it seems to be," one of the nurses answered. In those first few moments of life I was still an "it." It takes a while to become a human being.

"All the fingers and toes and everything there where it ought to be?" -- the second normal question.

"It has ten fingers and ten toes," said the nurse. "But..."

"But what?" my mother asked feebly, still weak from the ordeal.

"But..." said the nurse, "it has ten fingers."

"Perfect," said my mother. "I am so happy."

41

"But, they're not all the same," continued the nurse.

At this point my father joined the conversation. "What are you talking about?" he asked the nurse.

Well, they were talking about my fingers.

I have to interrupt my story for a minute to say that my mother never told me anything about these details of my arrival, and my father didn't tell me until after Mother died, nineteen years later. I was prodding him out of curiosity to explain it to me, and I have tried to reconstruct these early conversations out of what he remembered, not just what I remembered, which was practically nothing, considering how young I was at the time.

You see, although I was born with ten fingers and had one thumb on my left hand, like most other people, I had two thumbs on my right hand like... well, like me. It seems that in the hospital there was quite a little debate about what to do, if anything, with this freak that had suddenly appeared upon the scene, healthy and normal in all respects but one, or should I say three... thumbs, that is.

Mother apparently wanted to cut off one of my thumbs, and the nurse took her side. "Do you want him to have three thumbs like... a freak?" was their argument. We'll just circumcise the second thumb on his right hand. He's so little he won't know anything and it probably won't even hurt him much," they said.

Nobody gets the opinion of a patient this small, And," she added, "if we cut off one of his thumbs, he will never miss it: he will never know he had it."

My father and one of the doctors took another view. "Well then, do you want him to have nine fingers, like... a freak?" So, the debate was on.

It seems they finally compromised by agreeing to a minute structural and functional examination of the two thumbs on my right hand to determine, if one of them was to be removed, which one it should be.   Often, when unusual things sprout in a human body, like a third tit, they are not really functional, and little would be lost with their removal.   If, as some of the doctors suspected, closer examination revealed that one of the thumbs was a useless, poorly connected appendage, it would be removed, leaving the stronger, more normal, thumb free to grow and thrive. The surprise came when the results showed both thumbs fully functional and operational, identical as far as could be determined, and, if one were to be removed, the choice would be a toss-up.

Several more doctors were called in for consultation, while still others heard about this unusual case and, because they knew so little about it, were eager to volunteer their opinions. My father was strongly opposed to gambling of any sort, and accordingly insisted that the process of choosing the appropriate thumb for removal would be just that -- a gamble. Most of the doctors agreed with him, and one of them apparently reminded the other doctors of their mantra to "Do no harm," or, as he put it, "If you don't know what you are doing, better to do nothing."

43

So, that's the way they left it, or left me. Because they did not know what to do, they did nothing. Fortunately.

Frankly, I cannot imagine what life would be like without my two thumbs on my right hand, and when my father related these details of the close call I had had in those early hours of my life, I was sick from picturing the frightful image of what might have been, and at the same time very thankful that I had come out of it all unscathed. It is definitely unfair to scathe children when they are too young to know what is happening to them.

I actually had one less bones than most people. Or, I should say, one fewer bones to be grammatically correct. You are supposed to use the word *less* with quantity and *fewer* with number. That's the school-teacher coming out in me. Interestingly enough, a thumb has only two bones, called phalanges, where other fingers have three, in spite of the greater utility of the thumb. Of course, the thumb's greater utility comes only by way of its unique ability to cooperate with other fingers, or another finger. By itself a thumb is just, well, just a thumb. Being all thumbs would probably be no better than being all fingers — fingers of the common, three-phalange, variety, that is. My first thumb, or the thumb on the end, can cooperate with any of the three regular fingers, but usually works with the "ring" finger, second from the other end. My second thumb works best with the finger right next to it. It is the middle finger of the five, and it's what I think of as my index finger, but I have to be careful when I hold up a finger to signify "one" to avoid being misunderstood. So usually I hold up my first thumb to mean "one," like they do in Europe. Maybe our European ancestors all had two thumbs per hand, for them to have retained the atavistic habit of counting "one" with their thumb (so as to avoid the unintended signal which could be sent by an index finger in the third position).

The first glimmer I ever had that things were different, and by that I mean realizing that my left hand and my right hand were different, must have been when I was still a baby. I know that I preferred my right hand over my left hand when it came to sucking something, and it was my right hand that I held to my face as I went to sleep. My second thumb on my right hand was my thumb of choice for sucking. That was because I could suck it and gently caress the underside of my chin, at the same time, with the other thumb.

Of course, thumb number one had its advantage too, because when I sucked that one I could stick thumb number two up one of my nostrils -- either nostril -- but especially the one on the right, because it was more in line. And that was a very pleasant and comforting sensation too -- for a baby, you understand. But still, as a regular routine I preferred the arrangement whereby I could caress the bottom of my chin with the first thumb while gently sucking the second one. I didn't actually suck it, but held the tip next to my upper gum and the soft pad of my thumb, where your fingerprint is — that part — against my upper lip. I think I must have been weaned prematurely to have had these drives and to have such a lasting memory of my early oral-digital inclinations.

I remember the first time I ever ate in a Chinese restaurant. I was only about nine, and was with my uncle, who had lived in China, and loved everything about the Chinese, even their food. As we were going into the restaurant, he said, "You know, the Chinese eat with chopsticks; they are a little bit tricky to use at first, but I'll show you how to use them."

Well, I could understand how it might be a little clumsy to use chopsticks with your left hand, where you only had one thumb, but if you held them in your right hand, like I did, it was as easy as duck soup, so to speak. I held each stick firmly in two places with a thumb and a finger, and there was, as they say in today's vernacular, no problem. It crossed my mind that the ancestors of today's Chinese also must have had two thumbs per hand, like the prehistoric Europeans, to have invented such a manner of eating. Needless to say, I was immediately better at handling the chopsticks than my uncle was, with all of his experience, but I tried not to show off or rub it in.

I could have been a great criminal or identity thief, for I always had a choice of thumb-print whenever it was required for a license or ID card or anything like that. I could have had an alias with his own identity, and could have proved it. But I am an honest man and I wouldn't want to tell you anything that wasn't absolutely true.

Growing up, when we were old enough to start comparing body parts, I was the most popular kid in the neighborhood. They laughed at first, but then were envious when I showed them some of the things I could do with my right hand that they couldn't do with their right hand, or left hand either.

46

For instance, when we got to grade school I could shoot rubber bands with one hand, and roll the best spit-balls you ever threw, with one hand yet. I could ring the bell on a bicycle without taking my grip off the handlebar. In Sunday school, when they let us take turns passing the plate, I could hold it with one hand, without a tremor. And I usually needed only one hand to open the screw top of one of those little plastic water bottles we carried to school with our lunch. In chemistry lab in high school I could take the cork out of a test-tube and put it back with one hand. Later on in life I realized other people needed two hands even to use a piece of dental floss or to hold a pair of binoculars while adjusting the focus, things that I take for granted because they are easy for me to do with one hand as long as it is the right one. My right hand, that is.

And something else. Two of my friends always had trouble telling left from right; some people are like that. You tell them to take a left turn and they take a right turn. Well, I never had that trouble; I could always tell.

Guitars were popular among the kids when I was in high school, and one of them let me strum his one day. And some of those guys who had accused me of being weird really changed their tune, in a manner of speaking, when I showed them what I could do on the guitar. I mean, I used two picks and could pluck two strings at the same time with the picks. After that they thought I was pretty cool. To me it seemed as though guitars must have been designed to be played with two picks in your right hand. The guys that could only hold one pick seemed handicapped. And, speaking of music, when Carmen Miranda's Cuban style was popular in the 40's and 50's, I got a pair of castanets and found I could play them both with one hand — my right hand of course – while simultaneously playing my mouth organ which I held with my left hand. I don't do that much anymore; I admit it was rather childish.

But besides the guitar and rubber bands and spitballs, I was also a stand-out with the girls. With one hand I could caress them as no one else ever did. I could even pinch them twice at the same time in two different places, if they weren't too far apart.

Everybody is the center of his own little universe, and by that I mean that one's own self is usually one's standard. If you are five feet ten and you live in a country where most of the men are around five six, you think of them as being short. You don't think of yourself as being tall. If you think of skin at all, you think of your own skin color as being normal. Other people are pale, or swarthy, or light or dark, but always in comparison to you. You are the standard. In this country we think of the color of hair as being blond, or brunette, or maybe "brownette," or black or red. In a Swedish passport there used to be a place to check hair color; the choices were light blond, blond, dark blond, and other. We see the world from where we stand. If you like calves' liver and know other people who don't, they are the odd ones, not you. To me, having three thumbs seems very normal. I am normal. I am me.

When, as a young child, I first noticed that my right and left hands were different, I wondered why I didn't have two thumbs on my left hand too. However, I soon got used to having just one left thumb, although two thumbs on the right hand seemed natural.

There wasn't much that "ordinary" people could do that I couldn't do. I even took some violin lessons when I was young, before I ever picked up a guitar, and remember thinking it was a good thing it was my right hand that had the two thumbs. It was easy to hold the bow, and besides, two thumbs on my left hand would not have worked very well, leaving only three fingers on the strings above the finger board. I guess I would have had to learn to play left handed. I saw a left-handed violinist play once -- really weird looking. Think of how different violins might be now if Stradivarius had had three or four thumbs. Or even if he had just been left handed.

But all in all, I can't imagine life without a right hand with two thumbs. I have told that to doctors and psychologists and curious people and organizations that have even asked me for interviews on the matter. I should think it would be obvious to anybody. Well, I guess you can get used to anything, even having only one thumb on each hand.

So, that's my background. Now I am grown, married with wife and two children, all healthy, with six thumbs distributed evenly among the three of them. And I have a good job as vice-president of a small engineering company. Or ONE of the vice-presidents, I should say. There are a lot of vice-presidents in a company like ours, and in fact if you are not the president or a vice president you are just a wage-worker or hired help.

Anyway, at a company policy-planning meeting the other day, the question of opening a new facility in California came up for a vote. It involved a relatively small investment, but projections indicated it could increase our production by 30%. It was a good idea and we needed the expansion, but it was resisted by our overly conservative financial officer and some others, including the vice president for product design, who I think feared a threat from new blood being brought in. I was strongly in favor of it, and so was the president, as it no doubt would have added to his importance and possibly his annual bonus as well.

"I'm all for it," he boomed loudly, pounding his elbows on the table and holding up his two thumbs. "Let's have a vote. All those in favor, thumbs up!" he bellowed. "Those opposed, thumbs down. Mr. Secretary, count the votes."

Whether the president had forgotten about me, or wasn't aware that I was a freak, I never knew. What I did know is that it's a good thing I was there. There were ten of us present and voting, and, as you have probably guessed by now, the measure carried 11 to 10 when all the votes had been counted.

THE END

Happy Hallowe'en

This story is true, and you can believe it or not. We were seven years old, my brother and I – we are twins – and it was the first Hallowe'en that we were allowed to go trick-or-treating without our parents. As long as we stayed right in our own neighborhood.

It was a pretty big deal to us, almost like getting your driver's license when you are sixteen. We didn't believe in ghosts or witches or any of those things, or so we thought, but we did believe in candy and cookies. So we took our black and orange bags with us and set off down the street collecting goodies. We had to be home by 6:30, but by then our bags were full. It was just getting dark when we went back to our house. We weren't supposed to have any candy until after supper, so we wanted to eat early.

We went into the house but there was nobody there. Then all the lights went out, and we heard a spooky voice coming from outside, going WHO... WHO... WHO...! By now it was really dark. We were sitting in the living room and didn't know what to do. We didn't even have a flashlight, so it was pretty spooky. Then there came a knock on the door. Three knocks: BOOM... BOOM... BOOM...

I opened the door a crack and saw this ghost standing there, and that's the truth, making this WHO -- WHO

51

sound. I slammed the door shut and had to go to the bathroom because I had wet my pants. It was pitch dark there in the house, but I was able to grope my way back to the toilet.

Just then the lights came on and I heard Dad's voice call out, "Billy and Johnny, are you there?" Well, that is one time I was really glad to see my Dad, but then he started laughing, and Mom came up from the cellar and was laughing too.

The ghost was Dad dressed up in a sheet to scare us, and Mom had gone down to the basement to make it worse by turning off the lights at the master switch.

My Dad is kind of a nut. He then said he would give me and Johnny 25 cents for each piece of candy we had gotten, so I made $36.75 because I had 147 pieces of candy. Johnny made about the same. It was the most money I had ever had in my life.

Then my Dad threw all the candy into the garbage but two pieces of butterscotch for each of us. Dad's a dentist, and said it was bad for our teeth and all that. Then he got a watermelon out of the car and some grapes and bananas, and that's what we had for dessert. After that we started calling my nutty Dad, "Casper, the Friendly Ghost." What a nut.

THE END

Run, Run !

Have you ever had that dream where you have to run because you are chasing someone or someone is chasing you, but your feet are in a quagmire or a swamp and are sticking every time you try to pick them up and make them move? You try as hard as you can to run, but all you can do is painfully slog along at the speed of a slow walk. It is horrible frustration.

Well, I used to have that dream occasionally when I was young, and then, after I grew up, the dream came true -- sort of.

What happened was that when I was twenty-four years old I got poliomyelitis, or what they used to call infantile paralysis. Well, for me there wasn't anything infantile about it. I was laid up for several months, and when I finally got out of the hospital it was with the aid of a pair of crutches and later a cane. After that I did get better, but running for me was never an option. I could still dream about it, but the best I could perform was an energetic-looking shuffle. Later on I even learned to play a little tennis, but was careful never to tell my opponents that I couldn't run so they wouldn't know how easily I could be beaten if they merely hit the ball from one corner to the other.

Then one sunny day in springtime, many years later, I went back to my home town for the sixtieth reunion of my

53

high-school graduating class. I was seventy-seven then; all of us were over seventy-five at least. Usually you only have to be sixty or sixty-five to be considered a senior, or even fifty-five in some places, so we called ourselves the Super Seniors. Our real nickname though was The Beavers.

Unbeknownst to me, the reunion organizers had planned a baseball game between us Super Seniors and a similar team from the Johnson High School Wildcats, our traditional rivals, who were, not surprisingly, also having their own sixtieth reunion celebration at the same time. Both schools were pretty small: our class had only about fifty back then when we graduated. And of course many of our classmates were unable to attend the reunion now because they were in nursing homes or had already died or had some other excuse. So that Saturday afternoon it was all we could do to put together nine old men to make up our team. I was prepared to watch with amusement from the sidelines. However, to the dismay of all concerned, we were only able to field eight players.

The others came to me and said, "Dan, why aren't you playing too? We need you."

Now, I had never actually told anybody I couldn't run. My family and some of my friends knew, of course, but never talked about it much, probably for fear of embarrassing me, and I never felt any particular need to talk about it either. It was like our own little "don't ask, don't tell" policy. If people didn't know, what they couldn't see wouldn't hurt them. I was always quite happy to let people, especially the girls, think I was perfectly normal, if they could. At least as far as walking and running were concerned. But now it had to come out. In the open. No more pretending or hiding.

"I can't run," I said.

"What do you mean, you can't run?"

"I mean I can't run. It's as simple as that."

"None of us can run much; we are all just as old as you are."

"It's not that I can't run much; it's that I can't run period. I can't get two feet off the ground at the same time, which is the Olympic definition of running. As opposed to walking."

"Well, we've gotta have you. If we can't come up with nine players we forfeit the game to the damn Wildcats. Do you want the Beavers to put their tails between their legs and go and forfeit the game?"

"No, of course not. But... "

"Well, be a sport and get on out onto the field. You can play first base where you don't have to run much. The Wildcats are just as old as we are. Just do what you can."

"But what happens when I have to bat? You can't run to first base if you can't run at all."

"Sure you can. You stand up there at the plate and maybe you get to walk on four balls, or maybe you get hit by a pitch and get to go to first base at your own leisurely pace."

"Yeah," I said, "but even if I get to first base what do I do then? If the guy next up behind me gets a hit, he might get to second base before me, and then we would both be out wouldn't we? Or just me? Or is he the one who would be out? No, I don't think it would work."

"You worry too much. Their pitcher might walk the next three batters, and you could score without having to do anything. Or the batter behind you might hit a homer, and you could score strolling in with your hands in your pockets."

"I think you are being overly optimistic."

"You have to look at it positively. You know, at the brighter side of things. Come on, let's go."

We were the "visiting" team, so we were up to bat first. And would you believe, they had me lead off. Hoping, I suppose, for a lead-off walk. It happens sometimes. My own idea was that it would be more honorable to go down swinging than to disgrace myself on the baselines, so I took a mighty cut at the very first pitch of the game, intending to strike out as soon as possible but trying to look good in the process.

As luck would have it, I connected solidly and sent a scorching roller that went right up the middle and got almost half way to the pitcher's mound. I started hobbling off toward first base, pulling my feet up one by one out of the dream-like sticky mud, knowing that I would be promptly thrown out. In fact, anybody would have been thrown out after an easy ground ball like that. Looking on ahead at the first baseman, I kept expecting to see and hear the ball smack into his mitt, ending my agony so I could head on off to the dugout. But no... he just stood there with his foot on the bag and his empty glove in the air, with a look of dismay sweeping over his countenance.

"Run, run!" I heard people shouting. So I kept on slogging away at my top speed of 3 MPH, and when I finally got to the base all safe and sound I turned around to see what had happened to the ball and what possibly could have been going on behind me.

There was some confusion and apparently arguing going on in front of the pitcher's mound, but strangely enough no one from our team seemed to be involved. As my friend Freddy described it to me later, both the pitcher and the catcher had run to pick up the ball I had hit, each one eager to become famous by scoring the first out of the game. It seems they reached the ball at the same time and both of them got their hands on it, but neither felt he could shirk his personal responsibility for supporting his team and making the play. So that's what the discussion was about as I stood there on the bag looking back. And they still had the ball.

Now what? Another infield hit will be embarrassing for me; any hit, in fact, unless it clears the fence. How am I going to get to second base? Me, a guy who can't run? It will take me a while, I thought. Maybe I'd better start now. Yes, that's what I'll do.

The pitcher had gone back up on the mound, and was examining the ball that he had finally retrieved from the catcher, apparently counting the stitches in each seam. So, while he was doing that I put my hands in my pockets and started walking down toward second base as though I were going to ask their shortstop to lend me a wad of chewing tobacco or teach me how to spit.

You may have noticed in life that it is sudden movements that attract attention. If you pass by a rattlesnake or an angry dog, the best thing to do is just act nonchalant and pay them no attention. I learned that from my Boy-Scout manual. So, I acted nonchalant, as though I knew that what I was doing was perfectly okay, and by the time the pitcher had figured out where to put his fingers on the seams and started his stretch, I was standing on the bag at second, with my hands still in my pockets, as though I had been there all morning. The pitcher looked over to first to check the runner before making his delivery. Alas, too late: no runner there. No walker either, for that matter.

That pitcher wasn't too happy when he realized I had fooled him and taken second behind his back, so to speak. In fact, he was madder than hell. So mad that he walked the next batter on four straight balls. Heck, I thought. All my clever base-stealing for nothing.

But now my fears returned; once again I had to hope against my own team; no hits, please, unless it is a home run. Oh, I thought, if only we had a pinch runner, like the big leagues have! Well, we don't. And those Wildcats weren't going to let me walk to third this time, that's for sure. Or were they?

Their pitcher still had not cooled off from his double blows of the ball-struggle with the catcher and my walking steal from first to second. You could see he was still mad just by looking at the back of his head. Anyway, this time he got the count to one and two, and wasn't going to give the batter anything good at that point. So he gave him a high fastball inside, but a little more inside that he intended. The batter turned away, but the ball caught him behind the left shoulder in a glancing blow.

Bases loaded. Now I'm on third with no outs. This is going to be most embarrassing. Horror of horrors, I'm in a position to score the first run, and I know I can't do it. In case you forgot, because of an old affliction, I CAN'T RUN. How I got this far was only by a series of freakish miracles. My best accomplishment of the day was doubtless my quiet steal of second base, and I thought how nice life would be if only I could have died there of a heart attack or something, and gone down in history as a devoted and outstanding member of my class's sixtieth reunion baseball team. But no, I had to live on, doubtlessly destined to face the impending disgrace that was to be my fate.

At least, thought I, as long as I am alive I should try to make life as miserable as possible for my nemesis, the opposing pitcher. When he took his stretch and looked over to me at third before his delivery, I could tell by his eyebrows that he still didn't like me very much. Then I did a silly thing. I stuck my hands in my pockets and stuck my tongue out at him, and turned to face home plate as though I were going to take another sixty-foot walk. Although I was only eighteen inches off the bag, a distance that even I could handle in an emergency, he whirled and made as if to fire to the third-baseman.

Oh oh.

But he had already started his motion toward the plate before I distracted him.

BALK!

I walked on home, but in order to show respect to the opposing team and to high-five my teammates, I took my hands out of my pockets.

I had scored the winning run. It's the only time I have ever won anything in my life. And now, when I dream about running through a sticky marsh, I don't dream just about TRYING to run, but dream about SCORING runs.

THE END

Happy Thanksgiving

I am a company commander, out here in the boonies where we have been stuck for eight months. Infantry. Some battles, some wounded, some killed, lots of dirt, mud, heat, wet, cold, stink, mosquitoes, leeches, ticks, sores, aches, always on the go, patrols, alerts, keep moving, dragging on, tired, tired, tired. Tired of fighting, tired of the war, tired of this hell hole.

Can't let the troops know how tired I am. Or how hopeless I sometimes feel. Gotta keep their spirits up. When the spirit goes, the man goes. Here since March. Now it's November. Time to think of Thanksgiving. Try to think of something to tell the troops they should be thankful for. The opportunity to serve their country? Worn out. The college tuition the Army will help pay for when they get back to the States? Already used. The fact that they are still alive? That's something we can be thankful for. And our buddies. That's what we are really thankful for, thankful we have buddies. Of course, as Company Commander, I can't afford to let myself get too buddy-buddy with the troops. Could lead to a loss of discipline and respect.

One of my PFC's doesn't seem to have any buddies either. Kid from Alabama, named Joe Billy MacKenzie. It seems as though most of the kids I know from Alabama and places like that have two first names, usually in backwards order from what you would expect. I had a sergeant, Henry

61

John Campbell, from Tennessee, who was killed back in July. Joe Billy had enlisted, although most of the others in my company were drafted. He is pretty much a loner, doesn't talk a lot, keeps his rifle clean and tries to keep his boots shined -- a nearly impossible task out here. I often feel he is watching me, seeing what I do, and sometimes he just follows me around when he has free time.

Joe Billy came from a family of poor sharecroppers. I learned he had no parents and had lived with a deaf aunt who died when Joe Billy was 11 years old. He left the orphanage when he was 16 and tried to join the Army, but of course he was rejected -- too young. He never graduated from high school but began studying toward a GED while working in an auto garage, at first waxing cars then helping with paint and body work, jobs that didn't require much in the way of communication skills. Then he tried to join the Army again, and this time made it. I don't know whether he had to lie about his age to get in; I guess that happens on occasion, but I never investigated it in his case. Anyway, he must have had a pretty miserable childhood.

As I was saying, it was getting on to Thanksgiving. The best the mess sergeant and I could get from the battalion supply officer beyond our usual C rations and K rations and that sort of stuff was 144 miniature cans of potted turkey meat and forty pounds of flour that hadn't gone moldy quite yet, and twelve cases of O'Doul's beer, non-alcoholic. Now, I like a can of beer as much as the next man, but I had no desire whatsoever to get the real thing for the troops, even if I could have done so -- too dangerous with the enemy lurking about, five or ten miles away, or sometimes five or ten yards away.

62

Fortunately we had a couple of men who liked to sing, and, I thought, if I could get them to lead some singing, the boys might forget how pathetic this Thanksgiving was. So after we finished eating the miserable turkey pâté on toast, and downed most of the imitation beer, we started in singing some Thanksgiving songs, like "Now Thank We All Our God," and "We Gather Together," and even "Praise God from Whom All Blessings Flow."

I was proud of my men who took the feeble Thanksgiving effort in good spirits, some of them even with tears in their eyes. Then, just before I was ready to turn in for the evening, PFC Joe Billy MacKenzie came up to me, saluted, and said, "Sir?"

"Yes," I said, "what is it?"

"Sir, this has been the happiest Thanksgiving I've ever had."

THE END

Louis Valois. Born 1423, Bourges, France, son of King Charles VII. Became King Louis XI in 1461. Died 1483.

Jacques Rocher Grimpé. Born 1443, Paris, France. Became Astrologer to the King in 1466 when 23 years old. Was 39 years old when Louis XI died in 1483.

The Astrologer and the King

Modern governments and presidents are not the first to have conducted national policy with the aid of astrologers or soothsayers. Here's an example from the 15th century. Jacques Rocher Grimpé was Court Astrologer to King Louis XI of France from 1466 until 1475, a period of almost ten years.

Yes, many kings in those days had astrologers, like Jacques. They also had prisons. Jacques knew a little about prisons -- he had been in the infamous Galliard Dungeon for a short while when he was younger, but now he was almost forty at the time of this story, and doing very well. So you can understand how startled and horrified and dismayed he was when one sunny day the County Sheriff and some other energetic authorities came pounding on his door to tell him he had to go back to prison.

"Back to prison? But why?" He babbled.

"Things have changed," came the reply. "We have a new King now."   -   -   -

Jacques had to think fast...

But first, let me tell you how he got into this awkward situation.

When he was very young, growing up in Paris, Jacques Grimpé decided he wanted to be a soothsayer or astrologer. As it turned out later, he was one of the happy few who are able to do what they want to do in life, and also make a living at it. Most people who just do what they want to do are either no-good bums or Bohemian artists, or else they are rich people living on inherited money, or nobility and royalty parasitically sponging off the labors and taxes of the poor downtrodden peasantry.

Even as a child and teenager Jacques was interested in people. He was interested in knowing what people were thinking and what they wanted. Everybody has thoughts and everybody wants something, even kings and generals and idiots and imbeciles. Jacques realized that you can learn a lot about people by listening to them and by just looking at them. Maybe he had a special talent for it, but he found he could tell a great deal from a person's face, from the wrinkles in his brow, the way he lifted his eyebrows, and the way he turned the corners of his lips or stroked his ear or chin with his fingers while he talked.

Jacques learned about people's habits and their inner fears and wants. As he grew, these things became more and more obvious to him. As Sherlock Holmes would say in later years, if a man had mud on his boots, he probably had been out walking in the mud. But some people can't even see that. Jacques began to realize that a lot of the forces that determine both the present and the future course of events in people's lives are revealed right there in their faces and body gestures where he could see them just by looking.

66

When he was still a teenager he could amaze his school friends by telling them about forthcoming examinations, for instance. He could look into the future and tell them that some exam questions were going to be harder than others. He told them they would have to get more answers right than wrong, in order to pass. He could predict that confident students were going to do better than nervous ones. He could also tell which of his friends were falling in love or breaking up with their girlfriends because he read it in their faces. Things like that were all quite clear to him, but the other students thought he was a genius, or a "psychic" or "soothsayer," as some of them said.

Yes, Jacques had an understanding of human nature in general and a sense of people's feelings and aspirations in particular. And, being a garrulous and gregarious fellow (if you know what those words mean), he was quite willing to talk about what he saw coming over the horizon. People then, as now, loved to believe things that smacked of the miraculous or the supernatural, so Jacques's friends and acquaintances generously credited him with having psychic powers and the ability to look into the future.

Jacques reasoned that if people could look up into the sky and see chariots and archers, and dogs and bears, then in their mind's eye they might also be able to see and believe almost anything he fed them. Any hooey at all. People in those days were no different from people today who will believe anything, from impossible supernatural religious miracles to alien UFO's. People and the human race change but little over the centuries.

At first, Jacques didn't know much about professional psychics and soothsayers, but when he thought about these things he realized that being a soothsayer might be an interesting and rewarding career.

Also his admiration and ambition lay upward on the social scale, toward the aristocracy, even in those days when social mobility was a rare and difficult process. And he was determined to get to wherever it was that he was destined to go, by using his brain instead of his muscles. Peasants used their muscles. Not Jacques.

Jacques became very popular by telling people what they already knew or believed, and they loved him for it. "If that's what they believe," figured Jacques, "why should I disabuse them of it? He made a hit every time, and thought, "maybe I can make something of this." That's when he decided once and for all to become a soothsayer. He visited his local library and other libraries in Paris, reading up on the history and techniques of soothsaying. He studied the psychics, the prophets, and the Gypsy fortune tellers through the ages, as well as the history of astrology, ultimately concluding that it was all a bunch of hooey. But he also knew it worked. "I can do that," he said to himself. "I'll bet I can give out hooey as well as any of them. All you have to do is keep a straight face, don't laugh, and tell them what they want to hear."

His opening began during his final year at school. Because he was the best math student in his class, he was chosen to give a talk on a subject he didn't know anything about. It was set up as a colloquium or symposium or something like that. He was supposed to discuss farming problems and the outlook for next fall's grape harvest and the quality of the wine that would be produced. Now, there were farmers and wine growers present at the gathering, and he could see worry and concern in their faces. So in his speech he told them they should be worried and concerned about the forthcoming crop. Of course in his talk he used a lot of big words and beautiful phrases, and put on a very knowledgeable tone to his voice. As it turned out, six months later, at harvest time, would you believe, the wine growers were worried and concerned, as always, but they gave Jacques credit for having special powers to predict the future.

As luck would have it, word of his perspicacious prowess even got to the King's Privy Council, who were still upset about some poor decisions the King had been making recently.

"You should get a new Court Astrologer," they told the King.

"Yes, but who?" said the King.

"We have one in mind," came the reply.

So that is how Jacques Rocher Grimpé, when he was only twenty-three years old, became Court Astrologer to King Louis XI. It was as easy as that. Needless to say, he was delighted with the appointment. He liked the job. A lot of influence and no responsibility. Ideal. And he liked the official term "Astrologer" better than "Soothsayer." It sounded more scientific. More high-tech.

Now, the King of France in those days, Louis XI, was by nature very unsure of himself. He suffered from a condition that today would be called an inferiority complex. He didn't become King until 1461 when he was already 38 years old and had almost given up on ever making it. Until then he had divided his time between quarreling with his father, King Charles VII, and chasing pretty women around Paris and across the countryside. As one of the local journalists later put it, he left few footprints, and those were mostly in ladies' bedrooms and boudoirs.

When he finally became King, Louis was still unsure of himself. He spent many hours praying on his knees, but was not sure whether prayers at the chapel or at the cathedral would be more effective, so he prayed in both places, alternating back and forth regularly. He covered himself with medals to give himself fortitude, and made the entire royal court, even Dukes and Counts who were his brothers and cousins, bow and scrape and call him "Sire." But still his insecurity dogged him. Like his father, Louis had to have many mistresses to try to convince himself of his manhood and satisfy his need for solace. And, in a further effort to adopt a macho image, he sent out his armies to subdue uppity peasants in Brittany and Burgundy or to confront various coalitions of English, Spanish, and Austrian forces threatening his security and peace of mind.

So he needed an astrologer to help him plan his military strategies and his taxation policies, and face many other decisions. What would the effect of this new tax law be? (Complaints.) How much will this project cost? (Too much.) Will people find out my secrets? (Yes, there are always leaks.) What will happen to my ratings with the populace if I let them know what I am doing? (Down. The more they know, the more your ratings will go down.)

Louis was never sure that his official decisions were the right ones. Or his unofficial decisions either, for that matter. Never sure which Colonel to promote to General, never sure which Chamber Maid to promote to Mistress of the Royal Bedchamber. (If you want to know which Colonels to promote, ask the Majors. If you want to know which Majors to promote, ask the Captains. If you want to know which Chambermaid to promote, ask the Stableboy.)

Things like that. So you can see why Louis needed a good Court Astrologer to rely upon. And when the new Astrologer, Jacques Rocher Grimpé, got installed, Louis consulted with him regularly, right from the start.

Now, Monsieur Jacques was careful never to tell the King directly what to do. For the most part he limited himself to fancy words and phrases that said what the King wanted to hear or already knew. If he was called upon to predict the result of this or that possible course of action, Jacques always made sure his predictions had plenty of ambiguity about them that he could fall back on if necessary. But the King thought he was a wise and useful fellow to have around.

71

"I never give advice, Sire. I only tell the truth," said Jacques.

For instance, since the King always fell in love with every beautiful woman that caught his eye, Jacques safely predicted that, if he fooled around with one particularly attractive and ambitions courtesan named Marguerite de Sassenage, he would promptly fall in love with her, (everybody did), and she would soon be bossing him around all over the place. Is that what he wanted? So, just as predicted, and not his intention at all, the King did fall in love with Marguerite. Now, the King had loved a lot of women in his time, but didn't much cherish the idea of being IN love, but there it was. Like people who like to drink too much wine but don't like the idea of BEING a drunk. He tried to hold Jacques responsible. Jacques could only say, "I told you so, Sire." But Marguerite gave Louis comfort and solace, as well as a couple of lovely illegitimate daughters, Jeanne and Marie. Although Marguerite was not able to see into the future as Jacques could, she still held King Louis in the palm of her hand, so to speak. Almost as the infamous Agnes Sorel had held Louis's father, Charles VII, in the palm of *her* hand. Anyway, Jacques's position was still secure.

Jacques the Astrologer and Louis the King were a perfect fit for each other. The King had what Jacques wanted. Jacques had what the King needed. And he did well in the job; all Jacques had to do was tell the King what he wanted to hear. And of course keep any predictions ambiguous.

In time, Jacques got a little bolder and was tempted to make a few more predictions. He learned that, if he were wrong, people would often forget by the time the event had come and gone, or else his predictions were ambiguous enough to let him off the hook, like the Greek oracles of old. If he were careful, he could make predictions that were right no matter what the outcome was. He even predicted that the price of salt, like the stock market, would fluctuate. Of course, it did.

Jacques may have gotten a little too sure of himself and perhaps began to feel he really did have some psychic powers to predict the future. He no longer just told the King what he knew the King wanted to hear. He began to give him something more -- some truths -- as he saw them. And as we all know, sometimes it is the truth that hurts. And it hurt the King.

Indeed, one day Jacques really did look into the future, although in this case almost anybody could have done so. But Jacques forgot one of his most important mantras, namely, "Tell them what they want to hear."

It so happened that at that time King Louis's forces were deployed along the eastern front, stemming the threat of aggressive Austrian terrorists. Jacques predicted the King's army would lose the battle. It was all so very clear: outnumbered forces, poor morale, bad positions, unfavorable wind and weather. Even Dr. Watson could have seen the debacle coming. Jacques knew that the King's army, badly situated and commanded by a nobleman general who drank too much and was distracted by his wife's exorbitant spending habits, was doomed to defeat. And he said so.

73

But that was not what the King wanted to hear.

Four days later King Louis's forces suffered a disastrous defeat as predicted. The angry King had Jacques brought into his throne room, on to the carpet, as it were, and lashed out at him.

"YOU did it! It's YOUR fault! You were the cause of the defeat of my army at Liège!" screamed the King.

"I'm just the messenger, Sire. I bring you messages from the Gods and the Stars who, like yourself, are all powerful and control the universe."

The King was furious, but what to do?

"Look what you did! You made my men die in battle!"

"With all due respect, Sire, I have no power whatsoever to alter the course of events. My meager abilities are limited to seeing what is happening and what will happen."

"I don't believe you," bellowed the King. You are a Witch! Son-of-a-Bitch Witch! Wizard! Warlock... whatever it is... Anyway, you're a Scoundrel...! Guards!

"I'll have you thrown into prison! In this day of infamy, 2,900 of my troops are dead at the hands of those terrorist Austrians, plus my best General and three mediocre Colonels. Gone! You are so smart, and know so much about other people and other people's lives, now tell me, how long do you think YOU are going to live, you rascal?"

74

"Sire," said Jacques serenely, knitting his brows in pensive fashion and looking off into his crystal ball beyond the horizon, "I shall die exactly one week before you die, Sire. Seven days before you."

"You are just saying that."

"Oh, yes, Sire. I am just saying that. Because it's true. You will see, Sire, that I am right. Or rather, France will see that I am right, because you will be dead and gone."

"I don't believe you! You are a scoundrel and deserve to die."

"Very well, Sire. Anything you say."

"Off with him," screamed the King in fury. "Put him in the Galliard Dungeon."

So that was that.

But the King didn't sleep very well that night. The next morning he sent instructions to the Galliard Prison to give the new prisoner the best non-smoking dungeon room available, and to make sure he stayed warm and dry, and to give him the best choices on the prison menu, including extra helpings of healthful fruit and vegetables, like orange juice and spinach and broccoli -- things with plenty of vitamin C and vitamin A. In the past, many inmates had died at the Galliard of vitamin deficiency and colds and flu caused by bad diet and drafty corridors.

75

Of course, the King didn't want to believe the dire prediction of his own death so closely following the death of this scoundrel. But why take the chance? The King realized it would be best to keep Jacques Rocher Grimpé alive. Yes. No point in taking unnecessary chances. I don't really want him to die, do I? What good would that do? Maybe -- just maybe -- he is right. Better to keep him healthy. But the infamous Galliard did not have a reputation for the longevity of its residents, even those receiving special treatment. Prison life is not healthy -- not healthful either.

So, although he was still quite vexed with this astrologer, just to be safe Louis called his Minister of Special Interior Operations and together they decided what they had to do to assure that the astrologer would live a long long life.

Then they wisely had Jacques taken out of the Galliard Prison and placed under minimum security house arrest in a pleasant, medium-sized chateau outside the town of Rouen. He was given servants to take care of him, and an entry permit to the Royal Forest for free firewood to keep him warm in wintertime. Don't want him dying of a chill. Some people did in those days, you know. And they didn't have Aleve and Vicks Cough Syrup to temper the dark agony of imminent death.

The chateau had only a very small moat and a very small drawbridge, just big enough to keep out the riff-raff, but the household was provided with a full staff including cook, butler, stable-boy, gardener, and two French maids. There was a little chapel right in the chateau where Jacques

76

could have conveniently prayed had he ever wanted to, or even just given thanks. The King's instructions to the Provincial Governor and the County Sheriff were to spare no expense in keeping Sir Jacques healthy and happy. Especially healthy. He would also be wealthy and of course was already wise enough.

You can imagine how delighted Jacques was with his change of fortune. He now had reached the heights of his youthful aspirations. Had it made. Life was A-okay. Life was beautiful. He was practically nobility, living in his own chateau. Aristocracy, anyway. There is a fine line between aristocracy and nobility. You have to be an insider to see the difference, and Jacques was almost an insider himself now.

Jacques found it easy to get accustomed to the soft life. He was especially delighted to find he had a full Social Security pension and a lifetime healthcare plan, all paid for by the Government, or taxpayers, if you will. Further happiness and solace came from the two French maids, especially the Upstairs Maid, a young girl of considerable competence. You could see that she had outstanding talents even when she was bending over to dust the furniture or sweep the floor.

Jacques joined the local hunt club, took violin lessons and art lessons, and got his chateau on the annual Homes Tour sponsored by the Historic Normandy Foundation, a local tradition and institution, although most of those who came through on the tours were descendants of Germanic invaders from the North, who did not understand all of the peculiar institutions in the countries to their southern borders. Jacques was in Seventh Heaven. Who said soothsaying doesn't pay? He had it all.

For a while. For a number of years.

Then one day the County Sheriff came back to Jacques's place bringing along an emissary of the King, none other than Louis's old Minister of Special Interior Operations, with the news that Jacques had to vacate the chateau and go back to the Galliard Dungeon.

"But why? What's up, Doc? -- if you will excuse the expression," asked Jacques in dismay.

"I'm afraid the jig is up, Sir, if you will excuse the expression. We seem to have reached the limit of your cleverness. You know King Louis XI is dead? We have a new King now, Louis XII."

"I have heard some rumors to that effect."

"The new King doesn't feel bound or obligated by policies and arrangements made by the previous administration. And we don't think our poor departed King Louis XI would be happy in his grave if he knew you were living on in luxury like this after he had died and you were supposed to have predeceased him. So I am afraid it's back to the Galliard Prison with you... Sir."

"Just a minute," said Jacques, knitting his brow slightly and doing some fast thinking. Then he took on a very serious countenance and continued:

"I am terribly sorry. I have an apology to make. I meant to tell you: When I didn't die last month and the king did, I knew something was wrong. I opened my eyes and I went back to read the stars again. I soon realized my mistake regarding what they were saying. In actual fact the stars were saying that I will die one week before King Louis XII dies. I'm not very good at math, and I get my numbers mixed up sometimes. Ex Eye looks a lot like Ex Eye Eye. There's only an iota of difference. I'm awfully sorry about that. Do tell the King, for me, won't you?"

THE END

You'll Love It

They say that opposites attract. I won't deny it, but...
maybe yes and maybe no. You certainly see a lot of odd
couples when you look around you. Sometimes you see
couples that seem beautifully suited to each other, who
have been married for a number of years and have even
begun to look like each other, as well as look like their
dogs. And then sometimes you see couples that you cannot
imagine could ever have gotten together. You may know
two or three couples like that whom you would like to
rearrange, pair them up differently so that they would make
better matches.

Schools and colleges are one of the great mixing pots, if
not melting pots, for people of different natures and
different backgrounds. I am now thinking of one particular
couple who met each other when they were students at City
College. Beth Davidson was a city girl through and
through; I don't think she had ever been farther east than
Riverhead or farther west than Scranton. Felipe Campbell
was a country boy who grew up on a little ranch his father
owned near the Caribbean Coast of Central America.
Maybe the different backgrounds and experiences of these
two is what made them initially interesting to each other.

They could talk about things they had known and done
without ever being boring. They found each other
endlessly fascinating, full of new insights and tales of

81

strange events and exciting activities they had known. Felipe was intrigued as he learned about the complicated inner workings of the big city through Beth's eyes. At the same time, he charmed her with his stories and images of life growing up on the western shores of the Caribbean Sea, the warm sunshine, the quiet beaches, and healthful outdoor activities like swimming and surfing and boating and fishing that he had known as a boy. "You would love it," he would say, thinking of one particular place, as he looked deeply into her eyes and into her heart. "The food is superb -- endless quantities of fresh fish, shrimp, and lobster, and piles of tropical fruit like pineapple, papaya, and bananas and cocoanuts, plus oranges and watermelons and anything else. And it's all quiet and secluded," he repeated. "You'll love it," he insisted.

And Beth told Felipe some things she knew about the City, the most exciting place in the world, she claimed. The throb of life was everywhere; the vitality of humanity pervaded the atmosphere. Art and culture surrounded one on every hand, with theaters and concert halls and libraries and art galleries and discothèques nearby whenever you might want them. All you needed was money and you could do anything -- buy anything, eat anything, wear anything -- in New York that you could do or find anywhere else in the world. "We have South American restaurants and tropical fruit right here in New York, you know," said Beth, not speaking defensively but nevertheless rather proudly.

Meanwhile, Felipe was adapting rapidly to his new urban surroundings. He already had his favorite restaurants and bars; he was enchanted by the ice skating at Rockefeller Center (which he tried, unsuccessfully), and he found the evening view from the top of the Empire State Building "out of this world."

Felipe was majoring in International Finance, and after his Junior Year he got a position as a Summer Intern in a New York investment firm. He was almost becoming a New Yorker.

Beth was an English major. She had had several poems published in the school paper, and one published in a national magazine, but her ambition was to write a great novel. "I will someday," she thought.

So these young people spent the final two years of their time in college charming each other while telling about their different views and experiences. In so doing, they fell in love and decided to marry as soon as possible after graduation. It was as simple as that.

For a honeymoon, Felipe planned to show Beth his country, and in particular a little Caribbean paradise on a tropical island he knew about. He would briefly introduce her to his family and friends on the mainland, but for most of their visit he had reserved accommodations at a tiny hotel, or "Bed and Breakfast" as it was called, on a little island just off the coast.

"It's quiet and secluded," Felipe explained.

So, that's what they did. They got married as soon as they graduated, and headed south, visited Felipe's parents, and then went on to Felipe's island paradise.

Sadly, though, when they got to the little isolated island with its beaches and seafood, it wasn't nearly so exciting to Felipe as his childhood memories had pictured it. After New York, he soon found himself getting bored.

"Beach and seafood -- seafood and beach," he repeated. "I can't imagine why I thought it was so great. I'm sorry I brought you out here."

"Oh, no," said Beth. "I love it." I love the deserted beach and the quiet, with just the sound of the ocean breakers at night. And I love the fresh leafy aromas from the tropical foliage, the row of hibiscus and the old almond tree trunks covered with wild orchids on the path to our little lodging, and the little bridge over the lovely hidden pond with its still, black waters, stained dark by the mangroves. And, something you didn't mention, the delightful friendliness of the people who live here. I think I could live here forever."

"That's ridiculous," said Felipe. "You will turn into a vegetable if we stay much longer. I'm making reservations for us to go back to New York on Monday."

"What are you saying? I'm perfectly happy here; I don't want to leave. I'm staying, even if it means staying alone."

"You're crazy," Felipe said, the first time he had ever raised his voice to his young bride. "What would you do here alone?"

"I want to write a book -- here, where it's quiet."

"All this quiet is getting on my nerves. We're going back to New York."

"Well, I'm not," she said. "I have an 800-page novel in mind, and I'm going to write it right here. It's about a girl who lost her bikini on the beach. It's called, BIKINI ON THE BEACH."

"Well, I'm going back to New York," insisted Felipe. "They have offered me a job at the firm where I was working last summer, and I plan to take it while I can. We may have to put off having a family for a while."

"Yes, I guess we may. That is very possible."

"Maybe I'll come back next year and see if you are still here."

"I'll be here."

"What on earth ever gave you this crazy idea, anyway?

"You did. You said I would love it here... and... I love it here."

THE END

The Millionaire

or

How to Make a Million in the Small Boat Building Business

A classmate of mine from college, named Arthur Hamilton, loved boats more than anything else. Maybe even more than women. I remember that in school he was always drawing pictures of boats on the back covers of his notebooks, or talking about the America's Cup Race, or telling us about somebody that had sailed around the world, like Joshua Slocum or Robin Knox Johnston. I never knew Arthur very well back then; he was on the sailing team, whereas my main interests were horses and electronics -- besides women, of course. As a student Arthur was rather quiet, and certainly was not the sort of person you expected to become a mover or a shaker or a big CEO. After graduation I never saw him again. Not for thirty years.

I spent most of my adult life overseas. I worked for a company that had major contracts with a big US government agency to design, construct, install, and maintain various types of electronic surveillance equipment all over the world. I liked my work, but it was demanding and never seemed to give me the free week in May or June I needed to toddle back to the old campus for fun and games.

Finally, in 1998, at our thirtieth class reunion, I saw Arthur at one of the dinner parties. My memory of him was at best very vague, and without seeing his name-tag I never would have recognized him. This was only the first class reunion I had ever attended, and to be honest, almost half of the guys there, that I had known before, I wouldn't have recognized. It made me wonder how much I had changed too. At gatherings like that you always feel that it is the others who have changed, not you.

"You're the fellow who used to love boats so much, aren't you?" I opened the conversation.

"Sure," he replied. "Still do, although I am not into boats as a career anymore."

"Boats were your career? Were you in the Merchant Marine, or maybe the Navy?" I asked.

"Oh, I was only in the Navy for five years during the Vietnam War. When I say boats, I mean sailboats, from fifteen feet to fifty."

We chatted on, much to my enjoyment, mostly talking about boats, which was a subject I too loved. Arthur had been retired for five years, and had a forty-eight-foot English style sloop that he and Uffa Fox had jointly designed. He owned a piece of land and a cottage in the Bahamas, where he was living the life of a millionaire.

Somehow Arthur seemed to radiate an air of prosperity. For the special occasion he was wearing a beautifully tailored suit, Italian moccasins, and a nice suntan, although it was still early in the season. And impeccable table manners, not like most sailors.

Then he went on and told me some more of his story. Seemingly without much ambition after college and his time in the Navy, he went into the business of boat building. He bought a piece of land in the southwest corner of Cape Cod Bay, about halfway between Plymouth and Sandwich, in an area that, at the time, was not too heavily frequented by tourists, who preferred the warmer water and beaches on the south shore of Cape Cod or The Islands. He built more than 180 boats in the ensuing 25 years, most of them in the 25-35 foot range, but a few 40- and 50-footers as well. All wooden boats, typically oak frames with mahogany or larch planking and decks. Over 20 of his boats had sailed in the Newport-Bermuda races, and four or five of them had sailed around the world.

"You must have done pretty well building boats, then, to have retired as a millionaire."

"No, the business wasn't always so good. Wasn't bad at first, but then people started drifting away from the classic wooden boats into these horrible IOR fiberglass Clorox bottles. I was barely breaking even, and then, for the last two years in the business, I was losing about one or two thousand on every boat I sold."

"But I don't understand."

"You mean, how could I have I retired as a millionaire?"

"Well, yes, something like that."

"I sold my business."

"But who would buy it if it wasn't making any money?"

"Oh, it was forty-seven acres of waterfront property. During my years in boat-building the value of the land went up and up and, when I sold it, it was worth over $30,000 an acre. Sort of sad, but true. They have some beautiful condos there now. You ought to see them. Actually, though, my wife and I like Eleuthera in the Bahamas better."

"Oh."

THE END

Harmony

CONFLICT RESOLUTION: A wide range of methods of addressing sources of conflict, whether at the inter-personal level or between states, and of finding means of resolving a given conflict or of continuing it in less destructive forms than, say, armed conflict. It may include non-violent methods.

Non-violent methods may also be used by a party to a conflict as a means of pursuing its goals on the grounds that such means are more likely than armed struggle to lead to a resolution of the conflict.

- Civil Resistance and Power Politics, Oxford University Press, 2009

* * *

I can remember my grandfather always liked to sing. He used to come and visit us sometimes when I was a child, and would often sing to himself. One of his favorite songs was called HARMONY; It was written by Johnny Mercer; at least the lyrics were. (I don't know of any songs that Johnny Mercer actually wrote himself. He wrote lyrics. He also sang some of them -- in his way.)

What I remember best was the last part of one stanza that ended like this:

Would Rigoletto sound the same
With no quartet..?
It's Harmony,
You bet !

I liked that.

Anyway, my grandfather didn't stop with the song, but used to tell us kids that harmony was one of the most important things in the world. Lack of harmony was what caused wars, and caused the gap between rich and poor, and racial unrest, and riots like the ones we had in Detroit and Washington in the sixties, as well as marital problems and divorce, divisions and arguments within businesses and corporations, bankruptcies and breakups of companies, and loss of jobs for hundreds of people. Why couldn't there be more harmony in the world of national affairs and human affairs, he used to say. We all should turn a deaf ear toward people's complaints and bickerings. Harmony is what we need in this world.

I was fifteen and a sophomore in high school when my grandfather died. I felt a great loss, but the memory of his singing and his theories on the importance of harmony and the idea of turning a deaf ear toward people screaming at you stayed with me for many years.

In college I majored in physics because it seemed easy to me, but even before I graduated I realized I didn't want to pursue physics as a career. I liked the theories and the math, but I didn't care for the lab work. What I really didn't like was the constant bickering that went on in the Physics Department, especially in the laboratory, where the other students would quarrel and scream at one another when they thought someone was plagiarizing from their experiments or taking too much time using the new high-speed centrifuge or the old spectroscope. That sort of thing.

There was always some bone of contention, even among the faculty. We had three physics professors and they used to have seminars to present and discuss their theories. They would form a panel, but then their presentations usually degenerated into noisy arguments among themselves and vituperative accusations about who was right and who was wrong, or whose idea it was. I really didn't like my department, but I stuck it out and finished college and got my degree and got out of there as soon as possible. So, upon graduation I didn't have any definite plans for my future. No plans at all, in fact.

My father had served in the Army for a short while during Vietnam, but had gotten out soon after the war. I was never very close to my father -- not like my grandfather -- but I did respect him and even admired him. So, because I had nothing in mind when I graduated, he suggested that a hitch in the military wouldn't do me any harm, and I signed up. And because I now had a physics degree and the Army needed physicists, I was able to get a direct commission as a Second Lieutenant, AUS, thinking I would go to Aberdeen or Redstone. However, with its infallible inscrutable logic, the Army assigned me to the bureau with responsibility for personnel management and general administration.

I was given an exciting sounding job, with the title of Assistant Personnel Systems Management Officer, in the Division of Personnel Systems Management. According to the TO&E, I had responsibilities for personnel requisitioning, reassignments, re-enlistments, promotions, casualty reporting, eliminations, and awards and decoration,. My job also included the management of activities of personnel operational elements providing specific support to organizations, headquarters, and individuals. And there was even more, although of course I wasn't the only one doing this. There were other Second Lieutenants and First Lieutenants and even some Captains doing it too, and of course the Adjutant General himself, in charge of it all.

There were normally a lot of things going on, and, while it was not quite a constant can of worms, there was often excitement and always confusion. Even though I was only an Assistant, what my day-to-day job boiled down to was to serve as an expert in personnel resources and human relations. I was supposed to provide recommendations for the development of common understanding and cooperation between vastly different types of people and units with vastly different objectives for themselves and their vested interests in their particular corners of their particular organizational divisions. Even as a Second Lieutenant I was responsible for making initial recommendations for officer assignments and transfers of Majors, Colonels, and even Generals. I suppose they figured that, if I had been a Colonel myself, I wouldn't have been objective. Amazing.

The people involved never agreed on my recommendations -- neither the losing organization, nor the gaining organization, nor the individual or individuals involved. Perhaps, if you want to get people to agree, you should give them a subject none of them know anything about. But everybody is a personnel expert, especially if the case at hand involves him personally.

I went on for some months making intensive efforts to understand the pros and cons in every case of conflict or difference of opinion between quarreling sections and interests, and in due course I found my own best avenue for conflict resolution. It was to let all interested parties have their say. Encourage them to talk it through and encourage them to give even more comments and testimony than they had intended. If they become tired and weary with the drawn-out process, so much the better. Sometimes if you draw out a process long enough the problem will disappear of its own accord, or will be OBE, as they say (Overtaken By Events), or all the people involved will forget what the problem was. Otherwise you quietly summarize your own initial recommendations, and you present a succinct proposal for the Commanding General to sign, preferably on one of his busiest days just before quitting time.

I was in the Army during the Reagan/Bush years at the time of our invasions of Granada and Panama, operations that I am glad to say I was not personally responsible for. Neither I, nor any of the others in my division, who were supposed to be experts in developing "common understanding and cooperation," were consulted or even apprised regarding these ventures. There was no harmony between the planners and the do-ers. Frankly, I believe we should focus more on our own problems here at home in the United States and not try to intervene with our military in foreign countries that we are not in harmony with or whose leaders and policies we don't happen to approve of. That is not our business. It didn't work in Vietnam, and I wasn't proud of our Panama incursion. That is when I decided to quit the Army and end all the fun I had been having.

But then, with my outstanding military record and experience in human resources management and personnel relations, I promptly found another cushy job back home in my State Government, working in the Office of the State Administrative Officer.

My new job was Personnel Relations Analyst, a staff position, and without authority for hiring or firing, and consequently without much real responsibility -- just analysis and recommendations. However the work looked easy and even interesting, and was right up my alley, considering my experiences with human resources in the Military.

After a few months working in the State House, I was given the task of examining and reporting on the degree of cooperation among the sections and individuals within various organizations and agencies throughout the state. I was to prepare analyses and recommendations with a view toward improving morale and eliminating the waste of time and money caused by conflicts of interest and methods, and personnel differences and altercations. Almost what I had been doing in the Army.

My first investigations were directed to the various law-enforcement entities within our state; after that into the hospitals and health care systems, and then on into the Department of Transportation and even the Department of Health and Environmental Control. All of those are long stories unto themselves, all terribly involved, amazingly full of conflicts and people pulling in different directions and screaming at each other and at their underlings and even at their bosses. My general technique was essentially the same as the one I had developed in the Army, namely let all parties to a conflict write memos and speak on and on, putting forth their views. I would of course give the appearance of sympathetically paying strict attention. Let them talk and scream at each other until they are tired of it, and then make the recommendation you were going to make in the first place.

My most recent assignment has been with the Education Department, and it has taken me through most of the institutions of higher learning in the state. Here the lack of cooperation, the lack of harmony, has been as evident as it always was everywhere else I ever worked. People always bickering and yelling at each other. The supervisors and department heads consistently complained to me of the frustration and trauma they were suffering because the people they were responsible for, or responsible to, were constantly screaming at them from all sides.

And that's the way it was when I first got to McKenzie College, a small branch of the State University way upstate. The Math Department didn't like the Chemistry Department using its computers because they left a bad odor. The Spanish Department didn't like the noise coming through the walls from the English Department because it upset their train of thought. And everybody wanted more space.

The new young French teacher wanted to teach modern slang which the older established teacher resisted as degrading and insufficiently literary. And they argued and yelled at each other so that all the school could hear them, even though they were screaming in French. Of course no one could understand them, but, even irate as they were, they made it clear to everyone that they had differences of opinion. The head of the Department of Foreign Languages was at her wits end; she was frustrated by their endless arguing, and both sides attacked her for trying to take a middle ground.

And the athletic coaches – even the coaches, mind you -- would loudly argue about who was to get some outstanding freshman athlete; the football coach wanted him on the football team, and the soccer coach wanted him on the soccer squad, and the vociferous vituperation was driving the Athletic Director bonkers. The basketball coach and the baseball coach could not even decide when Spring Training for baseball should begin; did it have to wait until the basketball season had been completed, or could it overlap? They brought more headaches to the Athletic Director and the School Principal. People all over McKenzie College always seemed to be at odds with one another, everywhere, screaming and yelling throughout the school. There was very little peace and no harmony whatsoever.

Except for one department, the Music Department.

Now in the music departments of other schools I had visited, I had seen great lack of harmony -- not just discord but syncopated cacophony, as intense and bitter as the internecine wars in any other department. Perhaps even more
so, for it may be that artistic people are most ready to reveal their testy inner nature when their opinions are questioned or given less respect than is their due. The strings wanted practice time away from the piano and horns. The woodwinds didn't like the program selections. The drums were two slow. The orchestra had no oboe, so the clarinets

had to set the pitch, and various ambitious clarinet players would vie for the honor. These were the sorts of complaints and raucous bickerings assailing the ears of the music directors in all the other schools I had visited, driving them almost out of their minds.

But not McKenzie College, where the Music Director was the remarkable Miss Angelina Markowitz. The Music Department was very active, comprising several divisions, called "activities." There was the band, the chamber orchestra, the jazz ensemble, the glee club, the McKenzie Chorale, and one or two other irregular groups of school musicians. There was enough material here for as many conflicts and differences of opinion as I had seen anywhere, but in the reports from the Music Director to the Head of School it never appeared that she had heard of any problems or conflicts within the Music Department.

Miss Markowicz oversaw all these activities with quiet authority and unruffled composure. She never complained when people hollered at her. She was never upset by the cacophonies that drove other people up the wall. The cellos played next to the violas without annoying her. The drums pounded away without ever bothering Angelina. She let the clarinets have their way. Angelina was an angel. She smiled when the horns played with the flutes and the violas played with the bassoons.

I was impressed. Indeed, amazed. Everything in harmony. She seemed perfectly happy with the classical music, the chamber music, the jazz and the swing, the rock and rap, the full orchestra and solo performances. Always content, always satisfied. If people ever screamed at her she never let it bother her.

How could Miss Markowitz remain so calm and collected in such a position? I had never known anything like it. I was so taken by the gentle equanimity of this lovely music director that I had to make a comment to the Head of School.

"Your music director is a most unusual person," I said, filled as I was with admiration. "She is so calm and she always seems to maintain such a gentle equanimity. She never lets any dissention or discord within the orchestra and the music groups bother her. I don't know how she does it."

The principal turned and said simply,

"Miss Markowitz? Oh, she's deaf."

THE END

100

Disappointment

If you can't rely on your family, your own children, who can you rely on? I always wanted what was best for my two boys when dey was growing up. I sent dem to the best schools so dey could get the education I never got myself. When dey finished school I arranged to bring them into the family business and give them jobs of reasonable importance -- you know, with responsibilities. At least I was able to get my youngest son, Georgio, to come into a place in the company that I made for him.

My oldest, my first-born, Enrico, wouldn't take the job that I had for him. He wanted to go out on his own, he said. Wanted to prove that he didn't have to rely on his inheritance or his father to make good in the world. Noble ambition, but stupid strategy. I guess I tried to put a little pressure on him. Maybe I pushed him too hard toward where I wanted him to go, which was into the family business. Anyway, it didn't work. He always had the most independent nature of anyone in the family, and there wasn't anything I could do about it. He resisted the efforts that I was making for his own good; he had to be himself, be his own man.

Well, I had to do that too, when I was his age, but I never went so far as to ignore my family or completely let them down like that. Now I was running the business that my father and grandfather started right after World War II.

101

Besides Georgio, I had a couple of cousins working for me and about thirty other people, but that's not like having your oldest son in the business where he could grow up getting to know all about how it works and finally take over the operation when I am old. Georgio's heart was in the right place, and I loved him for sticking with me in the business, but Enrico is the smart one, and he is the one I wanted some day to be the top boss.

I guess Enrico couldn't stand my pressuring him. Anyway, he left town and I didn' see him at all for some years. He would write sometimes, nice little notes with his beautiful prep-school handwriting, not saying much, just saying he was well and doin' what he wanted to do, and hoping me and Momma and Georgio were all right. But he didn't say nothin' about what he was doin' or who his friends were, and I was gettin' worried that he might have fallen in with the wrong kind of people. Some kids do, you know.

Meanwhile the business was doin' good. We was in the export-import business. The trade. All right, so we were tradesmen. We ain't so hi-falutin' that we have to look down on anybody dat's engaged in the trades, like some of them Park Avenue snobs does. They got their money from their grandfathers who got it by screwing poor people like my grandfather, who didn' have nuttin' when he came here from Sicily after World War I. I make mine by working for it, by working deals and using my brain. Things musta really been bad in the old country to make my grandfather wanna leave it. I was back there for two weeks last year, and let me tell you, Sicily is really beautiful. It's even more beautiful than Brooklyn. And the wine is better and cheaper too, as well as some other things I know about and sometimes import to the USA.

The way you hafta make money in this society -- any real money -- is by buying and selling: buy low and sell high, like the big boys on Wall Street will tell you. Look at Walmart and CVS Pharmacy. They don't make nuttin' really -- no stuff, I mean -- but they do make money. They buy and they sell. Their territory is all over the USA, and my territory is just New York City. That's big enough for me. I'm not greedy. I keep an honest relation with my suppliers and distributors and don' tolerate no foolishness. Business is business, and you gotta keep your nose clean and watch out where you stick it. Once or twice I stuck my nose where I hadn't should of stuck it, and got it burnt.

So, like I was sayin', Enrico went off and I didn't know where he was. The Company had been doin' real good, and I was sorry Enrico didn't have his rightful place in it. He could of been makin' good dough here with me, and taking some responsibility in the family corporation, the business that he and Georgio should be taking over some day. I was worried about him -- no idea of where he was now or what he was doin', and I was really afraid that he had fallen in with some bad types. There are a lot of people in this world that you wouldn't want to associate with, and some of them are right here in New York. Quite a few, in fact. How could I have let him wander off from the family like that? What did I do wrong? Families need to stick together. What could he have gotten into? All sorts of terrible possibilities entered my mind.

Then something happened and there were some problems. It was all over the newspapers, the damn scandal sheets.

A coupla months after that I saw Enrico again, the first time in over four years, and I had to look at him through the bars at the county jail. My Enrico. My oldest son, named for his great-grandfather, Enrico Calamari, one of the most important men in Palermo before the bully boys took control of Sicily in the twenties.

I thought we would have a lot to tell each other. We didn't. All I could think of to say, seeing him there through the bars, was, "I'm disappointed in you, *figlio mio.* You've let me down. I never expected this."

His rather rude response was, "Yeah, I know... Well, I guess that's tough, Pop." He used to call me "Poppa." Now I was just "Pop."

And with that he turned away and put his policeman's cap back on his head and went on off down the corridor.

THE END

Remember the Brain

I am an M.D. research neurologist and an intern at the Stanford Medical School Hospital, Stanford California. I earned my M.S. at Georgetown University, in biochemistry. I'll bet you didn't know you could get an M.S. in Bio-Chem from Georgetown -- amid the diplomats and cookie pushers -- but you can.

A few years ago I read an account of a surprising scientific study that stimulated my interest in the remarkable abilities possessed by some of the holy men of Tibet. The study detailed the results of an inquiry into allegations of unusual powers of certain Tibetan monks, called Bonzes, and was conducted by a group comprising several doctors from the Harvard School of Medicine plus a few neuro-scientists and other top US scholars. Articles on this subject subsequently appeared in several issues of the Harvard University Gazette, including the issues of April 18, 2002 and December 18, 2008. The study group that was the subject of the articles was led by Dr. Herbert Benson, Associate Professor on the faculty at the Harvard Medical School. So it was a serious undertaking -- nothing fake about it.

After gaining permission from the Dalai Lama himself during his visit to the United States back in 1979, Benson and his group set out to prove, or disprove, the veracity of tales about some of the reclusive Tibetan Bonzes, who were said to be able, by thought, meditation, or intensive

105

concentration, to significantly influence their "involuntary" body functions. Besides breathing rates, the modification of which should appear fairly simple and obvious, some Bonzes were able to raise or lower their rate of heart beat and their blood pressure significantly, apparently just by intensely thinking about it, that is, by concentration and meditation. In this manner they could also raise or lower their body temperature by as much as eight or ten degrees. The Harvard Gazette reported that:

> In a room at 40 degrees F with a yoga technique known as G-Tum-mo (deep meditation), Tibetan monks, draped with wet sheets at 49 degrees, dried them in an hour by raising their body temperature. Benson called it the relaxation technique. He studied G-Tum-mo for 20 years.

The bonzes were also reportedly able to bring their heart beat down to the low thirties or even the twenties, almost to a state of hibernation. Benson and his scientific team of inquiry were astounded to find that these reports were absolutely true. It was no hoax. Bonzes clearly had unusual mental powers. In short, the monks were able to expand the area of the brain responsible for voluntary control, until it encroached upon the brain area normally responsible solely for the control of various involuntary functions.

As a young child, I detested fairy tales and make-believe stories of talking animals and flying children -- things like that. I was literal. I wanted to know what was real. I was mechanically minded and physically minded. Even when I was six years old I used to wonder what was happening inside my head when I had various different thoughts, whether I was playing soldiers, or flying gliders, or trying to add and subtract. I "knew" that there were particles in my brain that were doing different things, depending on what I was thinking. There had to be. I knew for certain that there were tiny bits and pieces in there that were somehow arranging themselves in different ways according to what I was wondering about or visualizing at the moment.

I instinctively knew brain activity was physical. And I knew that everything that happened around me must affect me and my brain in some way. In later years I learned this was also the view of the rather discredited French philosopher Henri Bergson, who had held similar views around the turn of the last century. I felt that just being aware of the presence or existence of any other person or thing must somehow have its tiny effect on some little particle inside my head. I did not get far with these theories around the house or in grade school: I was told there was absolutely nothing physical about thought or memory, and after that I just shut up. But I still knew in my own mind that thoughts must have physical manifestations and effects, although at my tender age I had no words to describe this idea.

Many years later I was delighted to feel a sort of vindication when I learned that modern machines were showing that brain activity comprised tiny electrical currents and impulses flashing among the neurons in the brain cells. So there was a physical manifestation of thoughts and memory after all, just as I had felt.

Naturally I was immediately excited when I first saw the Harvard Gazette articles a few years ago, and read about the Tibetan monks who, just by thinking, could significantly raise and lower their body temperature and heart rate. I then heard about one Bonze who, not only could do these remarkable things, but was also said to be able to sense people's thoughts, and even their memories. Both these things had physical manifestations in the brain, said this Bonze, whose name was Thich Thach Thong. Just what I had unsuccessfully believed years before, as a child.

Maybe some Gypsy fortune tellers have this power too. I do not know. I am generally skeptical about Gypsies and other people claiming unusual or supernatural powers, but, then again, I sometimes see astounding true facts and abilities where least expected. Sometimes people apply the term "Extrasensory Perception," or ESP, to such abilities. I would use a different term: "Extra *Sensitive* Perception" might be a more appropriate description, as I shall explain.

Take animals, for instance. Some animals have an extremely keen sense of smell. Maybe sharks can sense a drop of blood a mile away. Some animals may have unusual sensitiveness to subliminal sounds. Whales are sensitive to subsonic sounds and are said to be able to communicate with each other hundreds of miles apart in the ocean. There may be many tiny little physical differences in our environment that human beings are unaware of but which specialized animals can readily detect. Some animals are apparently able to detect magnetic fields, which they can use for direction. Some species of migrating birds seem able to do this.

We have now learned that human brain activity is carried on with electrical charges. Brain waves and thoughts have their corresponding tiny electrical impulses. These impulses must affect the surrounding field, just as an electric current in a wire or a coil affects the magnetic field surrounding the wires. Every little electrical current, even your flashlight battery lighting the keyhole of your door at night, causes electromagnetic waves and has an effect on the surrounding electromagnetic field, small though the effect may be. How extensive is this field? The field is infinite, although of course only measurable by our present-day instruments in the immediate area. All forces and movements of particles have their effects on other forces and particles throughout the human body, the environment, and the universe. As to how these forces interact, there is much we do not know.

When I first heard of Thich Thach Thong, I was more excited than I had ever been before in my life.

I don't know how much Thich knew about science. He was just a Bonze who, like many others, had a religious background, and doubtless knew the power of meditation and contemplation. However, he apparently was able to bring these powers together to enable him to do even more than influence his body temperature and metabolism rate. He seemed to have a remarkable ability to directly draw meaning or understanding by sensing another person's brain waves. How he did this was the core of my quest.

Before my departure for Nepal I studied everything I could find about Thich Thach Thong and other Bonzes, although I was never able to find that there were any others quite like him. He had developed, or had inborn, abilities that, so far as I knew, no one else in the world possessed. And now his health was beginning to fail. Even with his remarkable powers, which some might call super-human, Thich would not live forever. I felt it my duty to humanity and to the human race, as well as to my own penetratingly inquisitive nature, to discover and save the secrets of this remarkable man to the extent possible. I must see him before his secrets disappear forever -- before he dies.

Now, let me tell you some remarkable things about Thich, who lived the solitary reclusive life of a hermit in the Himalayan foothills.

Thich had learned English in a most unusual way -- by befriending and caring for the young son of an English officer killed during the revolution.

The child was an orphan that the Bonze had found when it was twelve years old. The child then grew up in relative isolation in the Bonze's remote hillside cabin. The young boy had an unusual affliction, or handicap as we would call it today. He was mute, and had never been able to speak, because of a birth defect and infection damaging his glottal reflex and vocal cords. He could eat and swallow only with difficulty, but was never able to talk. However, he could hear perfectly well, and he had learned English through listening -- hearing his father and others all about him speaking English. And he had also learned to read.

Now the Bonze and the child each had something the other lacked. Although the child could not talk, it did know English, while the Bonze did not. The child of course still thought in English, and the remarkable thing is that the Bonze was able to learn English from the child, through being constantly with him and absorbing his brain waves.

Maybe it is like a dog that knows what you are thinking. If you are thinking of going out, your pet may go to the door and wait for you there, perhaps even before you yourself have made your final decision. Perhaps he senses your brain waves.

The Bonze, Thich Thach Thong, had this ability to sense brain waves a thousand times over, having intensively studied animal communication behavior and personal thought-control processes throughout his lifetime. Occasionally people from the nearest village came to him, sometimes to tell him what was on their minds and sometimes to hear what he had to say to them. At times he would sit quietly with them, sometimes for many minutes, and then would tell them what they were thinking and what they wanted to hear, or sometimes what they were worried about and *didn't* want to hear. He had apparently absorbed their brain waves while they were in his presence, sitting quietly, not saying anything.

However, the village and district authorities soon began to distrust Thich with his ability to delve into people's thoughts and memories. They rightly feared he had powers of the Devil that would have enabled him to extract their political motives, reveal their nefarious schemes, and leak confidential information and state secrets, had he wished to do so. Did his power come from a mixed diet? Perhaps strange fruit and organic vegetables and herbs? Or was it the product of a concentrated effort to develop and utilize latent powers hidden in the brains of every human being? No one knew.

Incidentally, Thich also preached love. Usually love between two people, as he put it. He never specifically said a man and a woman, just two people. I don't know whether this was his way of showing tolerance for liberal views regarding homosexuality and same-sex marriages or anything like that. The thought never came to me at the time, and perhaps never came to Thich either. This of course was several years ago.

Sublimation was a word he sometimes used, along with Urdu words like *tasseed* and *tazeeb* that he often repeated. I knew from school that sublimation in the scientific sense is the evaporation of a solid, such as ice, directly into the gaseous vapor state without passing through the intermediate liquid state. And that thought certainly seemed consistent with his ideas -- the idea of an unusual jump from one state to another, from one state of mind to another, if you will.

Thich never wrote down his technique for developing and exercising his power to absorb other people's brain waves. But he did welcome my visit and seemed delighted to find someone as interested as I was, who believed in him and in his work. Hard as it may be to imagine, there were people who considered him a fraud or wanted to bring him to trial in court on charges of witchcraft. Such unfounded accusations and attitudes dogged him through much of his life, and served to push him deeper into seclusion as an isolated hermit.

112

Now I would be the one to bring him out of it. I would connect with him, and I would elicit his techniques and ultimately reveal them for the benefit of mankind. But first I would develop, for myself, the greatest memory in the world. With Thich's secrets, I would be able to tap into the knowledge that thousands of great people carried in their memories. I would win quiz programs, write New York Times bestseller books, and displace Marilyn vos Savant as the person with the world's highest IQ. I would be famous.

But now Thich Thach Thong was sick. He had to have a twenty-four–hour nurse to care for him. He was dying. I needed to act promptly. I had to get the formula on tape. I wanted to know all I could about this power, what it was, how it worked, how he acquired it, how it could be used and maybe even created or developed in other people. Especially how I could gain it for myself.

His nurse granted me a one-hour interview. Thich talked in a subdued voice, mostly in English, or English sometimes mixed with Urdu. He seemed pleased to have a sympathetic ear at his side, and even more -- he told me -- a sympathetic brain. His words sent a shiver of excitement right through me. He said he felt he was "in tune" with my brain. Although he had learned English from the mute child, he had rarely spoken it, and I had to concentrate intently to understand him. The child was of course now an adult and his whereabouts were unknown. Thich would resort to Urdu and a dialect of Chinese occasionally, when he was concentrating, deep in thought. The few words of Urdu that I had hastily learned in Cambridge during the last two weeks before my departure did not carry me very far.

With Thich's consent and strong approval, I taped our conversation -- everything he was saying. I didn't understand much of it at the time, but of course I would be able to figure it out at leisure in my office or studio back home, if necessary with the help of an Urdu interpreter for the parts I didn't get.

So I set up the recorder, punched the start button, heard the wheels start turning, and then leaned back and concentrated on listening to what Thich had to say. I was fascinated for an hour while he explained the complicated process. I only occasionally interposed a question; Thich's explanation was too involved for me to comprehend at one sitting, even if I had been able to understand all his words.

I knew I would have to go over the material on the tape many times to analyze it and make sense of it and learn to be able to use it. A good thing I brought the recorder. What a wonderful, useful invention. What would I do without it? I would be helpless.

Then he died. I respectfully stayed for his funeral.

Then, when I got back home, I was most excited as I set up the recorder and got ready to analyze the tapes. I turned on the machine, rewound the tape, and pushed "play."

Alas, only silence.

I must have forgotten to punch the "record" button along with the "start" button when I turned the darned thing on at the old man's bedside. Damn.

THE END

114

Before He Ever Died

"It's where my husband and I were married," she said, "before he died."

I almost burst out laughing at this ingenuous remark, perhaps picturing in my fertile mind what it would be like for a woman to marry a man who had already died. I might imagine it in a one-act Puccini comic opera or a macabre Edgar Allen Poe tale, but at the time I thought it was the funniest thing I had heard all week.

Fortunately I had been well brought up as a young man and was able to cork up my mirth and politely maintain my straight face as I looked at the elderly woman there on the bus next to me.

I was in Viareggio, Tuscany, where I was spending the summer studying Italian at a little language school, twenty minutes by bus from my boarding house. Every morning after breakfast I caught the bus on the corner at 8:25. It was summertime, and the ride from the suburbs of this coastal town into the center was always pleasant and interesting. The bus twisted through shady streets, past old homes, the Garibaldi Park, the Church of the Resurrection, across the canal, past the central post office and through the banking district, to the Strada dalla Torre. That's where I would get off and walk half a block down a side street to my little school on the second storey of a rather nondescript office building. Little language schools all over Europe are to be found in places like that.

We had classes every morning, Monday to Friday, 9:00 to 1:00, with optional recreational activities in the afternoon, and I rode the bus into town every morning, Monday to Friday. However, before the end of my first week at the school, I was regularly beginning to work on the Italian language somewhat earlier than 9:00 o'clock. In fact, I was soon working on my conversational competence beginning about 8:28 weekday mornings. You see, on my third day I noticed that an elderly woman, quite alone, took the same bus into town regularly, and that there was usually an empty seat next to her. The following day, and every day thereafter, I sat next to her. The seat was near the front of the bus, and there was a good view.

To be assimilated, a foreign language must be used; especially it must be spoken. Schoolwork is not always enough to develop spontaneity and an easy fluency, which was precisely my objective in coming to Italy. When I sat down next to this lady I decided I would endeavor to engage her in conversation at the first opportunity. However, she preempted my intentions. Noticing that I had on a clean shirt and seemed to be a nice enough young chap, she opened the dialogue by asking where I was from. Now that was one thing I did know, even in Italian, and in school I had learned how to give a fluent answer; so, with a certain degree of confidence in my emerging Tuscan accent, I replied, "*Sono degli Stati Uniti. E lei? Di dòve è lei, signora?*" politely asking, in return, where *she* was from. That seemed to give her a chuckle, and the ice

116

was broken. She came back with a torrent of beautiful Italian, including a few key words buried somewhere in the deluge mentioning that she was born in a tiny village in the hills outside of Lucca, and that Tuscany had always been "her country." Just as many Southerners in the United States used to feel, she felt a closer attachment to her state than to her nation. But I had found an inexpensive means of working on my Italian -- in fact it was absolutely free.

The lady was clearly of modest means, dressed in black from shoes to shawl, wearing the ubiquitous black that used to be worn everywhere by elderly Italian women of village and countryside alike. She probably had not had much education and knew little of foreign affairs or even Italian literature. However, I never cease to marvel at how uneducated people may often speak a beautiful language, especially in Italy, even if not exactly a literary one, and she was no exception.

She told me she had been taking this bus at the same time every morning for thirteen years. I noticed that she always got off at the same place, about three or four stops before my own bus stop. I didn't see any shops or office buildings there; indeed she was probably too old for any kind of regular office work, except perhaps cleaning lady, and she wasn't dressed for that, modest though her attire was. Her stop was at one of the plazas, or *piazzas*, you see now and then spaced out around the town, a pleasant square with diagonal walkways, some shade trees, flowers, and benches. Facing the plaza on the east side stood one of the many old churches one can find everywhere in Viaraggio, and indeed all over Italy. It was the Church of the Resurrection. It was mentioned in my guidebook, and was

117

said to have been designed in 1373 by a colleague or student of Giotto di Berdone's.

The woman told me her name was Signora Pocalini -- Mrs. Guido Pocalini, she said, although later, almost reluctantly it seemed, she added it was Adriana, not that I would ever have called her anything but Signora Pocalini. After seeing this woman, this Signora Adriana Pocalini, every day for almost two weeks, I felt I knew her well enough to ask her where she went every day at 8:40 o'clock in the morning.

"I go to see my husband."

"Oh," I said, somewhat surprised and not sure whether I was speaking an Italian or an English word. Then, to stem the encroaching silence, I offered, rather stupidly, "Does your husband live around here?"

"I see him at church," she said softly, "every day. It's the Church of the Resurrection, on the other side of the Piazza Philippa. You can see it from the bus stop."

As I only took the bus on school days, and not knowing how else to continue the conversation, I said, "Do you come to this church weekends too?"

"Oh yes," she answered simply. "I come here every day. Saturdays and Sundays are no different. I love him."

So,I had to laugh -- almost -- when she said, "It's where my husband and I were married. Before he died."

THE END

Mad

My wife Dotty has always been a little weird. Cute, but weird. I have known her ever since we were children, for we lived in the same neighborhood. When we were old enough, we went to the same school. Even then she always had dreams and always wanted to tell us about them the next day on the way to school, or in the hallway, or at recess. I know she added to them as she was telling me and the other kids about what she had remembered, for she could make the reports of her dreams last half an hour, always making quite a story out of them. She has an uncanny ability to make the most far-fetched tale sound absolutely true. Although she is kind of nutty, she might have made a good novelist or mystery writer. I should suggest that to her sometime.

But her behavior has gotten particularly strange recently, and I have really been getting worried about her.

Dotty and I got married because our parents and everybody we knew in our little town seemed to expect us to. We went to the same little church, and when we were in our late teens and early twenties we were practically the only ones we knew that were around our own age. Everybody else at our church was either younger or a good bit older. Anyway, we got married because neither of us had any good reason not to.

119

It was all right at first, but over the years Dotty and I haven't always gotten on too well together. We have a lot of differences, mostly small things, but small things add up. Besides, two of her best friends recently got divorces and have been telling her how much better life is without some man bossing you around all the time, someone you have to take care of and pick up after, and all that. In fact, the subject of divorce has come up a couple of times, but we didn't pursue it. I don't think she was ever unfaithful, and I certainly never was. We only raised our voices at each other once, the time she was mad at me about something insignificant, and blurted out, "Oh why did I ever marry you anyway? I could have married Archy Philpot instead of you, you know." (Archy Philpot was one of the friends who had recently gotten divorced.)

I couldn't help responding, "Yes, and you'd be divorced by now..." but that only added fuel to the fire and made her even madder. I changed the subject as soon as I could.

Although we both knew that things were never going to get any better between us, she was too lazy to pursue divorce, and I was opposed to divorce on principle, or for religious reasons really. As I saw it, we were married in church and had made our vows in the eyes of God. I took my oath seriously.

I think we are both responsible people though -- we don't smoke and we don't drink much, certainly not to excess, and we are not abusive, or even violent. We both came from nice homes, although her parents thought I was somewhat beneath Dotty, because they had more money than my parents did. I sort of felt it was the other way around, as I came from a family of educated people -- literary types and university professors. So on balance it was probably about even. We respected each other and each other's relatives, but none of the family relationships were particularly cordial.

But as I was saying, Dotty and I have different interests and inclinations, and not really a whole lot in common. I think I love her, or did love her, more than she ever loved me. Probably neither of us made a wise choice of a marriage partner, and little annoyances can grow into big annoyances. But still I do not feel that divorce is consistent with God's will and His plan for us.

However, strange things started happening around my house recently. Or to be more exact, around my wife, Dotty. It was almost spooky. I was worried. I didn't know what to do.

For instance, a couple of weeks ago I got up at 3:00 a.m to go to the bathroom. I heard something stirring about downstairs, so I quietly went down, and there was Dotty, walking slowly around the dining room table, touching each place setting with her left hand, moving gently, like Lucia di Lammermoor, in her long white nightgown. I was about to call out, "Dotty, what are you doing?" but realized she was fast asleep, although her eyes were open, wide open. She did not seem to be seeing anything, but was staring straight ahead and feeling her way along.

I waited until she was on the side of the table, moving away from me, then I quietly moved in close to the near end of the table so she would have to touch me to pass. And that is what she did. She looked at me and touched my shoulder as though I were a fixture or a newel post. I took her hand and she let me gently lead her back upstairs. Then she quietly went back to bed, never saying a word. I was going to say she went back to sleep, but I guess you can't go *back* to sleep if you already *are* asleep.

I didn't know what it meant, but was astonished the next morning when at breakfast she said to me, "Do you know you walk in your sleep sometimes?"

"What?" I said, unbelieving.

"Yes. Last night I had to go let the cat out, and you were downstairs walking around in the dining room."

"I must have been looking for my cigarettes," I said weakly, quite astonished, surprised, and worried.

You see, we don't have a cat.

At least I don't think we do. I think we had a dog once, but he must have run away or died or something.

That was the first of several strange things that began happening with Dotty.

I felt I had to find out more before I upset her with a confrontation.

A couple of days after that, on Thursday afternoon, she called me at the office to tell me something strange had happened. I think I was at the office, or maybe I was at the shoe store. She said she had been downtown and somehow lost her bearings and had a little blackout. When she came to, she said, she was driving back on the wrong side of Connecticut Avenue, against all the traffic, as though she were in a dream. That's what she said.

I was then quite worried about her, and when I got home my concern must have shown on my face. "Why are you frowning so? Are you all right?" she asked.

"What's all this about blacking out in the car and driving on the wrong side of the road?"

"I didn't black out," she said, "I was backing out of the driveway and had to stop for the postman delivering mail. He always comes over to the wrong side of the road to put the mail in the box so he doesn't have to get out. It's dangerous; you ought to do something about it."

I didn't know what to say, so I just said, "Well, be careful," and let it go at that.

But that's not all. Two days later, early Saturday morning, when I got out of bed and went down to the kitchen to put the coffee on as I usually do, I noticed that all the drapes on the ground floor had been pulled closed and pinned tight. When Dotty came down I asked her why the pins, and she explained that she "had to keep them out."

"Keep who out?" I asked.

123

"Them," she said, "keep them out."

"Them who?" I persisted.

"Any of them," she said slowly and calmly, with absolute conviction. "I can't talk about them now," she said, avoiding eye contact and looking at the far wall.

I was suddenly very afraid. Whether I was afraid of "them" or afraid of Dotty, I'm not sure.

Something was very wrong. I would have to do some finding out. But I felt I'd better not push the matter further, there at the breakfast table.

"I am sure it will be all right," I said soothingly.

I thought it best to change the subject.

"I have to go to the office for a couple of hours," I said. "I'll come back early, and then we can do something nice. Maybe go to the beach or take in a movie this afternoon, or even go by and see Ethel and Paul." (Ethel was her cousin who lived on the other side of town.)

When I got back around one o'clock, the first thing I did was look at the curtains. I don't know what I expected to see, but they were absolutely normal, no pins, drawn back about half open, as they usually are. I couldn't see any sign of the pins having been there. Of course, pins are pretty small. You can't always see a pin-hole. I went to the kitchen and out the back door; Dotty had a trowel in her hand and was languidly stirring up the earth around the geraniums in the window boxes on the edge of the deck, looking very normal in a tank top and sun shorts. It was a nice day.

She came back in and made us a couple of tuna fish salad sandwiches, which we ate in silence. I felt I had to learn something, test the waters, so I opened up, saying, "Our living room curtains are getting rather old and drab. Do you think we ought to be getting some new ones?"

"Why on earth would you say that? They are perfectly fine as they are."

"Perhaps I should have them re-hung so it would be easier to close them all the way," I said, watching her face intently for any reaction. But no, not a twitch. Nothing whatsoever. Absolute deadpan.

"Oh, Mark, you know we never close them. They are always left half open like that. It looks nice that way, don't you think?" She has an uncanny ability to sound convincing regardless of the situation.

"Sure," I said, "looks fine." And that was the end of that discussion. But something was happening. What was going on? Is Dotty going nuts? Does she think I don't know she pinned the curtains closed? Does she think I can't see? I knew then that there would be no point in accosting her about the pins; she would deny it and say it was my imagination. Possibly she did not even know she had done it. I began to think that that was likely. Like the sleepwalking. She was doing things but was not aware of what she was doing, and had no memory of them. She

125

must have been acting in some sort of trance with the curtains, like sleepwalking in the dining room the other time. She had already said that the curtains always stayed half open, hadn't she?

I had to talk to someone. Maybe her father. I had always had a good relationship with him, even though it was perhaps a bit more formal than cordial. Yes, he's the one I should talk to, I decided. So I arranged to meet him for lunch at his club at the first opportunity, to seek his help and support regarding this strange behavior of his daughter, my wife.

I carefully explained these curious events to him as we were having our soup and salad, even implying that I felt we might need a psychiatrist to help us out. He listened quietly before commenting. Finally he cleared his throat and I thought I was going to hear some helpful suggestions. "I think you two have a problem," and that was all he said. He wouldn't discuss it further. He wouldn't talk about Dotty's strange history of childhood dreams and tales, and he wouldn't pick up on my suggestion of the psychiatrist. Such an idea was unthinkable. I believe he felt there could be nothing wrong with any member of his family or his relations, with all that blue blood coursing in their veins from famous ancestors of whom he was so proud.

Well, I had tried. I went on and got the name of a psychiatrist from a friendly neighbor who had a crazy uncle that they finally had to put away. I set up an appointment for a week from Wednesday at the doctor's clinic. His name was Varney, Dr. Hewitt Varney, with a lot of initials behind his name. Varney said we both should come in,

126

explaining that in most cases of mental illness of a married person, both husband and wife were involved. Fine, I thought. I'd be glad to go with her. We would see him Wednesday afternoon.

I told my wife that we had an appointment to see someone I believed could help us with our marriage, not knowing what kind of a reaction to expect. She was non-committal, said "all right," and that was that. Wednesday morning I went to the office as usual. She said she was going to the pet shop to look for another cat, and that she would meet me at Dr. Varney's office with separate cars. She seemed very cool and matter-of-fact about it. I was delighted that she went along with it so easily. I had expected some resistance on her part to the whole idea of a psychiatrist, after the reaction I had gotten from her father. However, from the calm way she was acting now it might be a little hard to convince the doctor that there was anything seriously wrong with her, but something was very wrong. I knew there was, and I knew that she needed help.

I got to Doctor Varney's clinic twenty minutes ahead of time, thinking it would be a good idea to give him some background on Dotty's deranged condition before our formal consultation began. I was surprised to see that her car was parked out front. She was already there. She had gotten in to see the doctor before me. Well, that's fine. He is a psychiatrist; he will see that she has mental problems, that's for sure. He'll know what to do.

So I went on in. A receptionist ushered me straight through the waiting room into the clinic, where I was delighted to see two strong men dressed in white standing by

127

a litter, or gurney, on wheels ready to wheel Dotty away. Good, I thought. They are not wasting a minute; they will find out what is wrong with her and in time they will cure it.

At that moment Dr. Varney and my wife came out of his office into the clinic area, with blank faces that told me nothing. The doctor looked at the two men, nodded slightly, and gestured toward me. The men came quietly to each side of me and took me by the arms.

It was time for the doctor to speak: "Your wife has explained everything to me... I am sure you will like it here, although you will only be here for six months. Then you will probably be moved to another facility if your recommendations are good."

I looked at my wife, but her face was turned in the other direction.

THE END

Story Telling

Story telling can be fun and rewarding. And listening to stories being read to you can also be fun and entertaining as well as instructive and educational. Teachers and child-education specialists will tell you how important it is for children, in their young, formative years, to have stories read to them. Children love learning new words and expressions, learning about other people and situations, learning about life. They soak it up and crave more. Then they go on and do better in school and, no doubt, in life.

I met a woman at an art opening a while ago; she was perhaps in her mid-forties. I was sitting down, taking a rest, when she came over to me and we started talking. She said she was interested in art (not surprising at an art opening), adding that she had some ideas, but little experience. "Then you should paint and draw anyway," I said. "Paint and draw all you can."

"I'm trying to get my ideas together," she replied. "I would like to paint on writing." I didn't quite understand what that meant, so I pondered a moment before seeking clarification. But before I could do so, she asked, "What do you do?"

Now maybe I should tell you, this was a black African-American woman, decently but simply dressed, that had grown up in a poor family in the country, probably with a dozen or so little brothers and sisters. A small, rather

129

slight person, she acted rather shy and spoke quietly, but had a glimmer in her eye that flitted about, showing interest in what was going on around her.

I'm not sure why she chose me to engage in conversation. Perhaps she liked my grand-fatherly countenance and my relaxed, non-threatening smile.

"What do you do?" she repeated.

"I used to paint some. Now I write -- stories and things. Also little plays and sometimes translations. Things like that."

"What kind of stories?"

"All kinds. Love triangles, murders, stupid people getting in and out of trouble... "

"Sounds interesting. Published?"

"Well, yes. I've published three books of short stories and some books of plays. Subsidized stuff, like self publishing."

"I would like to see."

"You would?"

"Yes, I really would."

"They may have some of my books for sale here. You can ask at the desk."

So, she wandered on off, and I picked up my plastic glass of the cheap white wine that you get at those functions -- jug wine if you are lucky. Or else wine that comes out of a cardboard box with a push button on the bottom corner.

I didn't really expect to see any more of her, there in the crowd, but after a few minutes she found me again, and had a little book under her arm. It was my first published book of short stories, entitled BAKED ALASKA AND OTHER SHORT STORIES.

"Oh, you found it," I said, unnecessarily.

"Yes. I thought I would read it," she said, also unnecessarily.

"Tell you what," said I, "let me read you one of them."

I always like to read aloud to others, especially from my own stories and plays, and she was agreeable. So she pulled up a chair next to me, and that's what I did.

I read THE PRODIGAL CALF to her, slowly and carefully, to be sure she understood every word. It was a simple story, mostly fantasy but nothing off color. It was about a young cow who gets back at her human captors by burning down their barn, and more.

The young woman listened silently, and attentively, I was pleased to note. I could feel her eyes following my lips as I read. Now although many of my stories are merely

131

silly fantasy, I like to read them with a serious tone to my voice. Accordingly, I was delighted -- and quite surprised -- when, as I finished, she looked gently into my eyes, and quietly asked, "Did that really happen?"

"Well, no, not exactly," I had to admit, nevertheless taking her inquiry as a compliment to my reading ability if not to the verisimilitude of the story itself. "It was all really make-believe, but I do try to make it sound realistic."

"Thank you. I liked it -- I never had anyone read a story to me before."

THE END

Epilogue

I had to turn away to hide the tears that were coming to my eyes at that depressing thought. How sad, never to have had a story read to you while growing up in the United States of America.

THE FINAL END

The Window

"Wow! Would you look at that!" said Abigail, one of the old spinster ladies, as she peered out the window on a warm evening in August.

"Let me see," said Adelaide, her slightly younger sister.

"All right, all right. You don't have to push. There's plenty of room," said Abigail, as she moved over a bit to one side.

Adelaide was enthralled: "There he is -- I can see him! And he has taken off his shirt!" she said excitedly, looking across the driveway into a window of the house next door.

Abigail and Adelaide Allen had lived alone in their little home on North Crestview Drive for as long as anyone could remember. They both had been schoolteachers -- Abigail taught English and Adelaide taught history, but they were long since retired. Their joy now was to find, and pointedly correct, any errors the other might make in either of those disciplines. But all in all, they seemed to be happy enough in their quiet life together. They were very proper ladies who went to church occasionally, supported CODA and the ASPCA, the Sierra Club and one or two other good works, but otherwise didn't get out much anymore. For sustenance they relied heavily on local gossip and the news of current activities in the community.

The rumor around town was that long ago they had had torrid love affairs with a couple of dashing young men. The two girls made the irremediable mistake of letting the cavalier gentlemen meet, and the two gentlemen, so dashing and gaillard, immediately fell in love with each other, and, suddenly realizing how delightful the real thing can be, left the young maidens in the lurch, the cads. Bereaved and frustrated, the forlorn ladies shared solace and sympathy in their solitude for the next half century. Their weekly height of activity thereafter consisted of giving each other soothing back-rubs on Saturday night.

So you can understand that, when on a warm summer evening they discovered the window with the open shade across the way, it brought a thrilling new wave of excitement into their hearts and minds, perhaps stirring up the ashes of long-dormant, half-forgotten passions.

The ladies had been raised Roman Catholics, in a puritanical New England home and environment, and they took their religion as a matter of course, neither questioning nor analyzing their beliefs, but adhering to them religiously, so to speak. What Abigail did realize when she was growing up, soon after she was old enough to notice such things, was that she was always uncomfortable in the presence of the half-clad statues of young Jesus on the cross, wearing only a skimpy loin-cloth. That tiny piece of precious material seemed awfully insecure. What if it were to slip? The thought was most disturbing.

She subsequently found that the Presbyterian Church was able to survive and prosper without these disturbing crucifixes, and accordingly she became,

134

nominally at least, a registered Presbyterian. She passed her views and feelings along to young Adelaide, who forthwith dutifully followed in her elder sister's footsteps. But as a good Catholic, Abigail had learned about the purifying power of confession, and after looking out the window she felt an uncomfortable guilt accompanying her excitement.

The young man in the window was a medical student, temporarily lodging with her neighbor, Violet Knapp. And now, there he was, stripped to the waist, just as our Lord had been, on the crucifixes which made such a disturbing impression on her as a child in church. This remarkable view she was now beholding gave her ambiguous shivers and shudders of attraction and repulsion.

But Abigail and Adelaide firmly agreed, albeit tacitly, that the young man in the window was definitely worth watching. You never could tell just when he might take something else off, reluctant though each was to acknowledge her thoughts out loud, or even to herself. But they were in a dilemma: it hurt their sense of conscience to look; it hurt their sense of curiosity not to look.

Abigail even thought of going back to St. Joseph's Church in the morning and pretending she was a Catholic again so as to gain access to a confessional in which she could rid herself of the nagging onus of her sinful ruminations. But here and now, in the absence of a confessional, if she could somehow slough off some of the blame for her lusty thoughts it would ease her conscience and perhaps purify her soul a bit, maybe even making it easier for her ultimately to get to Heaven when the time came. You never know when you might save the camel by keeping that final straw off its back. Every little bit of purity that you can muster up or maintain in your life here on earth may help when the call comes from Up Yonder. You never know.

Otherwise, what was she to do? There she was, excited and aroused by the view, but also disturbed by the image of Christ, bare to the waist, that it conjured up in her mind. She was both fascinated and ashamed of her fascination. She needed an escape. She needed help. Finally she even discussed the dilemma with her sister, who sympathetically said she had felt some of the same emotions. After some more thought on the matter, Adelaide suddenly hit upon another, more practical, means of lifting some of the pressure from their sinful minds. The telephone.

"Call up Violet," she said, "Tell her she should do something."

"Good idea," said Abigail. "She's the one we should speak to. I'll do it." Abigail considered herself holier than Violet; she liked to feel that her respectable status gave her a slight edge, sufficient to allow her to look down upon her dear neighbor, especially in trying times like this.

She called Violet's number and got her on the telephone. "Violet," said Abigail purposefully, "that young man staying there with you... "

"Yes, what about him?"

136

"I can see him in his room, There, in the window."

"You can?"

"Yes, I can."

"And Violet..."

"Yes?"

"He took his shirt off.

"He did?"

"Yes, he did."

"You don't say."

"Yes, Violet, I do say," insisted Abigail, "and it's shocking."

"I think you are making something out of nothing."

"No, I'm not. It's true. Adelaide is right here by me, and she can vouch for me and can confirm everything I am telling you. That young man is there at his desk, with no shirt on, by the window, where you can see him plain as day. His window is directly opposite ours, you know. You ought to tell him to pull down his window shades."

"Why don't you pull down yours?

THE END

Friendship

"Oh my God!" she shrieked, her voice penetrating the silence of the viewing room at the funeral parlor. She was looking into the casket where the divided lid had been partially opened for viewing. "My God!   There's something in there!" she screamed again.

Of course there's something in there. The body of her 19-year-old son, who had suffered such an untimely death, was in there. Of course she was upset, but why such an outburst?

"Who would have done a horrible thing like that?" the woman's voice again, only slightly less strident this time.

*   *   *   *   *

The deceased was Irving Millington, son of Dallas Mayor, Jeremiah Millington, and best friend of Hank Plainfield. Irving had suffered for some years from a rare virus that infected his nervous system and finally evolved into spinal meningitis. Hank came from a poor family, but was in Irving's class in high school. Irving's cousins and even his father, who was now the mayor, had attended the finest prep schools before they went to college, but Mayor Jeremiah sent Irving to public school for the better political image it gave the family.

139

Children can be mean to one another, and many of Irving's classmates teased him and even bullied him because he was the mayor's son and because his athletic abilities were very limited. However, Hank Plainfield, who was six months older and sixty pounds heavier than Irving, took a liking to him.

The two young men found they had academic talents that merged nicely. Hank was not a good student at most subjects, but was a whiz in Math. Math was precisely Irving's weak point, while Irving was strong in History and English Grammar and Literature. The two helped each other with their lessons. Furthermore, Hank put an end to any bullying aimed at Irving. Any bullies would have to go through him first, and few dared. Hank had been first-string defensive tackle on the football team ever since he was a sophomore, and was respected for his physical prowess. As a Junior he was named Defensive Lineman of the Year for the entire conference. His reward was a football that had seen action in a Dallas Cowboys football game and was signed by Troy Aikman and Deion Sanders. That football became Hank's pride and joy. He kept it locked in his bedroom; at night he slept with it, and he looked at every day. Nothing could ever have made him part with it. A dealer in collectibles offered him three thousand dollars for it, which Hank indignantly refused, although he and his family could well have used the money.

Irving also loved football, although of course he could not play. However, he studied the game assiduously and gave Hank a lot of good advice and encouragement. Furthermore, Irving occasionally got tickets to the Dallas Cowboys, box seats yet, that his father was able to arrange. The Cowboys were Irving's heroes too, and several times

140

he took Hank with him to their games, much to Hank's delight, as you can imagine. This unusual friendship continued until the middle of their senior year, when Irving was seriously stricken and suddenly taken to the hospital.

Hank had to wonder why Irving was not in school that day, and, as soon as he learned that his friend was in the hospital, he skipped the rest of his classes and rushed off to see him.

"Are you his brother?" they asked him at the hospital admissions desk.

"Well, no. I... "

"Are you a relative?"

"Well, no. I... "

"Young man, all I can tell you is that Mr. Millington is a patient here, but only family members and others with special permission are allowed to see him. Perhaps his priest. People like that."

"Can you tell me how he's doing?"

"Sorry, That would be privileged information."

"Please tell me something. Anything. Anything at all! He's my best friend," pleaded Hank.

"Well, he's in Intensive Care. But I'm not supposed to tell you that."

141

"Intensive care, my God! So that means it's really bad, doesn't it?"

"Not good."

Two days later Irving was dead.

Hackensack Funeral Services were in charge of arrangements. Hank learned there was to be a viewing and vigil Friday afternoon and evening. He was afraid he would feel out of place there, with all of the political big-shot friends of Irving's father, fancy family members from both sides, as well as the school principal and some of the teachers. But when the time came he didn't feel that way at all. Irving was his friend. His best friend. He felt perfectly comfortable in his place there, as close to Irving as he could be. He wasn't even upset by the scream of Irving's mother. Let her scream, he thought.

And the scream went on. "There's something in there!"

The friendly funeral director rushed to her side and reached into the open casket; he found something brown and oblong tucked under the crossed arms of the body. He looked more closely.

"I think it's all right, Mrs. Millington," he said soothingly. "It's seems to be a football signed by Troy Aikman and Deion Sanders. I think your son would like that. I know mine would."

THE END

Connecting

You might not think this story very funny unless you have studied a little German or maybe one or two other languages.

One of the big problems that foreigners have in learning German is the highly inflected grammar, particularly the endings of nouns and their modifiers. For example, a simple word like the definite article, "the," in English, has as many as six different forms in German, depending on which of three genders the noun may possess, and which of four different cases the noun may fall into, all of which possibilities are doubled with consideration of singular and plural. Some people love complications. They are the ones who should study German.

For instance, there are certain prepositions that always call for their following nouns to be in the dative case, with appropriate dative case endings. Then there are some prepositions that always call for the accusative case (also called the objective case). A few even call for the genitive (or possessive) case. And then there are those prepositions that can take either the dative or the accusative case, letting the action of the verb decide, perhaps according to whether or not motion is involved.

So it behooves the student early on to memorize the list of prepositions that take the dative case, and the list of

143

prepositions taking the accusative case. I clearly remember, from my own first meager studies in that language, memorizing "*aus, bei, gegenüber, mit, nach, zeit, von, zu,*" the "dative" group.

* * * * *

I was spending a few weeks last year on an isolated Caribbean island off the coast of Central America, enjoying the solitude while working on a book of short stories I was putting together. One day I met a Swedish woman, a tourist apparently, who wasn't bad looking and even seemed interesting enough to engage in conversation. Unlike that of many Scandinavians and other northern Europeans, her English was only fair, even halting, I thought. Then she spotted the German book I had with me, for I had been trying to refresh my own halting German at the time. (I wanted to speak in their own language to the few peripatetic German hikers and wanderers who had discovered that remote corner of the world.) Seeing her glancing at my German book, I asked her, "*Sprechen Sie zufällig Deutsch?*"

"*Nur ein bischen*" -- just a little -- she replied, slowly and gently. "*Ich habe etwas studiert...*" Then, showing that she had indeed studied a bit, she continued, in her lovely, lilting Swedish accent: "*Aus, bei, gegenüber, mit, nach, zeit, von, zu.*"

I laughed out loud, and replied, "*Bis, durch, für, gegen, ohne, um,*" the "accusative" group.

144

Still laughing, we settled for having a -- mostly silent -- cup of tea together. Fortunately we both knew what *eine Tasse Tee* meant. Two different cultures connecting in one language that belonged to neither of them.

I never saw her again, but I hope she is still laughing too.

THE END

Point of View

My forebears were from Vermont -- Vermont, New Hampshire, and even Massachusetts -- 'way back. I don't know how they stood it. I mean, it gets COLD up there. I spent part of one winter in Burlington, where my grandparents lived, and later a couple of years in Boston in school, and let me tell you, New England gets COLD. My nephew grew up in Burlington, and later worked in Iowa and Kansas, which he said were even colder than Vermont in the winter. I don't know how that could be possible; it must have REALLY been cold out there. I don't know how people can stand those places.

I lived for a number of years in Washington, DC, working for the government, and that was cold enough for me. Too cold. The first thing I did after I retired was to move SOUTH. I found a pleasant little spot on the water near Beaufort, South Carolina, that I could afford. I love swimming, especially in salt water. I could swim in the creek there behind my house for six or seven months of the year, and the winter months were never so cold that you couldn't play tennis or golf occasionally, at least two or three times a week.

But as I got older it seemed that the winters, even in South Carolina, were longer and colder than I liked. They probably were not really getting any colder; I was probably getting older and more feeble and sensitive. Anyway, I

147

decided to get out of the South Carolina winter for a few weeks and find some place where it was nice and warm.

After methodically checking atlases and climate statistics and weather reports, as well as airline connections and fares, I decided on a little island off the Caribbean coast of Nicaragua, and now this is the fourth time I have been here. The climate is delightfully pleasant, just what I wanted and hoped for. The ocean is warm, around 78 degrees. It is mostly sunny, with occasional ten percent cloud cover or a little tropical shower. Air temperature also averages 78 degrees, sometimes getting up into the middle or high eighties in the afternoon and falling to the low seventies at night. Oh, how delightful it is to be warm in January while the poor folks back in the United States and other places are shoveling snow and struggling with freezing temperatures and ice storms.

Yesterday I met a fellow with an interesting accent who had just arrived to stay here at the same little beach-front lodge where I am staying. Being perfect strangers, we naturally began to talk of the weather. We agreed it was ideal here.

I told him I was from South Carolina, and explained where that was. He was from Cordoba, Argentina, northwest of Buenos Aires. Then I thought: Argentina... that's way down there in the Southern Hemisphere, about as far south of the equator as the United States is north of it. Down there their seasons are backwards from ours, of course. I counted up mentally, adding six months in my head. Here it was early January; down there it must be like early July, as we know it. Early July in most of the United States is usually pleasant and warm.

Just after I had told this fellow that I was here in Nicaragua to get out of the cold back home, I went on to say, "But your place in Argentina -- it must be summer. It can't be cold there now."

"That's right," he said. "I came here to get out of the heat."

THE END

The Beauty of This World

The Beauty of This World

Some people will tell you that a great composer, or a great poet, or a great artist, has to suffer, or at least should suffer, as he climbs the parlous path to greatness and fame. I wouldn't know. But I do believe that we don't always appreciate what we have until we lose it. Or maybe until we die. But then...

Beauty and fresh air and peacefulness certainly are things we don't appreciate until we don't have them.

For example, I didn't sufficiently appreciate my wife until after she died. Then I appreciated her. Also, by then we had no more disagreements. And my childhood -- I have enjoyed my childhood more looking back on it than I ever did going through it. And music. I always knew I loved music, but I didn't realize how much I loved music until I started to go deaf in my seventies. Now I can only hear the tubas and the double basses and the drums in the eat symphonies. I have tried to follow the score of Beethoven's Ninth, written when Beethoven had already lost his own hearing, but reading notes is not the same as hearing them. It is nowhere nearly so much fun.

But one great thing about great artists, whether they have suffered or not, is that they are supposed to be able to see things that ordinary people are not able to see. Like poets, and maybe composers as well, artists interpret the world for us less well-endowed, less perspicacious, ordinary human beings.

151

How many times have you looked at a haystack in the late afternoon twilight and seen the colors that Claude Monet saw? Or seen the beauty that he saw in a stagnant pool of water sprouting a mass of lilies behind your house or alongside the golf course in that gated community not far from your home?

Beauty and fresh air and peacefulness are things we don't appreciate -- until we don't have them.

* * * * *

In 1748 a young man was born in Paris who, from the time he first wanted anything, wanted to be a painter. His name was Jacques Louis David. Maybe you have heard of him, or seen some of his famous paintings of Napoleon and other notables. Of course, being born in Paris was a good start for a fellow with an ambition to be a French painter. Michelangelo, the sculptor, was lucky to have been born in the shadow of a mountain in Tuscany made of marble. Mozart got a good start merely by being born at the right time and place for his music -- Salzburg in the eighteenth century. Paris was a good place to be born in, in 1748, if you wanted to be an eighteenth century French painter.

When Jacques was growing up, his father sent him to the best schools. The lad was fascinated by things of beauty, like poetry, music, and art -- but especially art -- including the paintings of the old masters. He didn't care much for Latin and mathematics, except for an interest in geometry -- for the proportions and ratios and angles it dealt with, and for the beauty and balance it showed him.

152

Proving the Pythagorean Theorem was less interesting to him than just looking at the 1.62/1.00/0.62 rectangle, the rectangle with the perfect ratios so beloved by Leonardo Fibonacci and the ancient Greeks, for its ideal proportion and balance, a thing of beauty in four straight lines. (If you were to cut a square from a perfect rectangle, the remainder would be another, smaller, perfect rectangle.)

To young Jacques, art was the path to deeper insights and greater understanding of life and love and beauty and nature -- indeed, the world. The finest artists, by means of their beautiful oil paintings, were able to go deeply inside worldly objects and worldly people. They could elicit and reveal to the onlooker the essence of fascinating subjects that were unfathomable to the eyesight of ordinary human beings.

Jacques might have felt these things, but he did not really think about them while studying art. Art to him was a captivating mistress. He was only really happy when he had a pencil or a brush in his hand, and could yield for a moment to his creativity and the driving force within him to put what he saw on to paper or canvas. No, that is not quite correct. Not only what he saw, but also what he felt, what his involuntary emotional reaction was, his reflexive response, his brain activity as stimulated by his vision. Although he would not have said it, and maybe did not even know it, what he was doing was interpreting what he saw and preserving it and its existence and meaning.

His art studies in school had given him a solid knowledge of the techniques of preparing canvasses, grinding colors, mixing paints, turpentine thinners, fixatives, varnish glosses -- all the mechanics of painting. But the inspiration for the creation of something beautiful did not come from studies in school -- it came from within.

Like all fine artists, Jacques was a master at drawing with pen or pencil, although his love was of course painting. His interests and studies took him to Italy as a young man, where he made numerous pencil sketches of his surroundings -- street scenes, landscapes, and people, but he soon realized that his forte was painting people, namely portraits. He was fascinated by the realization that an artist could paint not just what he saw in a subject's face but what he saw in his heart and soul. He was fascinated by the power that resided in an artist's hand -- the ability to reveal the truth, so often hidden from ordinary people whether through ignorance or by design. He gained great expertise in Italy, and was an experienced portrait painter by the time he had to return to his native country.

Back in the land of his birth, his portraits were an immediate success. He was in high demand and painted portraits of many famous political and military leaders, with little regard for their politics or party orientation. Unfortunately, there was great confusion in France in those days.

Especially confusing in Paris were matters of government and politics. Political allegiances were intense and ephemeral. Opposition groups quarreled among themselves. Yesterday's leaders were in prison today. Notables and non-notables, thinkers and non-thinkers, were losing their heads right and left, both figuratively and literally.

Jacques had no deep political convictions -- his devotion was to his art. He was indifferent to politics. However, politics thrust its ugly head into his life willy-nilly, and the subjects of his paintings, whether statesmen, military leaders, or outstanding citizens and philosophers, got him into trouble -- deep trouble. Because his subjects included individuals of all political persuasions, he was accused, from all sides, of being a spy, a traitor, a political enemy.

It wasn't hard in those times to get connected with the wrong groups. Indeed, in Paris in the frantic days of the early 1790's, it was hard not to. It was difficult or impossible to know which were the wrong groups, who the Good Guys were and who the Bad Guys were. They all seemed to be wrong, depending on one's point of view. Today's Good Guys were tomorrow's Bad Guys and today's Bad Guys were yesterday's Good Guys.

Still uninterested in politics, Jacques let the political breezes blow him this way and that, until one fine day in the autumn of 1793 he was arrested, by the forces currently in power, because of his alleged allegiance to groups now out of power. In those hectic days there was no time for civil rights or due process of law or anything like that. David was seized and summarily thrown into prison in the Chateâu Luxembourg -- the Luxembourg Prison.

Now at that time there were lots of evil forces confronting each other, but it so happened that some of the individual prison guards had only meager political convictions. Some of the guards had been conscripted merely because they were available or because of where

155

they happened to be at the time, and not because of their political beliefs or orientation. Some of the kinder ones recognized Jacques for the famous painter that he was, and did what they could to make his time of incarceration a little easier, if not exactly enjoyable.

Life in prison was indeed onerous for the painter, whose heart and soul had floated freely and wildly across many beautiful countrysides and elegant salons. The isolation from the world of people and nature that he loved made his relentless incarceration ever so much more onerous than it would have been for ordinary people. Most prisoners were like a mouse or a rat in a box. An artist, a painter like Jacques, was a bird locked in a cage, unable to fly or even to stretch his wings, barely able to stay alive.

The days and weeks dragged by interminably. Jacques even thought of ending his life although, perhaps fortunately, there were no convenient means of doing so at hand. He only survived by closing his eyes and recalling what he had known in the past. He had to live on memories. He thought of his past freedom, and regretted that he had not consciously savored it more intensely. It was only in looking back that he realized how great had been his enjoyment of life and freedom at the time.

His thoughts were morose. In his mind's eye he saw only darkness and gloom. "Regions of terror, doleful shades, where peace and rest can never dwell, hope never comes..." were the mental images he shared with John Milton. /1

/1   Phrases educed from Milton's "Paradise Lost"

That was when some of his friends were able to arrange plans with sympathetic prison guards to bring Jacques some brushes and paints and blank canvases. Perhaps Jacques could make some portraits from memory, or put on canvas his impressions of the dank, cold, forbidding, redoubtable, immutable, adamantine, slimy walls of the prison. He needed something -- anything -- to help him fill in the hours; something to help him cling to life.

Jacques received the equipment with but little interest or excitement at first. His spirit was downtrodden after months of imprisonment. He felt he must have lost any skill he ever possessed. Furthermore, he had no interesting subjects like dukes or generals or princesses to pose for him. His only ray of light and life in this dismal cell squeezed in through a tiny window covered with bars and an iron grating.

In spite of his initial lethargy, and because he was not pressed for time right then, he began mixing some paints. The smell seemed to touch his inner reflexes and stimulated a renewed interest in creating something on canvas once again. A Pavlovian response.

So he did it. He made a beautiful painting like none he had ever done before or since. All of David's other great paintings were people and portraits. This was a landscape, the only landscape painting he ever made. The only other known landscapes of any sort to have come from the hand of Jacques David are some pencil sketches of the Tuscan hills and seacoast made during his year in Italy.

This was a new first for Jacques, this one-and-only item. It was an oil painting, 55cm by 65cm, in full color, of the Luxembourg Gardens in spring, filled with budding green foliage of the sycamore trees, brightly colored flowers, bees and butterflies spreading pollen and fresh growth all about, gently washed by warm sunshine pouring down from Heaven giving new life and energy to the earth below.

It is what he saw, looking through the bars of his prison window.

THE END

Epilogue

Some critics have described this painting, the only full landscape known to have been painted by Jacques Louis David, as being a precursor to the Barbizon School. It even suggested the coming Impressionist movement 75 years later. The painting is now hanging in the Musée d'Orsay, on the bank of the Seine, about half a mile from the Luxembourg Gardens and the prison where it was painted. Go see it the next time you are in Paris.

THE FINAL END

Fifty Cents

I am an old man now, and I have done everything --
well almost everything -- that I ever really wanted to do in
this life, including some things I was supposed to do, plus a
few things I wasn't supposed to do. Now I am tired. My
joints ache. Even the parts of me that are between my
joints -- or join my joints -- ache. My organs are also
slowing down -- most of them. All of me is wearing out,
and I am virtually a walking "One Hoss Shay," as Oliver
Wendell Holmes would have said, and as was explained in
an earlier story of this series. /1

I know I won't live much longer, and that is all right
with me. I have written my will, made my funeral
arrangements, fed the dog, changed my socks and put on
clean underwear, and instead of Christmas cards I have sent
out some postal cards to close family members and
relatives plus a few friends that I probably won't see
anymore. Postal cards are the ones you buy at the post
office, with the stamps already printed on them, not like
postcards, which need a stamp, and require a certain
amount of effort in tearing the sticky little things out of a
booklet or off a roll and licking them or peeling the backs
off them and sticking them somewhere near the corner of
your card or envelope. Your postal cards can also serve as
Christmas cards -- all you have to do is write "Merry

/1 See "Oh, All Right,"   SHORT STORIES FOREVER,
p 153.

Christmas" or "Happy Hanukkah" on them. It is possible that some of these people may see me again, especially if the funeral home lays me out in a half-open coffin for a couple of days and gives out public notice. But my friends are getting old too, and even if they come to see me, by then many of them may be too old to be recognizable.

I have one particular friend who runs a little restaurant not far from where I live. The food is good and the prices are right, so I eat there quite often. He specializes in seafood, and it just so happens that I have a taste for seafood: fish, shrimp, lobster -- things like that. I used to take my wife along now and then, back when I had a wife, before she died.

But now I suddenly thought of a little problem, a very little problem that most people would think hardly worth mentioning. Interestingly enough, the problem didn't arise when I had my wife with me, and wouldn't be arising now if she were still with me and going with me to Ellery's Restaurant. But she has died, so she does not live with me anymore. I am not sure where she has gone, whether up, down, or sidewise, but that's neither here nor there. Anyway she's not here. Let me explain:

I have always tried to follow socially and ethically correct behavior, being a properly brought-up young fellow. When I was young I was always taught that it is nice to leave a good tip for servants or waiters in a hotel or restaurant -- places like that -- but not if the service is rendered by the proprietor herself, or her husband. Now that is precisely the case that existed with Ellery's Restaurant.

You see, Ellery had sort of a quirk. He had all the prices on his menu ending in fifty cents. Thought it looked elegant. High class. And it always seemed that the total on my tab ended in fifty cents. Unusual, but nicer than the ubiquitous ninety-nine cents that is now so common. When my wife (RIP) was with me and each of our meals ended in fifty cents, the total would end in a round dollar and there would be no problem. "No problem," as young people all say today. The problem arose when it ended in fifty cents, because I don't like to carry change in my pocket. I would rather let it accumulate on the bedroom dresser. I wasn't able to round it off in a tip because I didn't tip Ellery because he was a friend and because he was the one who always served me. The result of all this is that sometimes I would leave Ellery's Restaurant still owing him fifty cents, and sometimes with his owing me fifty cents, which we would take into account the next time. I generally preferred to overpay him by the fifty cents, because I hate the feeling of owing people money. But fifty cents wasn't a whole lot, even back then, and my conscience was able to live with it, from one meal at Ellery's to the next.

I have a niece, a nice niece, who lives nearby and comes around from time to time to drink a can of Coca Cola or a glass of grapefruit juice from my refrigerator, check on me, and help a bit with some household chores that happened to have piled up -- that sort of thing. This morning when she came around, she stared at me and said I didn't look so good. Said I looked pale. Didn't say "deathly pale," but I could tell that's what she meant.

"What else is new," I replied rather smart-alecky. "I haven't looked good for twenty years, and have been pale for part of that time."

161

"I am serious," she said. "Let me take your pulse."

"All right, I said, take it, take all you want, but leave me some of it. I may need it."

"Ha ha, very funny. I told you I'm serious." So she took my pulse. Then she herself went pale, maybe almost as pale as I. "Your pulse is feeble," she said, trying to smile a friendly little smile. "I think you are going to die. It looks as though your time has come, Uncle Don. No one can live forever," she continued, offering a soothing philosophical insight into man's mortality that I was already aware of. "And you have already lived more than your allotted span." I knew all that -- she didn't have to tell me. But women like to talk, you know.

"That's all right," I said. "You know who to call when I go. First my lawyer and then the funeral home. I'm ready."

Then I thought of something.

"No!" I exclaimed, suddenly raising my head an inch off the pillow. "I can't go yet. You have to DO something!"

"Don't get so excited," she said. "It's bad for you. Now what is it? Is something bothering you?"

"Give me artistic restoration or a long-lasting aspirin repository or something! Quick! Don't let me die!"

"What on earth is the matter with you? Don't you feel well? I thought you said just a minute ago that you were ready to die. What's gotten into you all of a sudden?"

"It's Ellery," I explained.

"Ellery?"

"Yes, Ellery. I can't die now, dammit. I still owe Ellery fifty cents."

THE END

The Ransom

Tom Graystone and Jerry Lynch were cousins and good friends as well. Tom's father and Jerry's father were also cousins -- first cousins, as they had the same grandfather. They all lived in the same town and all grew up as friendly neighbors quite close to one another.

The two boys were a lot alike and did a lot of things together. Only four months apart in age, they played together as children, went to the beach sometimes with their parents, and when they were old enough went to the same school. They had many of their classes together, played softball and other sports when they were in the fourth and fifth grade, and even slept over at each other's home occasionally, especially on weekends. It was a good relationship, although a little one-sided.

Jerry liked visiting Tom at the Graystone's more than having him to his place. Tom's place was bigger, more things to do, more fun. It was in a better neighborhood than the Lynch's, and near the best public park in town, with a Jungle Jim and swings and slides and a big playing field with a cinder track.

Tom's father, Henry Graystone, made more money than Jerry's father did. Jerry's father, Phillip Lynch, loved Jerry as much as any father could love a son. He followed his schoolwork closely, played ball with the boys and their friends when he could, and gave Jerry the same weekly allowance of spending money that Tom got. It was a little more than he could comfortably afford, but he didn't want the boy to feel inferior in the presence of his cousin.

There were other neighborhood children who came from families where the financial gap was even greater. Some of them showed it; some didn't.

Now all this was happening a number of years ago when the kids in some of the fancier suburban schools not only dressed nicely but sometimes tried to outdo one another by the clothes they wore as well as by their prowess on the athletic field and in the classroom. This was common in many private schools, but also in some of the public schools, especially in Virginia and other Southern states.

The boy with the most expensive shoes and cashmere sweaters (and also the loudest mouth) in the fifth grade was Fiorello Petrini. However, he insisted on being called Buck, because he thought Fiorello sounded sissy, which it does. Fiorello's father was of course Jack Petrini, owner of the Petrini Chevrolet-Cadillac Automobile Agency, also known as Petrini Motors. The Petrini were a proud and prosperous second-generation family from Palermo. Jack taught his son that he was not only equal to any other American kid, but that he was better than most. Jack gave Buck a larger allowance than necessary, frequently augmented by rewards for good grades or athletic exploits.

When Buck was 11 years old and in the fifth grade, he heard about a summer camp for boys on a lake in New Hampshire where the rich kids from some of the socially prominent families in New Jersey and Delaware and even Massachusetts went for six weeks of fun and adventure in July and August. He thought it might be fun to go to camp because then later, back at school, he could brag to all his classmates about his adventures. He took the idea to his father, Jack Petrini.

Now just by coincidence, it so happened that Tom Graystone's father, Henry Graystone, also knew of the camp -- it was called Kamp KareFree -- for he had been there himself and loved it when he was a boy. He also thought the time was right and made arrangements to send Tom to camp too. Tom was delighted with the idea, thinking of the exciting things he could do. Like his namesake, Tom Sawyer, he would swim, and make a raft, investigate the woods, learn about different trees, and maybe even find a dead cat or a cave.

Of course he told Jerry about it, and got Jerry very interested too, but alas, when Jerry spoke to his father about it, he was told it would be too expensive. The family just could not afford it.

When Buck Petrini told his father he wanted to go to camp, at first Jack Petrini didn't like the idea. Italian families always stick together. But he did some research, and learned that some notable people had sent their children there -- basically Christians, some Lutherans, but mostly Episcopalians and maybe even a few Catholics -- perhaps

167

some Kennedy -- and no Jews or Muslims so far as anyone knew.   The Jewish kids had their own fancy summer camps, but not on the same lake.

So that's what they all did.   The Graystone and the Petrini, unbeknownst to each other, made their plans to send Tom and Buck off for the first six-week session of the summer, May 29-July 9.

Jerry was disappointed to think of facing half the summer without his friend Tom nearby, but swallowed his sorrow and took it like a man.   But he was definitely interested in what Tom would be doing at summer camp, and got Tom to give him a brochure outlining the schedule and the activities the campers would be engaged in.   They included sailing lessons, swimming contests, volleyball and softball games, choice of archery or riflery with 0.22 target rifles, crest design, chorale singing, and even art work and basket-weaving for anyone with talent or interest along those lines.   And the capstone: one week camping in the woods in isolation, a unique and dangerous experience for which Kamp KareFree was famous.

Campers were urged to bring at least one white shirt and a pair of long pants for the outdoor dance held annually with their female counterparts from nearby Kamp KareLess for Girls.   Parents were to rest assured the operation would be well chaperoned.   There had been only three teen pregnancies reported at Kamp KareLess in its twenty-three years of operation, and the last was almost ten years ago.   Furthermore, the boy involved in that case had repented and apologized for his wayward behaviour.

Although the campers were discouraged from making telephone calls to their families, for fear of their becoming homesick and upsetting the routine, as Tom was leaving, Jerry gave him his allowance in coins, entreating him to call once a week and let him know how he was doing.

One evening, sometime later, when Jerry was in the living room still mulling over the brochure with the pictures and schedule of activities of Kamp KareFree, dreaming of what it would have been like, his father asked to see it too. He had tears in his eyes as he realized the disappointment it had left in his son's heart.

"Buck got to go too," said Jerry.

"Buck? Buck Who?"

"Buck Petrini. His real name is Fiorello Petrini. Another kid in our school. He's a jerk -- the biggest loudmouth around, always bragging about how important his father is and how much money he has."

The words hit Phillip Lynch.

"I know Jack Petrini," he said. "He is the largest GM car dealer in the county. I bought our Chevy from him, fifteen years ago, before you were born. The only new car I ever bought. I remember, I had only had it for two years when the paint on the roof started peeling. It just happened to be a bad paint job. I went back with the warranty, a three-year warranty, and asked whether that covered painting. 'Sure,' Jack Petrini said. 'We'll make it look "factory new." You'll have to let us have it for two or three days.'

"Well, I never told you this, and maybe I shouldn't now, but it ended up costing me $940. Petrini said my warranty was for three years or 30,000 miles, but the car odometer had 32,700 miles on it, voiding the warranty. 'How do miles affect the paint?' I demanded. 'It's barely been two years.' But he was unmoved, adamant. I felt like pasting the guy. I even talked to a lawyer, but he said it was no use."

But it did seem unjust. Was unjust. That the other boys had been able to go, but not Jerry.

"Don't worry about Buck Petrini," said Mr. Lynch. "He's a fustian brat, a nobody, just like his father... crass social climber..." His voice trailed off as he bit his lip.

The next day, still filled with heartache, he picked up the Kamp KareFree brochure his son had dropped and idly let his gaze wander through it. Then he shut his eyes for about two minutes, as though thinking. When he opened them he said silently, to himself, "I think I have an idea."

What caught Phillip's eye was the part about the week in the woods alone, designed to "make a real Pathfinder out of each boy." Over the next two or three weeks, Phillip Lynch's idea became a plan.

* * * * *

The Ransom

On Tuesday, June 28, along with the early morning mail
that had come through the door slot at the office of Petrini
Motors, there was a plain white envelope with no stamp,
typed simply, addressed to "Jack Petrini, Personal." The
return address given on the envelope was merely "Kamp
KareFree," no zip code. Jack Petrini opened it
immediately. Inside was an unsigned letter with no
letterhead that read as follows:

TO GIACOMO PETRINI YOUR SON HAS BEEN
KIDNAPPED IF YOU WANT TO SEE HIM ALIVE
AGAIN YOU MUST TELL NO ONE DO NOT TELL
THE POLICE OR ANYONE ELSE NO ONE HE WAS
SEIZED MONDAY WHILE CAMPING ALONE ON THE
OUTSKIRTS OF KAMP KARE FREE NEW
HAMPSHIRE HE WILL REMAIN UNHARMED IF YOU
FOLLOW THE FOLLOWING INSTRUCTIONS
EXACTLY OTHERWISE YOU MAY NEVER SEE HIM
ALIVE AGAIN WITHIN THE NEXT FORTYEIGHT
HOURS ENDING NOON THURSDAY JUNE 30 YOU
ARE TO SEND A DEPOSIT OF TWO HUNDRED FIFTY
THOUSAND DOLLARS $250,000 BY BANK WIRE TO
THE UNION BANK OF SWITZERLAND ZURICH FOR
DEPOSIT TO THE FOLLOWING UNLISTED
ACCOUNT U2401772 REPEAT U2401772 UPON
VERIFICATION OF THE DEPOSIT YOUR SON WILL
BE RELEASED UNHARMED AND RETURNED TO
THE CAMP CENTER WITH HIS COMRADES AT THE
SCHEDULED TIME FOR THE END OF HIS OUTING
IN ISOLATION YOUR SON IS NOW SAFE AND
HAPPY AND BELIEVES THE KIDNAPPING IS PART
OF THE SYLVAN ADVENTURE DESIGNED BY THE
CAMP AUTHORITIES TO MAKE A MAN OUT OF HIM
A MAN NOT A CORPSE MISTER

171

PETRINI THIS WILL BE YOUR ONLY INSTRUCTION
AND WARNING NO FUNNY BUSINESS OR ELSE...
CAPISCE ?

"Holy shit... Madre Mia," thought Jack, who had little
education and few words in his limited vocabulary to
adequately express his great dismay. But what to do?
"They always say you should bring in the authorities as
soon as possible in cases like this, but, shit, $250,000 is not
much compared to the value of my son's life. I would
rather pay that than take the risk."

So he notified no one and sent off the bank wire as
instructed. He waited one more day beyond the forty-eight
hours so as not to upset the kidnappers, then called Kamp
KareFree to inquire about his son. "They are in the woods
on a week-long camping experiment," he was told.

"Experiment? My son...? Listen here! My son has been
kidnapped! I want to know where he is! I want to talk to
him."

"I am sorry, Mr. Petrini; we don't know anything about
that. Perhaps you are mistaken. You and Fiorello agreed
that he would participate in the wilderness-survival
experiment, and I'm afraid there is nothing we can do. You
signed the terms of his enrollment at Kamp KareFree,
which included one week incommunicado during a solo
camping experiment in isolation, camping in the woods.
You will have to call back tomorrow, after they return at
4:00 p.m."

172

"I'll call the police!"

"Very well, Sir. That sounds like a good idea. Sometimes the police like to know what's going on when people are upset. They may have some soothing advice for you."

Petrini was furious; he slammed the phone down. "Dammit! Dammit all," he said, making a mental note to get his lawyer to sue Kamp KareFree when he came back from vacationing in New Hampshire himself.

"Let me fix you a cup of tea, dear," said his thoughtful wife, Petunia, recognizing that Jack was becoming distressed and distraught and that he needed solace and soothing. "What did you find out? Do they know what happened?"

"No, dammit, they don't know anything, but they don't know that they don't know anything."

Thirty hours later, at 4:25 Saturday afternoon, Jack got Kamp KareFree on the line once again. "We don't encourage phone calls from parents, you know," said the bonhomous camp secretary sweetly, while Buck was being summoned.

"This is an emergency," Jack screamed, as was becoming his wont. "It may be a matter of life and death," he thundered. (Jack wasn't even his real name. His real name was Giacomo, but he liked Jack better because he thought it sounded more American and more high class.)

"Please hold your horses a minute, kind Sir. Your son has been summoned and should be here forthwith."

Hold my horses? screamed Jack silently to himself. They can't talk to me like that! "Well, hurry up," he reiterated loudly, still in his stentorian voice mode.

Finally Buck came on the line. "Hi, Dad! How's everything at home?"

"But you... are you all right, figlio mio? I mean, the kidnapping and all."

"Kidnapping? What kidnapping? What are you talking about? I've just spent a week alone in the woods. It was really fun there; it was neat with no one around telling me what to do or bossing me around all the time."

"I'll drive up there tonight and bring you home in the morning."

"But why, Dad? What are you talking about? We still have another week to go. Everything's fine; I really like it here."

Jack had a little trouble reorienting his head and the image he had built up, but after several minutes, when his temper had finally simmered down a bit, he said, "Well, if you are sure you're all right..."

* * * * *

Monday morning, now that Jack knew Buck was safe, he took the letter to the police and insisted they find the kidnappers, or threatened kidnappers, or whatever they were. "This letter is a little old," they said. "Maybe it was just a prank. What do you know about the kidnappers?"

"What do I know?" boomed Jack, still agitated and ruffled from the heart-wrenching days he had suffered through since receiving the letter the previous Tuesday. "You are the ones who are supposed to keep our streets clear of kidnappers; if you don't want to help, I'll go to the FBI. And if it was a prank, it was a prank that cost me $250,000."

"If what you say is true, Mr. Petrini, the FBI will be involved in any case, so to speak. They always especially enjoy getting in on kidnapping cases. You are lucky, though. Usually ransoms for kidnapping start at about two million and go up from there."

"Thanks a lot. Well, I want to file suit."

"Against who?"

"Against the usual suspects, or against the Police Department for non-performance of duty."

And so it went.

Fortunately for Jack Petrini, the Feds did get involved, because it is true that they do like cases smacking of kidnapping, and began an investigation.

They had few suspects. They tried working through Buck and his camp-mates and schoolmates. Buck's friends and acquaintances thought he was an egotistical egotist, and some called him paranoid, claiming he probably made up the kidnapping story for fun. So that got nowhere.

The FBI asked Jack if he had any enemies or if his company had any accounts with dissatisfied or disaffected clients who might feel vindictive. They spent several days going through his records, back through the years. They finally found that there had been an old altercation about a warranty covering a paint job on one of the cars the Petrini Agency had sold. The Feds are thorough.

Phillip Lynch was questioned and indicted. There was suspicion but no proof. The DA felt certain that Lynch was guilty, but had to come up with something in the nature of firmer evidence. He wanted a conviction; it would look good on his record. Then, just before the trial began, he got an idea. It might be bending the truth a bit, but he felt sure he had his man; a little cleverness would only be in the service of justice, even if not strictly legal.

Now it just so happened that back in the sixties, when there was so much unrest throughout the country, the procedures for issuing drivers licenses and other ID cards were significantly stiffened in many states. Some states began requiring a thumb print as well as a photograph on any ID card issued by, or sanctioned by, the state. A few years later, when DNA entered the scene as a means of positive identification, some states began building DNA banks and collecting samples of DNA whenever and wherever possible, for instance with the issuance of drivers licenses and automobile registrations.

"That Phillip Lynch fellow has been around here for a pretty long time -- at least twelve years that I know of," thought the DA. "Maybe we have his DNA on file." So he checked and, sure enough, they did. Then his idea rounded out. When the case came to court, the DA had his little plan ready. He would get his conviction for sure. He would confront Lynch on the witness stand and get him to confess.

* * * * *

"I haven't seen anything but circumstantial evidence," said the judge, addressing the District Attorney. "You are going to need something more than that to convict this man."

"We do have more, your Honor," asserted the DA. "Our forensic laboratories have analyzed the DNA contained on the flap of the ransom letter where the perpetrator licked the seal, and we have a positive match with that of the suspect, Phillip Lynch, which was collected for our data bank several years ago."

"Why wasn't this evidence brought to my attention at the preliminary hearing?" asked the judge, somewhat irritated by the late arrival of this telling evidence.

"The FBI was working on it, your Honor, and we did not have all the information at hand." The DA had to think of something; he couldn't say that he had only just now gotten his idea of how to convict the suspect.

"Very well then .... So," said the judge, addressing Philip Lynch, "if you licked the envelope, how can you deny your guilt?"

Mr. Lynch was quiet for a minute or two, apparently thinking. "May I see the envelope in question, your Honor?"

"I don't see why not. Bailiff, show the defendant the envelope." With that, Phillip Lynch looked attentively at the envelope, turned it over, then handed it back to the bailiff.

"Your Honor, this is interesting," said Lynch. "It appears the DA has trumped up the evidence that he claims is incriminating. What he says about the DNA match is impossible."

"How so? What are you talking about?"

"Your Honor, this is a self-seal envelope. No licking."

"Let me see that envelope," said the judge to the bailiff.

The judge looked the envelope over. "Mr. District Attorney," he said, with a bit of anger rising in his voice, "I would like to see the police lab report identifying the DNA taken from this envelope."

"I'm afraid I don't have it here, your Honor."

"No. You don't have it here, because it doesn't exist. There could have been no DNA from saliva on this envelope because, being self-stick, it needed no licking. Your nefarious ruse of falsifying evidence to get a conviction is despicable, facinorous, naughty, and un-American, as well as shameful and illegal. Your devious behaviour is a matter that will be taken up in all seriousness on a future occasion. I consider the evidence in this case unconvincing, inadequate, and falsified, and find in favor of the defendant, Phillip Lynch, NOT GUILTY. Case closed.

Everyone within earshot seemed pretty happy with the verdict, except the DA, of course. A day or two later, when the DA was back in his office, thinking over the ransom case and nervously pondering what sanctions he might face for falsifying evidence, he said to his assistant, "Say, Grunewald, how do you think that Phillip Lynch fellow was able to guess what kind of an envelope the ransom note came in?"

"Good question, Boss."

THE END

Epilogue

The next year both Tom and Jerry went to Kamp KareFree for a delightful six weeks of fun and games together on the lake shore and in the woods, May 30 – July 10. Buck was sent to a different camp, on a lake in Maine.

179

Apparently something about the people at Kamp KareFree made Petrini feel they were unreliable and he never trusted them again. The District Attorney was fined and given a year's leave of absence without pay. Phillip Lynch's wife now has a new car, but Phillip still has his thirteen-year-old Chevrolet, of which he is so fond. He has had it repainted for the second time, and it looks like new.

THE FINAL END

Depression Dandelions

I remember the Depression. Sometimes it was called the Great Depression, and sometimes just THE Depression. Depressed means down. THE Depression meant everything was down. Everything that had anything to do with the economy, or anything else, it seemed. Wages and salaries were down, and lots of people didn't have a job at all. So they didn't have much money. So they couldn't buy much, just a little food and a little milk for the baby if they were lucky enough to have that much. But no money for new cars or for extra clothes or toys or holiday trips. So the car stores couldn't sell their cars, and the clothing stores couldn't sell their clothes, and the toy stores couldn't sell their toys. So the car factories and the clothes factories and the toy factories and many other factories weren't making any money and had to close down, or at least cut wages and salaries. So wages and salaries were down, and like I said, a lot of people didn't have a job at all. So they didn't have much money.

My parents didn't have much money either. Some, but not much. My father was a soldier, and most soldiers got enough to live on, even though it wasn't a whole lot. Privates in the Army got $21 a month, but that went up to $50 a month around the time we got into World War II. Fortunately, my father was not a private and got a little more than that.

181

Nobody had enough money to let their children have all the things they might have wanted. Kids were supposed to take care of their old clothes and any old toys. If your pants got a hole in the knee, you were careful not to tear it any more until you could get your mother or grandmother to sew it up for you. If the wing on your old toy airplane got broken, you glued it back or taped it together; you didn't get a new one.

Some parents, including my own, thought the best way to handle the cost of any toys for their children, or other non-essentials, like pocket knives or wallets or baseball caps or movies or popsicles or chewing-gum and candy, would be to give them an allowance along with the responsibility for buying any such things for themselves. A thrifty financial measure for the parents and a lesson in economics for the children. That's what my parents did too.

I had two older brothers whose financial needs were presumed to be greater than mine. Accordingly, the formula for our weekly allowance was based on age. When I was 8 my brothers were 10 and 13. The formula for the weekly allowance was one and a half cents for every year of age. So I got 12 cents a week, Bill got 15 cents, and I guess Lyman got 19 or 20 cents, maybe on alternate weeks. By that time, the United States no longer used smaller coins than one cent, such as the half-cent coins that were discontinued in 1857, or the mil coins that some states issued, purportedly for use in paying sales taxes. A mil -- a thousandth of a dollar -- back then was worth almost as much as a nickel is worth today. About the only quote we see given in mils nowadays is in the inane pricing of gasoline at the pump. Absolutely asinine. You would need nine mills to pay exact change for a gallon of gas. Pennies and nickels are also useless relics of the past that could now be discontinued and abolished painlessly.

Our allowance wasn't much, but it may have been more than you think, if you were born after WWII. Movies then cost 10 cents for kids and 25 cents for adults. I could have gone to the movies with one of my brothers every Saturday if I had wanted to. And I would have had two cents left over, when one cent would buy you a lollipop or two licorice sticks, each nine inches long. Orange popsicles cost five cents, and they were usually made in separable halves, each half with its own stick. I could put up two cents if Bill would put up three.

By the time I was 13 and my brothers were in high school, we were getting a little more. The War was beginning and prices were going up. I think we got 25 or 40 cents a week then but had to buy our own pencils to keep us aware of the value of money. But sometimes we kids were offered extra money for doing extra jobs, beyond our regular chores. I think it was 10 cents for cutting the lawn, 15 cents for washing the car, things like that.

I was 13 when we moved to a new city where Dad had been reassigned. We had a row house that was big enough for all of us, but had just a tiny front yard. When spring came the following year, the dandelions came too. My mother didn't like the dandelions, although I thought they were "dandy." She offered me a job: would I like to dig up the dandelions? She would pay me. Sure, I said. How much? She surveyed the little patch of lawn there between the front steps and the sidewalk, perhaps no more than 15 by 20 feet. She said she would pay me one half cent for each dandelion I dug up, but I would have to carefully dig it up by the entire root, which was usually 6 or 8 inches long, or more. Dandelion tops or half roots would not count, because those dandelions might grow back.

Okay, agreed, I happily said, glad for the chance to make some change. Maybe I would take Anne Clifford to the Apex Theater with me Saturday.

I got out the trowel, or what was much better, a giant screwdriver twelve inches long, that was good for digging straight down the side of a dandelion and loosening it up. And then, if you were careful, you could wiggle it around and twist it gently and pull the whole thing up, root and all, unscathed.

I think my mother estimated that there would be forty or fifty dandelions out there, and I might have estimated that too, at first. But after I got digging, working slowly and carefully with the trowel and screwdriver on each plant to preserve the root in its entirety, I realized that there were a lot more than we had surmised.

I worked for over two and a half hours, and dug up 274 dandelions. I laid them out on the sidewalk with their roots parallel so you could see them all, lined up like

184

soldiers, in squads 5 by 10, 50 to a squad, 5 squads plus 24, for the total of 274. Mathematical whiz that I was, I figured that I had earned 274 times one half cent, or $1.37. I had never had that much money in my life. I was elated. Mom will be delighted too, when she sees what a good job I have done.

But she wasn't.

"Oh, I can't possibly pay you $1.37" she said. "Here's a quarter."

That's when I knew what Depression meant.

THE END

The Bridge

If you are old and living in a nursing home, living what life you still have, there, quietly, out of people's way, there are fewer exciting things for you to do than there were when you were younger. Fewer things that you are *able* to do.

And you see things from a different point of view now. Current world news seems less important than your family picture album. You don't worry about building up your muscles or increasing the strength of your hand grasp; you just try to maintain as much as you can of what you still have. You are more concerned about the temperature in your room at night than you are about global warming. World population is a problem that no longer concerns you, either intellectually or personally -- you have enough children and grandchildren already, even if they are all scattered far and wide where you rarely see them, fully involved and occupied as they are with their own activities and sprouting families. You don't have many friends anymore. Most of the friends you did once have have died and gone to Heaven, or Somewhere, and those who are still alive you rarely see or hear from. They are just as feeble as you are, maybe more so. And they rarely see or hear from you either. Everything you do is an effort.

Stewart MacFarland was one of these old men. He had just spent the winter reading *War and Peace*. It was quite an effort. He would read four or five pages at a time, and then had to take a nap to rest up before he could continue reading a few more pages.

He did not read it when he was young because he didn't have much time.

He was reading it now because he didn't have much time.

By the time he finished the book, it was spring outside his bedroom window, and Stewart realized it was easier to watch the activity outside than it was to hold a heavy book and turn pages, grinding his way through great literature, fascinating though Tolstoy was.

In his advancing years even simple things became more difficult for Stewart. Dressing himself was hard, particularly putting on a shirt or a jacket, getting his arms into the sleeve holes and shrugging it up over his shoulders. He had arthritis in his shoulders -- osteoarthritis. No cartilage in the joints meant painful contact of bone on bone. He needed a shoulder replacement, but his bones were not strong enough to allow the operation. His legs were weak from an old illness, and walking was difficult and torturesome, even with crutches or a walker. Everything he did was tiring and wearisome. He had to take a nap before his early supper to gain strength enough to go down the hall for his meal, and another nap after eating because the exertion had tired him so. There wasn't much he could do that was of any interest to him.

Then one morning he opened his shades and found great joy in the springtime activity that was going on outside his window. With minimal exertion he could lie in his bed and turn his head to look outside and savor the life and action he saw going on out there. Through the window he could watch the squirrels romping from one old oak tree to another, because the branches were almost touching, allowing them to jump across the gap between the trees. The branches formed a shaky bridge, but it worked. It was their private bridge. It went from where they were to where they wanted to go. They had a regular route they traveled, always using these same branches, and the old man found their frolicking fascinating. They were full of life, as they hopped from one great tree to another, crossing over by way of this long flimsy twig that was their private rickety bridge. Each time a squirrel came onto the long spaghetti-like branch, the old man had to hold his breath for a moment, hoping the squirrel wouldn't fall. They seemed to enjoy the challenge and the thrill of moving from one tree to another across this perilous parlous path.

As Stewart couldn't do much else anymore, it gave him something to look forward to every morning. He even had names for some of the squirrels. He eagerly woke up every day and promptly looked outside to see which of the squirrels were already out there, using the slender bridge.

Then good news arrived.

One afternoon the nurse told him the landscapers had been tidying up outside. They had sprayed Round Up around the lawn to kill the yellow spots of dandelions that were beginning to sprout up here and there in the morning sun. And he would have a much better view now that they had trimmed the bushes and trees and cut some branches that were in the way. The trees will look much better, she explained -- much tidier now that the scraggly branches have been cut away and removed.

However as a result of this arboreal manicure the squirrels of course would no longer be able to use their old familiar route from branch to branch and tree to tree outside the window. Too far to jump now; they would not be able to make the leap. No more bridge.

The following morning, making their rounds as usual, the squirrels came out onto their favorite branch in the big old oak tree, but the branch was shorter now, and when they came to the end of it, as they had been in the habit of doing to make their crossing, they promptly realized they had reached the end of the line. They turned around and didn't come back.

Stewart MacFarland never saw the squirrels again.

Three days later he was dead.

THE END

Good Cook, Tough Decision

"You really should do it, Greta," her grandmother said. "Go ahead and enter. Maybe you'll win the fifty-dollar first prize."

"Do you really think so?"

"Of course I think so. I wouldn't say so if I didn't think so."

Some of Greta's friends agreed with her grandmother. "Go ahead and do it. What have you got to lose?" they all said.

* * * * *

Greta Elsinore lived with her old grandmother, Nena, and was her principal care-giver, although she was only 19 years old and had a full-time job as well. She worked for a family, the Penningtons, that fortunately lived only a couple of miles away, so she was able to walk to work. Greta's mother, Ursula, had also worked for the Pennington family for quite a long while before she got married and moved to Florida three years ago. Greta didn't know her father.

Old Nena kept herself busy knitting scarves and baby clothes, which they could sell sometimes at the

191

church basement to help with their meager finances. She used to do crochetting and embroidering, and sewing as well, but had to give that up some time ago when it got too hard for her to see what she was doing. But she could still knit, almost with her eyes closed.

Greta was just a maid in the Pennington household. Mr. J. Carrington Pennington was an investment banker who had plenty of money but took the commuter train every day into the Big City to make some more. He was proud of his name and fond of his initials, even silently pleased when he overheard his subordinates occasionally refer to him as "J. C." A nice sound, he thought. Suitable.

Mrs. Pennington's name was Elaine, not that Greta would ever call her anything but Mrs. Pennington or Madame. Elaine Masterson Pennington's joys in life consisted in running the household like a Swiss watch and participating in some of the charitable organizations that other nice society people belonged to. For instance, she supported the Chamber Music Guild and the County Historical Society and had her name on the list of sponsors of the County Fair that was held annually just across the river.

Most of Greta's work was in the kitchen of the Pennington home. Charles Dickens or George Orwell would have called Greta a scullery maid, a word Greta had probably never heard. But she did the work. She scrubbed the pots and pans, washed the dishes, mopped the floor, took out the trash, dusted and oiled the furniture, set the dining room table, and did a lot of work helping to prepare meals for the Pennington family and their frequent dinner guests. She liked baking bread and biscuits, and even angel-food cake, but she also spent many hours preparing the meat and vegetables. She scraped the carrots and peeled the potatoes; she skinned the onions and sliced the tomatoes, separating out the old unsuitable ones and cutting off any soft spots in the good ones. She washed the asparagus and cut off ends that were too thick and tough. She trimmed the fat and gristle from the beef roasts and pork roasts. She plucked chicken feathers, cleaned their insides, cut off their heads and feet, and prepared them for roasting. She made coleslaw, careful to trim around the bitter cabbage core and remove it. She trimmed and chopped celery, peeled the cucumbers, and arranged the avocados.

Greta's work in the kitchen created a certain amount of garbage. But most of it wasn't garbage to Greta, who was perforce a thrifty person, given her modest salary and the financial needs of her dear grandmother's household. Potato peelings and carrot peelings were opportunities. Greta threw out almost nothing. Every evening she took home the potato peelings and the carrot tops, and the fat and gristle from the beef and pork dishes, and the necks and feet as well as bones, cartilage, and gizzards that came from making chicken pot pies for the Pennington's table. All these things Greta saved and made use of. She made stews and soup, but especially soup, for herself and her grandmother.

Home at night, she boiled the scraps she had saved, adding a wide variety of spices, a tiny bit at a time. Her precept was that if any particular spice stood out enough for someone to make an easy identification, it meant she had used too much of it. She didn't really have a formula for either the ingredients or the spices and flavors; it all depended on what was available. Her technique was: Taste As You Go. A tiny bit of this, a tiny bit of that. A pinch of salt, a dash of pepper. A little curry. Some oregano. A dash of thyme. Some dill. Oh, that's good! A little more dill. A dash of cardamom, very little, be careful, cardamom is strong.

Greta would let her concoction simmer for two or three hours. Then she would stir it, mash it, taste it again, several times, adding just the spices and flavors as necessary until it was just right baby. Then she would strain it and freeze it.

Her grandmother, who didn't have many teeth anyway, loved it. So did some of Greta's friends who used to come by on her day off, half-day every Thursday. That was when they told her it was so good she should enter it in the food contest at the forthcoming County Fair. She was hesitant at first, but they persisted and so she agreed to do it. She didn't tell Madame Pennington anything about it. Madame P. could find out about it later, if necessary.

So do it she did. She carefully and lovingly made the required two quarts, tasting every step of the way, adding bit by bit the right combination of spices and odds and ends she had saved, stirring as she went. When she was satisfied with the result, she took it off and froze it immediately in eight half-pint Pyrex bowls with snap-top lids. She was ready. On the day of the fair she got the Penningtons to let her off, even if it did mean the loss of a day's wages. The tasters were a select group of village socialites and county big-wigs, such as they were. Some were friends of the Penningtons. Greta had to pray and keep her fingers crossed that Mrs. P. herself would not be on the tasting board. That might create problems. Fortunately, as it turned out, she wasn't.

But it also turned out that Greta won! She was delighted, overjoyed. She had never won anything before in her life. She won in her category, which was "Inexpensive Homemade Soup." Inexpensive? Hell's Bells, it hadn't cost anything! Some salt and pepper and some spices, plus a little work and some TLC.

But Greta didn't think it would be wise to share her joy with her employer, Mrs. J. C. Pennington. Although they had plenty of money, Mrs. P. watched her kitchen expenses and use of food supplies and household supplies like a hawk. It was almost a game with her -- she was constantly checking the larder, and when they had guests for dinner she would always count the silver spoons before and after. Not accusing anybody, but just to be sure.

Poor Greta was afraid Mrs. Pennington might believe she had pilfered good food from the pantry to make her soup at Mrs. Pennington's expense. Greta had to keep the operation hidden.

Then something else happened.

195

At the same time that Greta was given her $50 prize and her blue ribbon, the organizers of the Fair asked her for her winning recipe. It would be published in the brochure to be prepared for next year's Fair, and in addition might appear in the local weekly journal, *The Village Voice*, bringing great fame, if not great fortune, to sweet Greta Elsinore.

"Oh dear," she thought. How embarrassing it would be to have to tell the world and all these nice people that she had only used garbage to make her prize-winning soup. "But if I lied and said I used real carrots and potatoes and chicken, Madam Pennington wouldn't like that at all, and I would be in real trouble."

"Oh, dear! What shall I do?"

THE END

Christmas Gifts

"What did you get for Christmas?"

"I got to go to Colorado."

"I mean, what did you get for a Christmas present?"

"Going to Colorado was my Christmas present."

"Why would you want to go to Colorado? -- what's so great about that?"

"I got a chance to visit my grandmother out there and tell her that I loved her."

"Where does she live in Colorado?"

"She used to live in Boulder, but she doesn't live there anymore. She died soon after Christmas, on January 6."

"Oh. So I guess your trip was pretty much wasted. That couldn't have been much fun for you."

"Yes it was, and my trip wasn't wasted. It wasn't wasted at all. When I told her I loved her, she smiled at me. She had a beautiful smile, although she didn't talk much this time. But she did smile. I'll bet she is still smiling on us now. She used to take me for walks in the woods when I was little. She said that the woods were like paradise, and

197

when I asked her what 'paradise' meant, she said she thought it meant heaven. Now I guess she knows for sure. Anyway, I still think of her whenever I'm in the woods, and sometimes in other places too."

"I've never been in the woods much."

"You might like it. There are a lot of woods around Boulder, and when it snows the woods are really beautiful. Every pine tree and spruce tree and fir tree is like a Christmas tree, only even prettier. They don't have to have tinsel on them or presents under them to be Christmas-y. That's what my grandmother said too, and she knew everything."

"Sounds cool."

THE END

Chemistry

Once upon a time there was a young couple that fell in love, both for the first time. The time was the middle of the 22nd century, and by then people had learned not to rush into romantic relationships in the foolhardy fashion so common in earlier centuries. Teen-age pregnancy was no longer popular, and many were holding off on the husband-wife thing until marriage.

She was two years older than her boyfriend, although they both were only in their early twenties, but they were so in love they couldn't wait. They went ahead and did the business. Now the lady had a younger brother who liked to play tricks on people, especially for fun. He thought it would be amusing to play a trick on the fellow, his brother-in-law to be. With his new 22nd century chemistry set, he sent his sister off to Alpha Centauri and back, to see if her boyfriend could wait. At the speed of light it took four years each way, eight for the round trip. Eight years the poor guy would have to wait. He waited patiently. He had no choice.

The boyfriend would go to their rendezvous spot every night till she returned. He was like a Shakespeare character in love. Well, he <u>was</u> in love. And it was a slow, arduous, painful process, waiting there for her all those long years when they could have been . . . well . . . doing things together. His sweetheart was worth waiting for, but still he felt like wringing her little brother's neck.

199

He thought that after eight years she would be a thirty-two-year-old woman with a middle-age sagging face and figure, and that he might have trouble recognizing her, but he knew he would love her anyway. Imagine his surprise and his joy when upon her return he saw that she had aged only eight months because of the time warp. He would still have a young bride. Now he would be the older one, an older man with a younger wife. Let his friends accuse him of robbing the cradle -- he didn't care.

But he couldn't get over the nagging thought that her nasty little brother had made him lose eight delicious years of togetherness with his love.

So he bought a bigger chemistry set for himself, and sent the little rapscallion off to Antares./1

THE END

/1 Antares, the brightest star in the constellation Scorpio, is some 600 light years distant from the solar system.

Cold Turkey

Some people think that, if someone is good in one thing, he must be good in anything, or that if he knows a lot about something, he knows a lot about everything. I remember reading a book by Albert Einstein no less, entitled IDEAS AND OPINIONS. I thought it was mostly vapid platitudes, nothing esoteric as one might expect, but indeed, on the contrary, rather commonplace, even exoteric.   Stuff I thought almost anyone could have written.

Our family doctor, Ives Taggart, is that way too. He wants to tell you what to do even in matters that don't have very much to do with health, like taste in food.

For instance, I have a friend on a farm who has his own smokehouse and smokes his own bacon and ham. Sometimes he lets me smoke turkey there too. And smoked turkey is really good for picnics on the beach, especially when eaten cold in sandwiches either with cheese or with lettuce and tomato and lots of mustard.

I'm sixty-six years old, and I've never had any particular problems with my health since I had my tonsils out, but I get an annual check-up every year anyway. This year Dr. Ives told me, rather forcefully, I thought, that I should "quit smoking cold turkey."

I don't know where Dr. Taggart gets his ideas and opinions from. He may be a good doctor, but he doesn't know what he is talking about when it comes to turkey sandwiches.

THE END

The Tiger and the Mouse

Brantley O'Bannon, or B.O.B. as he was known as, was also known as Big Bob. He liked that. Although he wasn't really very big, in stature that is, he liked having people think of him as big, like important.

Big Bob wasn't always big. He was the second son of Reilly O'Bannon, who had been known as Rob and grew up in a family of Irish immigrants in Boston. Reilly didn't have much education, and at an early age delivered groceries on his bicycle to help out with the family finances. Later on, he drove a panel truck and ultimately, when he was older, he got a permanent job driving 18-wheelers for the Mayflower Moving and Storage Company. It wasn't "permanent forever", however, but was permanent for almost 20 years, until he got both tuberculosis and lung cancer at the same time. Lung cancer from heavy smoking and tuberculosis from -- who knows where, maybe the exhaust fumes he was exposed to, or the unsanitary conditions of his childhood environment in South Boston. Anyway, after 20 years Rob was retired from Mayflower. Thereupon, on the advice of his doctor, he moved to Tucson, Arizona with his wife and two teen-age sons, where the cost of living was less than it is now and where he was able to eke out financially, living on social security and a token pension from Mayflower. Reilly was a good Catholic and had deep faith that he could always trust in God to take care of him and his family.

Reilly's wife, Maureen, helped God and Reilly by working part time for a sempstress shop. The O'Bannon's found solace through their faith and devotion to the Church and the Virgin Mary, to whom they prayed regularly, not only on Sunday, but sometimes on other days as well, when they were not even in church and didn't have to.

The two O'Bannon sons, Conner and Brantley, were now out of high school and had to plan careers for themselves. Conner loved cars and trucks and followed his father's footsteps. He drove trucks, saved his money, and ultimately bought three taxicabs and started his own taxi company, which managed to do fairly well, bolstered by the burgeoning population of Tucson in those years. He was not so active religiously or so committed to the teachings of the Church as were the O'Bannon seniors, but he was still a "believer," and considerably more devout than his younger brother, Brantley, ever was.

Brantley, or Big Bob as he liked to be called, considered himself more practical, or down-to-earth, as he put it, perhaps in contrast to heaven. In his view, God never helped anybody at all. The more deeply committed to God was your faith, the more miserable and poor it seemed you were. His parents were certainly devout, but they never had anything much besides each other and their illnesses and misery, as they scraped through life on the poor end of the scale. Conner, four years older than Bob, was plowing along with his trucks and taxi-cabs, doing the best he could, like an ox pulling a plow in a muddy field. "That's not for me," Bob thought, "I'm smarter than that."

204

So Brantley O'Bannon, with all his smarts, went into politics. He got himself elected to the Tucson Town Council, promising to see that all the city's dirt streets would soon be paved and that an outlying residential area would soon have its own neighborhood grocery store or supermarket. He also found that being on the Council gave him opportunities for improving his own pecuniary position on the side. "I like this," thought Brantley.

Accordingly he went on to become Assistant to the Mayor of Tucson, and later Mayor himself. He was on his way. He ran for a seat in the Arizona State Legislature, representing the South Tucson District, losing by only 800 votes. Two years later he ran again, increasing his political promises, and this time won with a comfortable majority.

His popularity grew with the people and citizens of the great state of Arizona, as he made grand promises of the great things he would accomplish for them. People have short memories though, and as long as his promises of future progress and prosperity were repeated often enough and loud enough, the people loved him. Bob O'Bannon even went on to national politics, wielding his power and influence along the way, often, as luck would have it, to his own financial advantage. For twelve dollars an acre he was able to buy 6,400 acres of dry desert land on the northern outskirts of Tucson, good for hunting jackrabbits and growing prickly-pear cactus, but not much else.

Miraculously, just two years later, the State and the Federal Government signed a joint agreement to fund a massive irrigation project bringing water to a portion of the dry lands surrounding Tucson. This section just happened to include Bob's parcel. The land he had paid $12 an acre for was suddenly worth $250 an acre, representing a profit of almost two thousand per cent. "And God didn't have anything to do with the deal," he said to his brother Conner.

Conner was distressed to see his younger brother coveting money so, and committing so many mortal sins, like lust, gluttony, avarice, sloth, anger, envy, and pride, besides failure to love his God and to honor his father and mother, not to mention love thy brother or do unto others as you would have them do unto you. "You'll never get to Heaven at the rate you're going," warned Conner.

"Heaven? Who needs Heaven when, with a little money, we can have Heaven right here on earth?" retorted Brantley, almost sacrilegiously.

In India the Bengal tiger is the only animal reputed to kill merely for the pleasure of it. All other animals are said to kill only for food or the defense of themselves and their families. In southern Arizona, with its strong Hispanic heritage, Brantley O'Bannon soon became known as "El Tigre."

* * * * *

Many years later, when he was an old man and his brother Conner had already died, Big Bob happened to hear a preacher on TV asseverating, with fire and brimstone, that "All you sinners out there will go to Hell unless you repent of your sins. Repent now, if you want to be saved, before it is too late."

Bob had to hear this hooey because he couldn't find the remote to turn if off, but the word "remote" suddenly made him think. "What if there were even a remote chance that they are right about this Heaven thing? Maybe I should consider even the small chance that there really is a Heaven. After all, it shouldn't cost anything to be a believer."

So he went back to church for the first time in many years, and he became a believer.

Two years later he was dead.

*   *   *   *   *

Unbeknownst to Brantley O'Bannon, a contemporary of his was born and raised on the other side of Tucson, across the railroad tracks that ran from El Paso to Los Angeles. Her name was Rosana Teresa Isabel Camacho y Álvarez. Yes, she was Hispanic, and her mother tongue was Spanish, although neither she nor her parents or any other ancestors of hers had ever immigrated to the United States or entered illegally. No. The United States acquired the Camacho and Álvarez ancestors when we annexed half of Mexico in 1848 with the Treaty of Guadalupe Hidalgo, to fulfill the manifest destiny of our great nation. All it took was a little military exercise we called the Mexican War, which was also a good exercise for preparing troops, Union and Confederate, to fight in the real war, the disastrous one, that began 13 years later, in 1861.

Little Rosana grew up knowing nothing of the joy of speaking English, until she got to high school, where she learned a little in a course called "English as a Foreign Language." But Rosana did remember, as a little child, going to church regularly with her parents and several brothers and sisters. Like the O'Bannon family, 2,800 miles away in Boston, the Camacho y Álvarez family also was poor. Rosana's father, Arnulfo Camacho, was a gardener. He had grown up on a little farm like his father and his father's father did, but Arnulfo now worked on a golf course in the summer to supplement his income. His wife, Maria Concepción, Rosana's mother, took in washing and ironing. Rosana and her sisters -- some of them anyway -- helped their mother. The boys had their school studies and sports activities to keep them busy.

One thing that Arnulfo Camacho insisted upon was that all the members of the family, including any visiting aunts or cousins, had to wash their hands and appear on time for meals. He would say the blessing, one that everyone now knew by heart. On Wednesdays, and sometimes on other days as well, supper would be early so the family could attend Evensong together at the church down the road -- the Church of the Redemption, it was. Of course, regular Sunday attendance was obligatory, but Arnulfo did allow the boys to go to an early Sunday morning mass if they wanted to get out earlier to go play ball. Working was not allowed on Sunday, and although Arnulfo didn't really feel that playing ball was consistent with keeping the Sabbath Day holy, he couldn't find anything in the Scriptures specifically forbidding it.

For her last two years of high school, Rosana was sent to a convent school. By then, because of her gentle, quiet nature, she had picked up the nickname "Ratoncita," or

208

simply "Ratita," which means little mouse in Spanish. She didn't mind if people called her "Mouse"; in fact, she preferred "Mouse" to "Ratita" because it sounded more elegant, more high class. Although the Mouse was not given the choice of whether to enter the convent school, it turned out that she actually liked it, even loved it. She loved the organization, the rigid schedules, the attentive, albeit strict, oversight by the straitlaced Sisters and Mothers. She loved the Mother Superior and several of the Inferiors as well.

At the end of two years, and after graduation from the convent school, the Mouse seriously thought of joining the order and becoming a nun herself. Her parents were all for it -- one less mouth to feed. Rosana felt that as a nun she could help people in both their religious and their secular lives. She had loved her schoolwork and knew that nuns make wonderful teachers. She would be a teacher.

But you can be a good teacher without having to be a nun, thought Rosana The Mouse. She realized she knew little of the big wide world, and was curious to learn more about it. Maybe giving up the chance to become a nun did not have to mean giving up her religious life and beliefs. She still loved her Lord God and His Son Jesus Christ as much as ever, and would always carry them in her heart regardless of whether she was to be a nun or a teacher or something else.

She set about getting a bit of financial help from a religious educational foundation, took a part-time evening job in a supermarket, and enrolled in the local community college, aiming at a two-year Associate Degree in Education.

For most of the rest of her life Rosana, the Mouse, taught children from pre-kindergarten through the ninth grade of middle school. She loved her work; she loved the children, and they loved her.

She never married; there was no need; her life was full and satisfying as it was. But she never forgot that it was her God and His dear Son Jesus Christ who had made it all possible. She took her parents to church when they got too old to drive, and continued attending regularly herself, perhaps with some neighbors or the parents of some of her schoolchildren, long after her parents died.

The years kept passing, and then it came time for her to pass too.

"I'm rather looking forward to getting to Heaven," she thought. "Think of all the wonderful people I may find there, all the saints and the angels and maybe some of the better behaved of my own relatives. I certainly shouldn't have to worry about getting in: the only two times I can remember ever being naughty were once when I raised my voice to my mother and once when I passed a beggar in the street without giving him anything."

And so, in due course, with these pleasant thoughts on her mind, Rosana Camacho died and promptly gave up the ghost.

* * * * *

She hoped she would be met with a warm welcome when she got to Heaven, although just getting in would be enough. When she got to the Pearly Gates, she knocked

210

and said, "May I come in?"   One of St. Peter's helper-angels took a look at her and, after referring quickly to her copy of the Judgement Book, replied, "Okay, you'll do," and waved her through.

"Well, anyway, I'm here," she thought.   Then a few days later -- or maybe it was a couple of weeks, it's hard to tell time very precisely in Heaven -- she heard a great commotion around the Pearly Gates.   People were gathering; some were looking ahead with their binoculars. A brass band had been formed.   It struck up and led off with "Dear Lord Forgive Our Foolish Ways."   The Mouse squeezed and twisted her way forward for a better view. Who on Earth could be coming to Heaven with all this fanfare?

Then she saw who it was.   She recognized him from his pictures in the paper and from seeing him on television. Believe it or not, it was Brantley O'Conner, one of the most egregious sinners Tucson or Arizona had ever known. Rosana was aghast.

She turned to one of the angels who was helping to control the crowd.   By chance it was the same angel who had opened the doors of Heaven for Rosana just a few days earlier.   "Why on Earth is that man getting such a warm welcome?   Why are you letting him in here anyway?   Do you know what a scoundrel and sinner he was back on Earth?   I didn't get any reception at all when I came in here, in spite of all my good works and my devout life and my religious devotions.   What gives?"

"Oh," said the angel, "we get lots of people like you. You are nothing unusual. What is really unusual is for us to get a powerful politician who has repented."

THE END

Lefty

We all have God-given gifts and God-given shortcomings. Or maybe our shortcomings are the work of the Devil. I mean, why would God give us shortcomings after he had gone to all that trouble creating man and creating the greatest human race, and races, known to man? Unless -- as some priests and people like that will try to tell you -- unless it is to make you stronger by having to overcome them.

In school our short-comings always showed up in the classroom. I guess that must be why we had a sports program, so any talents, or long-comings, we had could be developed and displayed on the athletic field.

Some of the little bits of philosophy and guidance that I remember from school seemed to pertain more to life itself than to academics. Things like, if you want to win the battle, "Git thar fust-est with the most-est."/1 Or, "It's not what you have that counts, it's what you do with it."/2 Or, "Take the cash and let the credit go,"/3 which I thought sounded clever but not very nice. Or finally, "If a man's reach exceedeth not his grasp, then what's a Heaven for?"/4

/1 Attributed to CSA Gen. Nathan Bedford Forest

/2 Common expression, source unknown

I had to ponder that one, but finally I figured it must have meant you should go on trying to achieve things even when they are beyond your ability. I'm not sure I agree with that idea; it's kind of stupid, because wanting what you can't have, or can't get, is the definition of frustration. Doesn't the Bible tell us to be satisfied with what we have? Don't waste time striving for the impossible, I say. Think! You should figure out what is possible and strive for that. It's best to recognize both your gifts and your shortcomings, and, as I started to tell you, I recognize that I have both.

I was smart in the classroom, got top grades, had a good memory, was rather good looking according to my mother, and I came from a loving and respectable family, almost distinguished you might say, with ancestors and relatives of all sorts that I could, and should, try to live up to. I was alert and observant, and had good eyes and hears.

But I also had some shortcomings. I was always rather skinny, too light for football, too short for basketball, and socially very shy. But among my shortcomings the one that bothered me the most was being left handed.

"What's so terrible about being left handed?" you may ask. "Lots of people are left handed."

Well, it's clear that you are not left handed, or you would never say that. Being left handed is the work of the Devil: We live in a right-handed world.

/3 The Rubaiyat of Omar Khayyam

/4 Robert Browning

214

The desks at our school were designed for right-handed kids, with the flat writing top attached to the right arm, and the ink well way up there in the right-hand corner. You had to reach way over there every time to dip your pen. Even handwriting itself, from left to right, was designed for right-handed people. If a left-hander writes in ink, his left hand naturally slides directly into his wet inky words before they have dried. It is terrible. He has to try to awkwardly twist his hand around underneath to miss the wet ink, or write upside down, as some left-handers try to do. Spell-check doesn't even accept the spelling of left-hander, suggesting it be replaced with "left-gander," or "left-sander," or, perhaps best of all, "left-hinder." I kid you not. You can look it up yourself. It is terrible being left handed. I hated it. I tried to learn to be right handed, but it didn't work. It's not a matter of choice; at least it wasn't for me.

People -- normal people that is, meaning right-handed people -- have no idea how miserable it is for left-handed people to have to live in this right-handed world.

If you are a boy or a girl

It is impossible to use the Boston Pencil Sharpener with the crank on the right side if you are left handed.

The bell on your bike, and the accelerator on your motorbike, are all wrong.

Most can openers nowadays are almost impossible for left-handers.

At the dining-room table, the knife and spoon are always on the wrong side, although the fork is usually okay.

And where are you going to get a left-handed violin? All right, so it's possible, but it's not easy. And when was the last time you saw a left-handed flute? Or bassoon? Or a piano where the left hand plays the high notes?

If you are young, preferably not over six months old, I strongly advise you to try to convert to being right handed if at all possible. You will be glad you did later on.

Gear shift on most cars is awkward for lefties.

At the gas station the nozzle is on the R side of the pump.

The slots at Vegas have the handle on the R side; also the shooter knob for the pin balls. It is almost impossible to use your left hand there.

Try shooting a 0.38 Colt automatic. The magazine release button is on the wrong side. The safety button is on the other side, the wrong side for it. Even rifle barrels spin the bullet to the right. Always. It's all part of a great complot against left-handers. Left handed means gauche, not right, two left feet, sinister.

Mostly boys

If you are left handed, the button on your Italian switchblade knife is on the wrong side, and when you press it, the blade shoots out the wrong way, sometimes cutting into your own hand or arm (don't try it.)

216

The twist on your Italian cork-puller goes the wrong way, and you have to turn it backwards to make it work when you open a bottle of Italian wine.

The handle on your antique moustache cup is impossible to use if you are a lefty.

Try putting a letter into your inside breast coat pocket with your left hand. It can't be done.

The zipper on your pant's fly is hard to find with your left hand, covered as it is by a flap that opens only to the right.

And dancing: if you are right handed and want to know what it's like for a lefty to do the waltz, try dancing with a girl the other way, with your right hand holding her left hand, and your left hand behind her shoulder blade. Or else let her lead.

The modern bow-and-arrow designed for hunting is no longer symmetrical, but is shaped for the right-hander.

Sickles and scythes are practically impossible to use left handed.

And polo. In polo you are not even ALLOWED to hold your mallet with your left hand.

Mostly girls

The angle on the edge of your new pancake-turner is cut toward the right. Try to find one cut to the left; you can't -- they don't exist. You have to grind it yourself.

217

The pouring spout on your frying pan for pouring off the stew juice or extra bacon grease may be on the wrong side and very awkward. Same goes for the little tin measuring scoops.

The old-fashioned meat grinder was designed for right-handers. Try it.

Most people, if they are right handed, don't even think of scissors as being R or L, but they are, believe me. If you are right handed, find a pair of L scissors and try to cut a piece of Saran wrap with them, and you will realize the standard problem faced by lefties using regular scissors. If you want to make a friend of people who are left handed, give them L scissors.

Synonyms for "right" include correct, fair, moral, and proper.

/// Synonyms for "left" include sinister, gauche, and abandoned.

"Go Right and you'll be Right.   Go Left and you'll be Left."

Maybe we should divert some of the energy that goes into ensuring racial equality and gender equality and put it into Left-Handed Equality. After all, there are almost as many lefties in this country as there are Blacks or homosexuals, about ten to fourteen per cent, and furthermore, even some homosexuals are left handed. We need an NAALP to be fair.

* * * * *

I wasn't much of an athlete, as I said, but I did play a little baseball, and, to my delight, there I found, for the first time anywhere, a place where being left handed could actually be an advantage. It was better being a left-handed batter against a right-handed pitcher (or being a left-handed pitcher against a left-handed batter) for the better angle on the ball that it gave you. Also, a left-handed batter, after a swing and a hit, was one step closer to first base than a right-handed batter would be, and was also facing in the right direction. And it is better for the first baseman to be lefty, especially if he is holding a runner on the bag.

I also learned early on, that a left-handed tennis player, like John McEnroe and Rafael Nadal, or Monica Seles and Martina Navratilova, has an advantage, simply because most tennis players have had less experience playing against lefties and are not accustomed to the service ball curving "the wrong way" into their backhand. I played tennis a little, and won a few games, but I certainly wasn't a star. I didn't know then that there were other sports where being left handed would not be a handicap, but might, as in tennis, even be an asset.

By chance, one Saturday morning, coming out of a shopping mall that I visited only rarely, I saw a new extension to Gold's Gym on the corner, where a sign said they were now offering lessons in jujitsu, karate, and fencing. I knew very little about jujitsu, or karate, and nothing at all about fencing, so I stopped for a moment to have a peek.

I frankly wasn't too interested in the jujitsu or the karate, but the fencing was something I had never seen before, and it pricked my curiosity. Through the big viewing window, I could see two students going at it precisely and seriously, behind their face masks and chess protectors. I was immediately fascinated. Their movements were quick and sure, and I could not take my eyes off them. I knew immediately that I would like to try to do that too.

So I did. I took fencing lessons that summer right after I got out of high school. I was even ready to talk my grandfather into paying for it, when he asked me what I would like as a graduation present. He was old school, doubtless having read "The Three Musketeers" and "Ivanhoe" when he was my age, and thought fencing lessons sounded like a gentlemanly thing and a great idea.

I loved it. My instructor, Serge Marovich, told me I "had some talent" and said I should "go on with it." I asked him what he meant, and he explained there were still a few elite colleges that had fencing as a varsity sport, and he thought I might even get a partial scholarship if my skills continued to improve. Was it my intention to fence when I got to college? he asked.

Until then I had only been fencing for fun and for the exercise, and for the excitement of feeling I was getting pretty good at it. "What do you mean?" I said. "Fencing in college? I never heard of that."

"Oh yes," was his reply. "Some of the best colleges recognize the ancient and honorable sport of fencing, and a small and rather close group still have fencing teams and inter-collegiate competition."

I was all ears, suddenly imagining what it would be like to go to college and be able to do something, and be a somebody in the world of athletics. And by then I had really gotten to like fencing. Marovitch continued:

"My own son, Igor, fenced in college, on a scholarship at Paramount University, and was captain of the fencing team two years running. Later he worked with me here, teaching fencing for almost four years, until he was killed last year in a motorcycle accident. Simply fencing was never fast enough for Igor."

"I'm sorry to hear that . . . I didn't know." What else can you say at a time like that? But I continued. "But Gee, it really would be fun, going to a college where they have fencing. I should look into it. I've already been accepted at State for September, but I don't think they have anything like fencing there. I've never heard of fencing in college."

Marovitch had some contacts in a few schools and colleges that had fencing programs, and he put me in touch with some of them. They were interested in me from the start. Apparently not many freshman applicants know much about fencing, and even fewer have any experience at all in the sport. I applied and was accepted at his favorite college, Paramount University, for September. I would leave my State application hanging for a while, as a backup. No need to disturb that arrangement -- not yet anyway.

I had attached a written recommendation from Marovitch to my application at Paramount. There was no overriding reason that I had to go to State, I told myself, but I was worried about the greater tuition costs at "the Mount." However, they seemed so happy at the thought of having me, with my fencing experience and the recommendation from Marovitch, that I figured maybe I should take advantage of it. I asked for an interview with the Athletic Director at P.U. and forthwith met with him and the school fencing instructor as well. Steven French was his name. I put on my long face and told them that, much as I appreciated their approval of my admission, I wasn't sure I could accept it because of financial considerations. I explained that I had already been accepted at State, where the tuition costs were much less. "If you are as good as Serge Marovitch seems to believe you are, I think we might be able to do something about it," said Mr. French. "Would you mind suiting up and giving us a little demonstration?"

A surge of excitement came coursing up through my veins, and the rest of my body as well -- that is exactly what I had been hoping for. I had almost included in my application an offer to demonstrate my skill with the epée, but I thought that might sound too pushy, as there was no blank spot for it on the application form. But I had brought my gear with me and had it out in the car. Mr. French, the fencing instructor, took me on himself, for a short bout in the gym that very afternoon. I must say he was a master of the art, beautiful to confront, and he made me feel embarrassed when he was able to get two or three "touchés" in short order, before I was able to get one. But apparently he was impressed enough to say, "I'll see what I can do." Anyway, the very next day I got a telephone call from the Admissions Office expressing the hope that I would accept a full athletic scholarship at Paramount University. "Well, thank you, " I said, "I think I can accept that."

Accordingly, perhaps not surprisingly, I made the Varsity Fencing Team at Paramount right away as a Freshman. My love for the sport continued to grow. I found myself watching old swashbuckling movies filled with swordplay by actors such as my heroes Errol Flynn and Douglass Fairbanks, Jr., and looking at some old videos of Olympic fencing. But I also worked at it. I was good, and I knew it. So far I could whip anybody I encountered with a foil or epée in hand, the only exceptions being Serge Marovitch last summer at the Gym, and Steven French right here. Nevertheless, I was still getting better, making more and more touchés, even fencing with him, as the early weeks of my first semester went by. Other Paramount students that I fenced against, also some kids from other schools, I was able to knock off like picking flies off the fly paper.

As I have said, I worked hard at it, wanting to be the best, to make up for my failures in football and basketball back in high school. But there was something more: I had one great advantage.

I was left handed.

I didn't know, ceteris paribus,/5 that being lefty would mean such an advantage in fencing, but other things are not always equal. Specifically, my opponents were not equally right and left handed, but uniformly and consistently right handed, so they had no experience fencing against a lefty. I won every match I ever entered.

/5 ceteris paribus abs (Latin) "other things being equal"

The coach arranged for me to compete in the State Fencing Championships that very spring. I was delighted: all my notoriety could only add to my personal satisfaction and importance, and bring more widespread attention and acclaim to Paramount University and its fencing program that had been such a boon for me.

So I did it. I entered the state-wide competition. It was, unsurprisingly, a great success. The competitors advanced by successive elimination matches, like the Wimbleton or the US Open in tennis. I won my first matches with ease against some of the best fencers in the state, with a match usually every day, or at least every other day, all that week. By the weekend I was in the semi-finals. My confidence and ego and self-esteem had risen far above that of the shy, retiring, misfit that I had been in back in school. I was in my element.

Then the semi-finals Saturday morning. I went in confident and unbeatable. I foresaw another win today, and began thinking only of the finals. I would knock this fellow off, and then go on to win the state championship Sunday afternoon, and after that, who knows?

But it didn't work out that way.

I lost right there, in the semi-finals. Badly.

I was taken completely by surprise. My opponent had tricks I knew of, but that had never been used against me in a match. When I gave the guy a double twist, he would not twist back in the normal way, the standard, acceptable, gentlemanly response, that all honorable fencers use, but

224

would twist back in the opposite way, a nasty, sinister /6 trick that I had never seen used by anybody else before, although I must confess that I had used it myself on occasion. Down I went in flames.

As by now you have surmised, he was left handed.

THE END

/6 Sinister adj. (Latin) "Left, Left handed"

Mongoose Mongoose

There is a little Caribbean Island that used to have a lot of beautiful tropical birds fluttering all about.

The main industry on the island, if it can be called an industry, was the raising of coconuts for the market. It seemed a stable economy; the work of caring for the coconut trees wasn't too difficult, and there was no significant competition in the market from the over-developed countries (ODC's) of Europe and the rest of the civilized world. The colorful birds and the coconuts seemed to get along fine together, neither interfering in the life-cycle of the other, and both apparently sharing certain bacteria and microbes in common as do most other living things we hear about in Environmental Biology101.

Then something happened.

A cargo ship from one of the aforementioned developed countries crashed on a reef one dark night, and promptly sank just offshore from the aforementioned little island. Fortunately or unfortunately, depending on how you look at it, it was close enough to terra firma for the scoundrels on board -- the rats that is -- to abandon ship like rats and swim ashore and survive. The bad news, from their point of view, was that the tasty boll-weevils and cockroaches that had provided their sustenance on board could not swim that far, and consequently went down with the ship.

227

But the lucky rats who survived found their pleasant new home gemuetlich and accommodating. They soon learned that bird's eggs and coconuts were tastier than anything they had ever eaten before, even better than boll-weevils and cockroaches. So they decided to stay on the island and make the best of it. And that's what they did, although they didn't have much choice in the matter.

There was only one problem. The people on the island, who were making their living watching coconuts grow, or growing coconuts for coconut milk and coconut coconut, began to suffer from the inroads of the rats on their industrial production. The more the rats liked their life there on the island, the more the natives disliked having them there. One of the islanders, who had been to school and had read read some stories by Rudyard Kipling, remembered that snakes are one thing that rats don't like, because snakes do like rats. Like to eat them, that is. As the lad was an enterprising young fellow, he got the Island Council to agree to import a covey of snakes from an African country that had more snakes than it needed and once had used snakes to cure a similar problem involving its own infestation of rats thirty or forty years earlier.

Ah! Success! Within just a few years on the little island, the snakes prospered and multiplied rapidly, to the chagrin of the rats, whom the snakes ate with relish. When they were out of relish they ate them anyway. About that time the fellow responsible for the importation of the snakes died from excitement over the success of his idea. However, his memory lives on in the form of a modest statue in his image that they built in the middle of the Central Square on the north end of the island. A few years later a group of revisionist old fogies on the north end of the island complained that the erection of the memorial structure had been premature. You see, the snakes had now taken over the island. Furthermore, as the population of rats decreased, so did the food supply for the burgeoning snake population. With fewer and fewer rats to feed this ever-growing number of snakes, cats and dogs began disappearing, for snakes like other small animals almost as much as they like rats and mice. Other household pets like guinea pigs and gerbils and white rabbits were also noticeably thinning out. Finally, it was apparent that, in their hungry desperation, the rats were becoming a threat to the little ones of the village, the tender tiny tots two or three years old. Even the lives of the four- and five-year-olds seemed threatened by the increased demand for snake food.

"This is unacceptable," declared the chairman of the Island Council. "Absolutely unacceptable." There was not a single voice from any of the other village fathers to be heard in opposition to this clearly stated, dogmatic position, only full bipartisan agreement from both sides of the aisle.

Perhaps for every problem there is a solution, and again the wisest people on the island turned to Kipling, who, someone remembered, had written the story of Rikki-Tikki-Tavi, the spunky mongoose who was unafraid of even the fiercest Egyptian asp or the most vicious Zanzibarian viper. Accordingly, any islanders who still had children under five years of age, or hoped someday to have them, pooled their meager resources and imported as many mongooses as they could locate. Many of them could be found only in the inner-city zoos of some of the advanced countries of Europe and the Western world.

Well, let me tell you: those mongooses had a field day with all the snakes on the island, and got fatter and more numerous by the day. The perspicacious reader may now surmise what happened next. Yes, the mongooses took over. Or mongeese. You see, mongooses prefer a diet mostly of snakes,, but when snakes are in short supply, as was the developing situation there on the island, they can eat anything that birds or rats or snakes or anybody else can eat. Most of the mongooses were too small to eat a whole human being, but the snakes had given them a taste of meat and a liking for meat, and the clever little fellows figured out how to get into the tents and straw houses of the natives and slowly eat the arm or leg of an unsuspecting victim there in his sleep. Like little blood-sucking leeches that in summer infest the ponds of Vermont and other New England states, this mongoose has developed an anesthetic solution on his front teeth which deadens the nerves and the feeling of any animal he bites into. This wonderful feature enables him to continue eating a limb of his victim with no discomfort or even knowledge on the part of the latter regarding the process. Until the next day, that is.

The Island Council had to meet again. They undertook some serious studies. Finally, they were dismayed with the conclusions of their research.

It seems the mongoose has no known natural enemies

THE END

The Sandbox

I like to travel. I always have. Fortunately I have a job that lets me travel fairly often -- makes me travel, in fact. My company has representatives and associates all over the USA and in several foreign countries. And we also have contacts and connections in a few more countries where we don't have direct representatives.

I especially like Europe, where the landscape, and the culture, and the language, change every few dozen miles, where, as we used to say, "Distances are short." Towns are close together. The countryside changes rapidly, even if you are just on a bicycle.

In much of Africa, Asia, and Australia -- places like that -- and even Nebraska and certain areas of west Texas, towns and centers of cultural interest are farther apart.

On one of my recent trips +to Europe, I found myself enjoying a weekend in Limerick -- yes, that's a town, as well as a racy bit of doggerel -- not far from Dublin, just over to the western side of the country. Ireland isn't much bigger than Pecos and Culbertson County Texas together. But Limerick is even greener than west Texas, and the beer is just as good as Lone Star and almost as good as Pearl. So there I was, heading over to the Bear Bones Inn after a gentle round of golf that Saturday afternoon. In Texas people go to bars mostly to drink and talk. In Ireland they go to bars – they call them pubs – mostly to talk and to drink.

It's a good place to find out what's going on, and have a short beer or hear a tall tale.

I ordered a mug of Guinness and soon found myself in conversation with an outgoing chap who was much more garrulous than most Irishmen. Well, he wasn't even Irish: he sounded to me more like an Englishman, maybe a London cockney, but it turned out he was Australian, or "Strine," as he put it.

I felt an immediate camaraderie with this fellow, for I had even more Australian relatives than Irish relatives, albeit relatives by marriage. You see, my wife was Australian. My second wife, that is -- my second wife and my best one she was, although she left me after 17 years, when I guess she found another arrangement she liked even better.

But having an Australian there at hand to talk to made me recall a story that one of my Australian wife's cousins had told me. So I decided to pass it along as best I remembered it. More often I am the one picking up ideas for stories in bars and places like that, so now it was my turn to pay back for a change.

First I told him how much I did love his country, and had loved my Australian wife, and how I admired Australians for their energy and thrift and clever inventiveness. "Oh, yes," he agreed, "we Australians have to be clever and inventive to survive in the Outback."

"That's what my wife's cousin Phillip used to say too."

Then I went on and told him Phillip's story about making money as a teenager.

When Phillip was a boy, kangaroos were more than plentiful: they abounded. And they also bounded about, everywhere. There may be preservation laws in place now, but there were none back then, so far as I know. Phillip and his buddies would go out after school on their bicycles and shoot kangaroos around Orooroo, on the edge of the Flinders Mountains. Just one kangaroo on a bike is a pretty good load. They would sell the meat mainly for dog food, but the money lay in the kangaroo skins. They skinned the kangaroos and dried the skins in the Australian sun. Then they stacked them in the back of their daddy's pickup truck and took them to the Orooroo Kangaroo Leather and Fur Factory, where they were further processed and made into a wide assortment of products, ranging from scatter rugs and fuzzy bedroom slippers and furry bedspreads, to kid gloves and leather boots and breeches and broad-brimmed hats. It was a good business.

They made their business a little better -- more profitable, that is -- by sprinkling a modicum of sand between the layers of skins going to the factory, surreptitiously increasing their weight, and hence their value, which was calculated at so much per pound. After all, kangaroos slept in the sand, and rolled around with each other in the sand, and hopped in and out of the sand, didn't they? So it's to be expected that there would be sand mixed in with their fur.

I explained to my new friend at the bar that I was rather surprised to learn that my Australian cousin-by-marriage had been making extra money by cheating when he was a lad, but was even more surprised that he now, an adult and a respectable businessman, would be so willing to reveal his youthful chicanery and, indeed, even be proud enough to boast about it.

233

I stopped talking then and had a couple of swallows of my beer, which was warn by now, even warmer than it was in the first place.

It didn't take my new friend long to respond: "Oh, I understand it perfectly well. Australians are an enterprising lot, as you said. Your story could even have been true."

It sounded as though that snide remark was his way of impugning the veracity of my story, but I let it pass without comment so he could continue. "It even reminds me of a very similar story, that actually was true, also about sand."

"Well, I guess there is a lot of sand in Australia. Tell me about it," I said, as I was comfortable there and in no hurry to go anywhere. "I'd like to hear it."

So he started in. He told me that he too traveled a lot, and that it was in Omaha that he heard an interesting story. Apparently a Nebraska company, called the Bradshaw Sand and Soybean Company, was selling soybeans in big quantities to a company in China. The arrangement had been working for over fifteen years and was apparently very satisfactory and reasonably profitable for both parties. It seems that when soy beans are harvested and packed for shipment, there is a certain amount of sand that may naturally get mixed in with the beans. It is really better not to wash them too much at first, because they have a little natural oil in their skin that helps protect and preserve the beans, so it's best to let a little normal sand stay where it was, for a while. Sand of course adds to the weight, so the contract between the companies stipulated that sand should constitute no more than four percent of the total weight of a shipment. That was a very generous limit, because usually the sand that came along with the beans was no more than about one percent. A couple of years ago the Bradshaw Sand and Soybean Company came under new management. They installed a new Vice President for Finance, who energetically started looking promptly for ways to increase the company's bottom line profits. Accordingly, he recommended that more sand be added and mixed in with the beans, amounting to approximately 3.5% of the total weight, a significant increase, but still well within the contractual limit and perfectly legal. Even in Nebraska, sand was considerably cheaper than soybeans, and readily available in almost unlimited quantities. Fortunately, the chemical composition of Nebraska sand was comparable to that of Chinese sand, so his recommendations were implemented.

The Chinese noticed the difference right away, the abrupt increase in the amount of sand they were getting, but said nothing and did nothing in response to the first shipment that had so much more sand. It was probably a one-time aberration they figured -- it had never been so sandy before. But they watched closely, and when the next two monthly shipments came with 3.4% and 3.7% sand by weight, as best they could measure it, they felt they should do something, even though they realized it was within the limit specified in the standing contractual agreement. They knew something had happened, but did not want to upset an arrangement that, even with all that sand, was still velly plofitable for them.

So with their characteristic Oriental politeness, they sent a simple request to the Bradshaw Company, saying:

"Velly honored Sirs Gentlemen: We muchly would appreciate you future sending us the sand in separate sandbox please instead of in soybeans mixed with.

"-- Your respectful trading friends, the South China Trading Company, Canton."

/Signed/ Ho Chow Mein, Vice Plesident

THE END

Red White and Black

It's amazing how the more we learn about history the more we realize it so often is not history at all, not factual anyway, but a well-written account of some so-called historian's opinion about history, and even his imaginings. Fake facts, even way back then.

The idea of one vote deciding a major issue somewhere seems to have captivated the imagination of historians and students alike. One case that comes to mind relates to something I was told concerning the German language. It was back in grade school, or maybe junior high school, where we learned about the Declaration of Independence and the Constitution and all that, and we also learned we only missed by one vote of having German be our national language.

Although back in the eighteenth century English was already being spoken more than German on the American continent, it is understandable that we so hated England after her years of colonial domination and the Revolutionary War that many patriotic Yankees wanted to epitomize their separation and independence from England by eschewing the English language along with the mother country that it came from. Accordingly, according to some history books and teachers, there was a vote in the US House of Representatives which, by only one vote, rejected a proposal to adopt German as our national language.

237

Of course, the deciding vote was cast by the Speaker of the House, one Frederick Muhlenberg, paradoxically a first generation German himself, who never liked his guttural mother tongue very much anyway. So the proposal was defeated by one vote. That was the story I got in school.

However, I learned later that, in truth, it was merely a vote on the question of whether to require our laws to be published in German as well as in English. It was turned into fake news from that time on.

There is another case in American history that not many people know about, involving one vote that decided a significant matter. It was early in the winter of 1776, and it was George Washington himself who cast the deciding vote.

You see, in 1776 the "Spirit of '76" was beginning to come alive, and the newly appointed Commander-in-Chief of the Continental Army, General George Washington, could see the war looming on the horizon. There were a lot of things that the Army would need, but among the most important was the need for patriotic flags, flags to identify your forces, and flags to salute and sing praises to, and marching songs, and flags marking whom to shoot in battle, or rather, in this case, whom not to shoot. I mean it was that important. Washington would need several hundred flags as soon as possible, and perhaps a thousand or two a little later.

The best known and one of the largest sempstress and upholstering enterprises in Philadelphia, and one that

General Washington had already heard about, was the famous Ross "Sew and Go" Yarn and Darn Shop, in the middle of the old downtown part of Philadelphia, although back then it was still so new that it hadn't gotten historic and famous yet. The proprietor was Mrs. Elizabeth Ross, a devout Quaker whom you could trust with a needle and scissors in her hand. So George hied himself over to the "Sew and Go" Shop on Arch Street to see what kind of a deal he could make with Mrs. Elizabeth.

He explained that he needed a lot of flags. Mrs. Elizabeth, understanding and competent businesswoman that she was, was able to work out an arrangement with George. "May I call you George for short?" she asked the General with aplomb, for at that point he wasn't very famous yet, more like just a person.

"Sure. May I call you Betsy?" Then he paused a moment, thinking ahead. "You may become famous," said George, "and Betsy Ross has a nice ring to it that will sound good in the history books, and easier to remember than Elizabeth Something-or-Other." And, as it turned out, he was quite right.

"All right," said Betsy, "but let's not get carried away prematurely. You'd better tell me what you want your flag to look like -- naughts and crosses, perhaps? -- for the mix of Heathens and Puritans in your little army?" she said with a twinkle in her eye that George did not fail to catch, keen observer that he was.

"I believe that it should consist of stars and stripes," said George, thinking of how euphonious "Stars and Stripes Forever" would sound.

"We can do that. But how many stars? And how many stripes?"

"How about thirteen of each, to represent all the thirteen colonies, if we count Rhode Island and North Carolina as well./1

"Fine. And how about the stars? How many points should they have? Six would be nice don't you think? And they would be easy to make."

"No, I think five points would be better. Six points might make it look a little too Jewish."

"And what's wrong with Jewish already?" contended Betsy, who, with her broad Quaker upbringing, held more liberal views than most Yankees and even Virginians.

"Oh, Jews are all right. Even some of my best friends are Jews," said George, unknowingly coining a phrase that would live for centuries. "But there is a place for everything, you know, and everything has its place." After a pause, he went on: "Now we have to talk about color."

"I have it all thought out," said Betsy. "It should be red, white, and black," she said in her positive tone of voice.

"Why do you say that?" interrupted George, feeling that she was getting ahead of him.

"They represent the three great races constituting this great country," answered Betsy promptly. "Red for the Indians, white for the Whites, and black for the Blacks, who will soon be an increasingly prominent segment of our country's population as time goes on," she added with her perspicacious foresight.

Now George knew about Negroes, as he and most people everywhere called them in those days, and he was very fond of many of them, even loved them -- some of them anyway -- although he could never look upon them as the social equals of the whites, any more than Abraham Lincoln could a couple of generations later./2

No, he thought, it wouldn't be quite fitting to plaster black all over our national flag like that. It would look too gloomy.

So he said, "No, I don't think so."

"Well then, what?"

"I think we should have red, white, and blue. Red to represent the Redskins, in the center of our continent, white for the Whites along the Eastern Seaboard and New England, and blue to represent the great Atlantic Ocean on the other side of us."

So Betsy was overruled. She was out-voted by one vote, the one vote that counted most, the vote of General George Washington. Betsy had no recourse but to go along with it. She needed the contract. The firm needed the work and needed the money.

But in her heart she knew that black was beautiful, and always regretted that, but for one vote, our national flag could have been three cheers for the Red, White, and Black.

THE END

/1 When eleven states seceded in 1788 from the nation as it had been formed under the "Articles of Confederation and Perpetual Union," which was ratified by all in 1781, Rhode Island and North Carolina still faithfully adhered legally to the original terms establishing the United States under the Articles. Thus they were left a de facto nation consisting of two independent states for a year and a half, until they were forced by severely coercive measures of tariffs, and economic and political pressure, to ratify the new Constitution and join the others. Interestingly enough, eleven is also the number of states that seceded seventy years later to form the Confederacy.

/2 In his debates with Steven Douglas in 1858, two years before he was elected president, Lincoln declared: "I am not, nor ever have been, in favor of bringing about in any way the social and political equity of the white and black races."

This is the end of Thirty Stories for All,, to be followed by A Novella: SUMMER FUN

SUMMER FUN

ADVENTURES
OF
JULIE AND DANNY

AND   FRIENDS

IN THE 1930's

Summer Fun
(Sullivans Island and Screven Hills, 1932-1940)

Page

THE END OF "SUMMER FUN"

FINAL END

Summer Fun

(Sullivans Island and Screven Hills, 1932-1940)

Dedication

This piece is dedicated to my cousin Julie, with love and thanks for the companionship and joy she brought into my life over the years, especially childhood summers from the time I was about four years old until I was twelve.

Prologue

The French Philosopher Henri Bergson said, around the turn of the 20th century, that every event in a person's life influences or changes him slightly, and that, at least to some extent, he is the product of all such events. I dare say that, at least to some extent, I am the product of the summers I knew, growing up in the thirties and forties. I guess we all were.

Background

I was born March 5, 1928. I have only the vaguest recollections of my mother, Helen Underwood Hoyt Daniels, who, as I was to learn later, fell ill with pneumonia around Christmas, 1929 and died some weeks later. Shortly thereafter my father, Robert Whiting Daniels, a bright and up-and-coming young Captain in the US Army, had the good fortune to meet and conveniently fall in love with a young widow lady from Savannah, only slightly older than he, whom he promptly married after the elapse of a discreet period of time. Her name was Jule Screven Willcox.

Miss Jule

Jule Screven Willcox (two "l's" please) came from a distinguished family of Savannah Aristocrats sprinkled with notable Mayors and Generals and businessmen of importance in the 18th and 19th century. She had been well brought up, or bien eduquée, as the French say, although without much public schooling or a college education. In those days proper Southern ladies didn't need college; college was for climbers. She didn't need to climb; she was already there. Or had been, until the Great Depression wiped out much of what little was left of the grandeur of the Old South after the War of Northern Aggression. While the devastation of the Depression hit the rest of the country as well, it was particularly upsetting and tragic in the case of the Willcox family, taking Jule's husband, Lyman Willcox, in its wake. So, finding a new husband, so soon after the Crash, even a Yankee, was a pretty good thing for Miss Jule, as well as for Bob Daniels.

She always had people call her "Miss Jule," in the old Southern tradition that recognized and honored the purity and virginity of proper Southern Ladies right through their years of marriage and motherhood. However, she wanted her two newly acquired step-children, me and my older brother Bill, to call her "Mother," which she felt would prove her loving nature and her complete acceptance by the new family. (A few years later I switched to the term "Mom," which she accepted somewhat reluctantly.) I also refer to her here as Miss Jule.

The Extended Family

Miss Jule's family and relatives, at least the ones I knew as a child, comprised her one son, Lyman, (5 1/2 years older than I), her somewhat younger sister May Bond Screven Simpson (later Rhodes) known as "Bonnie," and the three Simpson children, all roughly the same age as the three of us in the Daniels family, namely, Mary Screven Simpson, William Crayton Simpson, and Jule Simpson, in that order. At Miss Jule's idea, some of these names were modified in subsequent years to honor the illustrious old Screven name. Lyman, like his father, had been christened simply Lyman Willcox but Miss Jule later gave him Screven for a middle name. The others took up the suggestion: William, whom we knew as "Bubber," became William Crayton Screven Simpson, and the girls may also have done something similar; I don't know when Mary got Screven into her name. (Incidentally, Screven rhymes with "driven.") Dad was able to spend a week or so with us occasionally; I saw Bonnie only very rarely. I met Daddy-Billy (Simpson) only once I think, probably 1933 or 1934, in Screven Hills. I believe he died shortly thereafter.

Sullivans Island

First Plans

I was two years old and we were living at Aberdeen, Maryland when Mom (I now call Miss Jule "Mom") and Dad were married. They slipped off to a little church in the hills of North Carolina that Mom knew about, to do the deed. I wasn't invited. As soon as she had the chance, Mom wanted to show off to her Southern relatives what she had acquired out North (she always preferred "out north" to "up north.") A couple of years after the wedding, when things had settled down a bit, Mom took us three kids to Sullivan's Island to meet up with the others. This began an annual routine of half the summer at Sullivan's Island and half in the hills of North Carolina. Dad would come for a couple of weeks or so, when he could get leave.

The Cottage: Elmwood

My first memories of South Carolina were the great Cooper River Bridge and a little cottage called "Elmwood" on Sullivan's Island, a couple of blocks back from the beach, plus three more kids that I had never seen before. My memories of the little house are still quite clear, possibly enhanced by one of the b/w snap shots Mom was always taking with her ubiquitous Kodak box camera. (To Mom, every camera in the world was simply a "Kodak," regardless of its manufacturer -- like "Kleenex" in that regard.) I do remember that the little house was painted dark green with black and white trim. Mom's little photo I have in mind had a string of kids sitting on the porch railing, with me included.

251

New Cousins and Names

Julie

The two things I immediately loved about coming to this house were the sand everywhere and all the new cousins, especially Julie. It was said that she was named for her aunt, my new step-mother, Miss Jule. But we called her Julie, a name she didn't seem to mind then, although later in life, when she was probably near menopause and her aunt, Miss Jule, had gone on to Heaven so as to remove any chance of confusion, she decided to revert to "Jule" for herself. Because she thinks I am special, she still lets me call her "Julie" -- even though her husbands have always had to call her "Jule." In turn, I still let her call me "Danny," a privilege I don't give to many. (Mary's joke later on was, "If M-U-L-Y spells 'mule -- ee' what does J-U-L-Y spell?" The little kids were supposed to say, "Julie" and get laughed at with roars of mockery. I wonder whether Julie still remembers that.)

Mary

Most of us had nicknames, as you have already begun to see, but not all. Mary was always just Mary to me, although Julie, perhaps without realizing it, called her "Maire." When she was referring to both of her siblings, she had one name for them, one word, pronounced "Maire-Bubber." When we got together in the summer, Julie had to modify that, because Lyman and Bubber were the new inseparable pair, and their name was now "Lymbubber."

252

Bubber

The name "Bubber" was allegedly the closest that Mary, some fifteen months old when her brother arrived, could come to pronouncing "Brother." (It was years later that I learned, to my dismay, that the ugly word "Bubba" had been adopted by many Southern boys, often wearing backwards baseball caps and driving pickup trucks with a flag, a dog, and a gun in the back.) Bubber was the only Bubber or Bubba in the world to me. He tolerated the name Bubber without complaint until he was a grown-up teen-ager or maybe a West Point Cadet, at which time he decided that "Bub" was a more manly sounding pseudonym. Thereafter he was "Bub" to most of the world, for the rest of his life, to all but Mickey, his wife, and a few Army Generals who called him "Bill." When I first heard Mickey say "Bill," I didn't know who she was talking about. She would politely cringe whenever any of us said "Bubber." But all that was years later.

Lyman

Lyman had the weirdest nickname; he was "Tunk." Don't ask me where it came from -- maybe a story-book that his mother had been reading to him about African animals or little baby native boys. I never called him Tunk very often; I called him Lyman, which sounds more respectful. When he went to New Mexico Military Institute he became "Willie." I still called him Lyman; I idolized him, and would copy things he used to do, both clever and stupid. But more of that later.

Sullivans Island

Bill

Bill had to go through life explaining how he got the nickname "Bill." I may be the only one in the world who ever knew. Bill's father, who had the same first name, "Robert," had already usurped the sobriquet "Bob," removing it from contention as a nickname for his oldest son. My grandmother used to read aloud to us from a little pre-school picture book entitled, "Billy Robin and His Friends." I guess my brother liked it, and the association stuck. My grandmother started calling him Billy Robin instead of Robert. I remember when that evolved into her calling him Bill Robin, and that held for a time. In due course, Bill Robin was shortened to Bill, and stayed that way forever after. (Later. when he was State Senator in Vermont, his name on the posters and newspapers was always ROBERT V. ("BILL") DANIELS). I never heard anybody call him Robert.

Danny

The name "Danny" was all right with me. I never thought of myself as anything but a Danny, certainly not a "Daniel." Still, sometimes strangers, trying to connect, would say to me, "Daniel in the Lion's Den – ha ha ha." But that was all right with me too; I liked lions, and if I had had to be an animal, a lion is what I would have chosen -- the King of Beasts. But I didn't much like the other kids making up rhyming jingles about Danny-Panny, or worse, Danny Panny Wee-wee Wanny. Anything for a rhyme.

By the time I entered high-school (eighth grade to be exact) I decided the time had come to grow up and make a break. As no one knew me there in my new school, it was easy to change my name to Dan, and there it stayed. Miss Jule didn't like that very much, however; she thought Danny was much cuter. It took her many months to catch on, but no one else ever had a problem with Dan.

In later years, especially traveling in Europe, Daniel has been fun. In Spain or France, with accent on the ultimate syllable, it can be variously a Spanish or a French name, while in Italy, with the addition of an e, it becomes a beautiful Italian name, lending itself to a lovely drawn-out pronunciation of the penultimate syllable as though I were born and raised in the heart of Tuscany. The dictionary says that "Daniel" means "May God be my judge." I didn't know that when I was growing up, and maybe that was just as well; it might have been a burden.

Sand

On Sullivans Island there was sand everywhere: the front yard was all sand, with meager grass shoots along the edge, and some Lantana or other flowers struggling up against the porch. Sand, you see, was Heaven to a four- or five-year old. It was as though the whole place were one big sandbox, without even counting the beach. Under the house it was all sand. You could get up at 5:45 if you were quiet and go out to the sand under the house, and start your day. You took a few tootsie toys (tiny cars) out there, and maybe a kitchen spoon that you had snitched, and you could make roads, and tunnels, and bridges with twigs, and winding driveways up to the pile that was the Castle. It was Seventh Heaven. I remember there was a kid in one of the Booth Tarkington books, "Penrod and Sam" I think it

255

was, who liked to get up early, especially on Saturday. Someone told him he had to wait until 9:00 o'clock for something. "Nine o'clock! Why that's almost noon!" Five to seven were good hours in the summer. Then after a couple of days of such fun, someone found out about what you were doing under the house, and Miss Jule wouldn't let you play down there anymore. She claimed it was unsanitary or something, because some dogs might have been under the house, and there could be doggie-doo around there. But it was really because she didn't know about it and hadn't given her permission. Doggie-doo never bothered me, but after that I took a couple of toy cars and a little pail and toy shovel when we went to the beach and had my fun there, but you weren't allowed to go there by yourself. (Down South a little bucket is called a "pail.")

More Julie

Finding yourself in the midst of a family that had suddenly doubled in size was quite an exciting experience. They all seemed decent enough. Now I was the youngest of six, but of course I already knew what it meant to be the youngest, at least the youngest of three. I do remember that I was immediately attracted to Julie, the youngest of the Simpsons. Proximity of age rather than her feminine gender was probably the main reason for my sudden interest in her. At first she was just another kid near my own age; it was only later that I realized, with growing interest, that she was something more. She was female. She was a woman, or on her way to becoming one. She took an interest in me too, again because of our ages no doubt, rather than because of my good looks and budding masculine virility.

256

Now this Julie, you must remember, was the youngest of the three kids in her family. Like me, she had two older siblings telling her what to do and bossing her around for nine months of the year. When she found me there on the beach, offered up to her gratis, as it were, someone younger than herself, but not too much younger, she was delighted. She saw in me her own private toy, a live, talking, walking toy, eager to bow to her every command and fulfill her slightest whim. She had been pushed around and told what to do all winter, and now it was her turn to push someone else around and tell him what to do. Although it may sound as though I resented this horrible situation, constantly being dominated and ordered about by this new person in my life, it wasn't that way at all. In truth, I loved it. I guess I must have loved her attention at any cost, but I honestly think the fact that she was a girl had something to do with it too; she had a terrific advantage over me because of her gender. You see, I have always been putty in a woman's hands, and I was even then. Women do something to me. I want to hug and kiss them, and worship and adore them, although with Julie, at my tender age, I was too ignorant and too shy to reveal such devilish instincts. I don't think I knew I had them, and certainly didn't understand them in any case. Later in my life my weakness for women did not always stand me in good stead, but at the time it brought me closer to another person, this Julie, closer than I had ever been to someone before, and rarely since.

The Others
Bill

Bill, my own brother, was two years older than I but, with his penchant for precision, often gently reminded me and others that the difference was "two years, two months, and one day." Anything to keep me in my place. During the year, I adored and admired both Bill and Lyman, but Lyman was older, and Bill, who was a scholar and an intellectual from the time he was a baby, had interests of his own that didn't always include me or anybody else. Back home he always seemed more interested in drawing diagrams of steam engines and locomotives, or the military tactics that defeated Napoleon at Waterloo, or the river patterns of the upper Mississippi Valley, than in playing with me, so when he condescended to run around outside and play ball with me occasionally it was a special treat. However, I got -- no doubt justly – the reputation for "pestering" him. Here in South Carolina, he felt some pleasant relief to be among the cousins who merely by their presence helped to get me off his back. Now he wasn't the only person I could pester to play with me and my baseball or tootsie-toy cars in the sand.

However, Bill did like playing soldiers. We each had a few little "real" soldiers, store-bought soldiers, made of lead probably, about two or two and a half inches high, in uniforms, with helmets and boots and pistols and rifles, but a small handful of soldiers didn't make an army. Bill needed an army he could command with strategic wisdom, so he collected golf tees. He must have had several hundred, which he could array in battalion strength up the side of the sand pile. Sometimes he would assign some of his

258

troops to me to be his enemies, and we would prepare our arrays for the ensuing battle. We each were allowed one cannon, usually a piece of an old pencil or soda straw no longer in service.

Now Bill was faster than I in setting up his forces, and always won the battle. You see, the rule was that you were not allowed to aim your cannon until all your other forces had been deployed. Just as I had finished my deployment and was getting ready to aim my cannon, BOOM, his cannon, already placed and aimed at my cannon, went off and destroyed my entire artillery battery of one, before I was able to get off a single shot. Thereafter the overwhelming advantage of having a functioning cannon blasting against my exposed foot-soldiers was enough for his army to easily carry the day. I learned a lot from Bill, and although he probably didn't know it, I loved him dearly. Now, as I look back, it reminds me of a recent Dennis the Menace cartoon, in which Dennis is beating his little friend Joey at some game in the backyard. Dennis whispers aside to Margaret, "It's easy to win if you're the only one who knows the rules."

Lyman and Bubber

Lyman and Bubber, or Lymbubr as Julie used to call them, were almost like twins, born only ten weeks apart. Though cousins, they were, in fact, more like each other than their mothers were like each other, even being sisters. Bubber, living through the winter surrounded by two sisters and no brothers, relished the friendship and male companionship of having Lyman with him during the summer. I never thought about it at the time, but among the five of us

259

in the new Daniels family after the marriage of Miss Jule and my father, Lyman, being older, might have taken longer than the others to adapt comfortably to the new arrangement. Perhaps it was memories of his childhood in Savannah that were different from life in a northern city with a new Vermonter for a step-father; perhaps it was lingering memories of his own father and his tragic death that had a traumatic effect upon the boy, who could have been only about seven years old at the time, leaving him rather introspective and taciturn, even somewhat unsure and nervous at first.

I think Lyman and Bubber may have known each other even when they were toddlers, before the Daniels came upon his scene. Now, on the beach they would have little contests between themselves. Both were good swimmers, and it was always a challenge to see who could catch the biggest wave or body surf the farthest up onto the beach. I guess Bubber usually won that. Then fishing. Lyman was an avid fisherman, and I think he taught Bubber how to twirl a line horizontally around his head and heave it with sinker and bait some 30 or 40 yards out beyond the surf. He never caught much, but I do remember they caught a nice striped bass once -- Lyman it was I think who actually caught it -- and got Miss Jule to photograph it hanging halfway between them on the middle of a six-foot pole to make it look even bigger. It seems they both shared the credit. The fish was only about three pounds, just big enough to give everybody a bite. Probably too small to be legal now.

Bubber used to tell fascinating tales of wars with other neighborhood kids when the Simpsons lived in an area called Wales Garden in Columbia. He described vividly how he and other kids would throw clay-clods at each other, eliciting my rapt admiration and envy, although I wasn't sure what a clay-clod was, beyond being something you threw.

Others

There were still others: Aunt Claude, Ruth Steel, May Bond, and Dad, although Dad wasn't there with us very much and I saw May Bond only occasionally.

Aunt Claude

Aunt Claude was Claude Bond; she never married to my knowledge, and never changed her name. She must have been somebody's sister to be an Aunt, and I guess that somebody might have been a Bond lady that married the Screven that was Miss Jule and May Bond's father. The name Thomas Fineas comes to mind, or maybe that was an ancestor further back. I have the idea that the Bond blood came from out north, maybe Philadelphia, but never heard much about it. Maybe Mary or Julie knows, but when I was a kid she was merely Aunt Claude, and that was all. No, not all. There was also Trouvé, her lap dog.

Aunt Claude loved the ocean, although the bathing attire she wore into the water was more like a 17th century ball gown from the court of Louis XIV than a bathing suit. The guys typically wore fitted woolen bathing shorts called "trunks," usually navy blue, heavy wool. Wool is one material that can give warmth when wet. The ladies wore full one -piece suits, with bottoms sufficiently extensive to completely cover the part of their anatomy they sit on. Some had little feminine skirts or other frills, but they certainly looked much more comfortable than the skimpy high-rises or strings and bikinis you see on the beach today. I think the adults had two bathing suits each, and maybe some of the kids too. To Miss Jule a most horrible thought would be putting on a damp bathing suit to go swimming. That sounded silly to me; after all, the suit was going to get all wet soon anyway.

Swimming

I do remember that Aunt Claude swam with a side stroke, as it was called, with her left side up and her right arm reaching out over her head. She also loved to float. She would find a quite spot inside, or outside, the breaking area of the waves, put her head back among the fluttering ribbons and bows of her bathing costume, and float to beat the cars. Then she would try to get us kids to float. She would have us stretch out supine, face up in the water, while gently supporting us at the small of the back. Me, anyway. This is what I remember. So far, so good. Then she would slowly lower her hand, removing the support, and I was supposed to float. But I didn't. I sank. "Put your head back," she would say. I would put my head back and that sank too. "Relax," she would say. "You are not relaxing." Now I knew I was not relaxing, with the water now coming over my head and face as well as the rest of my body. I would stand up in the waist deep water, coughing and sputtering a bit, before trying again. "Now this time start relaxing from the start," she would say. And I would relax as hard as I could. "Relax more," she ordered, as I began to sink again with the removal of her support.

262

What my dear Aunt Claude didn't realize was that I was a skinny kid, mostly bones, with no fat at all, and that the average density of my body was probably about 1.3 (if sea water is 1.2). It was hopeless. I could sit on the bottom, in salt water. But I did learn to swim, but not by relaxing: I first learned to swim underwater. Yes. It seemed my natural element. I soon could hold my breath and swim fifteen or twenty feet underwater. Years later, when I was twelve years old at summer camp on Lake Champlain, I won second place in the underwater swimming event, only losing out to a sixteen-year old. Thank you, dear Aunt Claude, for teaching me to swim, even if you couldn't teach me to relax. In your memory, let me recall that the first surface swimming I ever did was, indeed, the side-stroke, with my right arm over my head.

Getting There

We Daniels were living in Washington, DC during the earliest years of our South Carolina summers. Dad was at the War College there, a feather in his military cap. Miss Jule would sometimes pull us out of school a couple of weeks early, to get a head start on the summer, to the chagrin of the school authorities. But we could always make it up. As I saw it, we were "moving" to South Carolina, as we had moved before, from one of Dad's posts to another in the Army. Although it is only about 600 miles, it took us two or three days to drive to Sullvans Island. No Interstate highways then, and the car was an old Chevvie flivver with a rumble seat. It had running boards, bumpers allowing another car to push it to get it started if necessary, and little triangular windows on the sides in front, for ventilation. I remember Dad telling Mom not to

263

drive over 45 miles per hour (although he allowed himself 50) and to use Kendall 40 motor oil, every 1000 miles. It was hard even to go forty-five on the narrow two-lane roads. (The nation's first four-lane divided highway came in the early thirties, in Delaware, but it was unique.) On two or three occasions we took a Chesapeake Bay steamer overnight to Norfolk to put 200 miles on our way. I loved it, and have loved boats and ships ever since. The line ran three vessels, the "Northland," the "Southland," and the "District of Columbia." Usually we got the "Northland." The car came on board along with us, for an additional fee that I think was twelve dollars. What fun to see Fort Monroe through the mist at dawn the next day and, an hour or two later, watch our car rumble down the gangway on to the dock.

I remember once stopping at New Bern and staying with old Mrs. Smallwood in her lovely place on the water near the Neuse River Bridge. She was some distant relative of Miss Jule's, I think, maybe through the Willcox connection. (The old historic home was later pulled down to make room for a slick new Holiday Inn.) The sleeping quarters of choice for the kids were in the boathouse, hanging out over the water, with a porch whence one could catch all the catfish and eels imaginable. (North Carolina exports quantities of eels, a delicacy, to Denmark and perhaps elsewhere.) An exciting afternoon had the three of us out in the river in the rowboat, with Bill's cat Tuzzy along (she went everywhere with Bill.) The Neuse River is brown with thick runoff of North Carolina clay. The day was calm, and the surface of the water looked as brown and firm as a country road. At least that's what Tuzzy thought. She decided to walk back to the boathouse and jumped overboard. She was as surprised as we were to find herself swimming. She swam like an otter, fifty or sixty yards, to the pilings under the boathouse, and wouldn't come out for the rest of the day. Mrs. Smallwood had a most helpful colored gentleman on the premises who baited our fishhooks for us and built the barbecue fire for our outdoor supper. We loved Mrs. Smallwood. The next year, I think it was, before she died, she gave Lyman a violin (which to my knowledge he never played much, but I did some). It had an unusual double inlay of ebony edging and a deep, gypsy-like tone. I don't know where it is now.

Other times we would stop at a "tourist home," where for a dollar or two we could have a bed, and a bath if lucky. At one of them, Hickory, North Carolina, perhaps, when we were all packed up and ready to leave, the cat went under the house and didn't want to come out. When alternate coercive and endearing words had failed, Lyman got the hose and squirted under there, to Bill's dismay and cries, "Oh, my Tuzzy." Tuzzy came scampering out without a drop of water on her, and we were soon on our way.

Burma Shave

We played games in the car, like "roadside poker," which consisted of counting animals that had various points, cows and chickens one point, sheep and horses two points, dogs five points, cats looking through a window, twenty-five points. But the greatest fun was watching for the Burma Shave shaving cream advertising signs. They are now museum pieces that you can see in the harleston Museum and elsewhere. Two of them went something like this::

Pedro told his girlfriend Molly
   That a beard would be quite jolly.
But what Pedro didn't know
   Was that his beard was hot tamali.
          Burma Shave

Keep to the right
   of the on-coming car.
Get your close shaves
   from the Burma Shave jar.
          Burma Shave

The Cooper River Bridge

The great Cooper River Bridge, with its two arches, one on each end of an island in the middle of the river, was a feature attraction of our summers, although we usually crossed it only twice -- coming and going. The bridge was quite new then, only a few years old, and it was a toll bridge. Unlike many toll bridges, the tolls were levied on a per person basis, not per car. Children under six were free; others were five or ten cents per head. I remember the year I was six and a half, and maybe even seven and a half, when I had to pretend that I was only five. I was told to scrunch down and "make myself small," for it was my duty to save the five cents that my full stature would have cost my family. Oh, I hated it. I was proud of my six or seven years, and I don't think I liked the deception. But there it was -- I was an accomplice to a crime, willy-nilly. Of course, this was during the Depression, and five cents was a lot.

The big bridge also provided great fun and amusement when Ruth was in the car with us. Ruth had, or professed to have, a great fear of water and a great fear of heights. The high bridge touched her on both of these sensitive points. As we crossed she would bend down almost on the floor in back, and cover her head with her jacket. We were supposed to tell her when the danger was over and we all were safely across. Of course the game required us to wait until the car was at the peak of the second arch (said to be the highest of the two), and at that point give the false "all clear." Ruth came slowly out of her shell, looked around briefly, and, playing her half of the game, gave out with the suitable shriek that we had all been anticipating. Dear Ruth -- we loved her and she loved us. More on her later.

The lovely old bridge was demolished around 2005 by spectacular explosions and replaced by an even bigger suspension bridge with modern radiating support cables.

Suntan and Beach

In those days having a nice suntan was a mark of pride. I can remember Bubber frowning at my pale Philadelphia skin as we arrived on Sullivans Island one June, and telling me with a mixture of pride and pity that his "little toe was browner than any place on my body." He showed me his little toe, and alas, it was all too true. I thought you had to lie down in the sun to get a tan; Bubber said that out walking was a good way to get a tan. Of course, all the South Carolina cousins had a great head start in the tanning department. Miss Jule wisely would not let us stay out in the sun long, especially for the first few days. She also kept a quart of Wesson Oil on the cottage steps, and anyone

267

heading for the beach had to get a complete coating of the gooey stuff. I don't know whether it really did any good or not, without any UV blockage component, but the flies loved us and you could always find a kid by looking beneath a swarm of flies and bugs.

And there were other rules. You couldn't just go out onto the beach. You had to go with others if you were a little kid. I don't know how old you had to be, but I wasn't there. And you couldn't go in the water for two hours after eating anything, even a peanut butter sandwich, even in wading. The great fear was stomach cramps, whatever they were. If you went in before your two hours were up, you were expected to get a stomach cramp and die, or drown, or both. It was that simple. If you were in the water with an adult who got cold, you had to come out. They told you your lips were blue, and so you had to come out. They told you your fingers were getting waterlogged and crinkly, and so you had to come out. Somebody was always telling you to come out of the water.

In retrospect I have come to realize I love, more than most people, to be in the ocean. In later years I am amazed at how many people go to the beach in Ocean City or Myrtle Beach and sit on their terraces and swim in their hotel pool. Yuck. As I write this on the shores of Corn Island, Nicaragua, I am staying on the edge of the ocean where often I am the only one on the beach when I take my daily afternoon swim. And I stay in for an hour even if my fingers are getting soggy.

But there were things you could do on the beach besides go swimming. You could build sand castles. I loved the "drip" method, where you could build towers worthy of Antoni Gaudi by letting sand and water drip off your fingertips. Every one a work of art; every one different.

Then if you had an old tennis ball or the like, you could play roly-poly, a game Dad showed us, consisting merely of two tennis-ball-size hollows in the sand that you would try to roll the ball into from ten or fifteen feet away.

And then you could carve your initials or even your name in the sand, or your girl friend's initials if you were a big kid and had a girl friend, neither of which was I. Lyman and Bubber started looking at other girls on the beach, and seemed to waste a good bit of time doing that. I couldn't see the point, but I suppose that in due course that changed.

I also wanted to play fox and geese, a beach version of a game we played out North in the snow, tramping out circular paths and zig-zags that you had to follow while chasing or being chased. I don't think that that one ever caught on very well at the beach. Breeches Inlet

Perhaps a couple of times a week we would go to Breeches Inlet. That is the water passage between Sullivans Island and the Isle of Palms, connecting with the back channel, which is part of the Intra-Coastal Waterway. I didn't know all that at the time; for us it was just "the Inlet" -- it didn't have a name.

But what it had was crabs. Oh my, yes. It had crabs. The sporting technique for crabbing was to toss out a chicken neck or a piece of old meat on a fifteen- or twenty-foot string, wait five or ten minutes (an interminable length of time), pull it in slowly to shallow water, and if a crab was coming along, you would signal for a big kid to come with the crab net to try and scoop up the crab. Scooping success rate was about 75% or 80% on a good day. It wasn't until many years later that I got to be a big kid one summer on Martha's Vineyard and could handle my own crab net; at Sullivans Island there was always a bigger kid handy -- bigger, taller, older, wiser, than I.

Of course, we would NEVER go into the water at the Inlet, with all those crabs in there, waiting to bite your toe off; and who knows what other denizens of the deep were ensconced in that little haven.

One unique plus for the Inlet was that you could play in the sand under the end or the bridge, where it was shady, so you didn't have to worry about an overdose of sun. I remember making a little car in the sand, digging out seats that you could get right into. I also remember the tar smell of the giant creosoted pine pilings holding up the bridge. Lyman went fishing in the inlet. I don't remember whether anyone else did;

Lyman was the fisherman in the family. He loved it. He had what was probably a well-deserved reputation for being the most patient one. I think he caught a few whiting and an occasional flounder. Dogfish, which are a species of miniature shark, were cut up and used for bait; shrimp made better bait, but cost money. Shrimp were sold in a little store on the other end of the bridge -- the Sullivans Island end. For five cents you got one handful of shrimp, and for ten cents you also got one handful of shrimp.

Bait-shrimp and eating-shrimp were all the same Three or four good handfuls of shrimp would be a foundation for supper for all of us. The technique was to send four kids in succession into the store with five cents each, to buy shrimp. Miss Jule needed to stretch her funds to the limit, and she knew how to do it.

The Beach

The beach was of course the focus of summer fun and activities. We didn't require lounge chairs or giant beach umbrellas or even sodapop and hamburger stands. We wouldn't have had money for them anyway. The beach itself was like a great voluptuous woman (in retrospect) lying there waiting to be taken, and to give. She was all anyone needed or could imagine wanting. Warm, inviting. Me, anyway. Pure fun, chasing the edge of the incoming breakers, or the outgoing line of white foam slipping back into the ocean before the nest wave came pouring ashore. Riding in on the curlers when the "surf was up" was superb. Sometimes with a good wave you could plane in for twenty or thirty feet, arms outstretched, holding your breath, until you washed up in six inches of water.

The Rocks

Then there were walks on the beach, especially walks to "the rocks." Down the beach a quarter mile or so was a sort of jetty composed of big boulders covered with seaweed sticking out a couple hundred yards into the ocean. I still do not know its purpose. It looked like a retainer to impede erosion of the beach sand, such as those you see in Ocean City and Rehoboth. But the Sullivans island beach

271

was not eroding; it was actually accreeting, or growing. (Years later I returned to look at the beach-front house we had known, and found that there were two new rows of houses, with parallel frontage roads, between our cottage and the ocean -- houses that of course had not been there before. The beach had grown out that much.) Anyway, the rocks were great fun to climb over and investigate, for in their nooks and crannies was a plethora of marine wildlife -- crabs, minnows, limpets, water-walkers and I don't know what all, surrounded by chattering seagulls, scampering sandpipers, and various other seabirds. The adults, which usually just meant Miss Jule and Aunt Claude, were strongly opposed to our climbing over and amongst the rocks. We were sure to get hurt. The thing with adults is that anything they can't do themselves must be dangerous or immoral, and so they didn't want kids doing it either. They judge everything against themselves as the standard.

Walks on the Beach

On our walks on the beach we would scour the shoreline for treasures washed up from the sea. Beautifully twisted pieces of driftwood in grotesque shapes, boards we surmised had come from a sunken pirate ship. Pieces of bottles and colored glass, tossed by the waves into a translucent smoothness, were definite collectibles. And then the shells, of course. The most common shells looked like miniature clamshells, between a half-inch and an inch in length. About half of them had a tiny pin hole near the hinge that served, as Julie taught me, to carry a thread so you could work it into a bracelet or a necklace. I didn't know that doing things like that was sissy or feminine; if Julie liked to do it, so did I. Prized among the shells was any kind of welk or spiral snail. I didn't know the word "welk" then, but I did know what spirals were. How about "chambered nautilus"?

I later learned that the pinholes came from predator snails who ate the miniature clams (cockles?), opening them by drilling with a sharp prong into the hinge muscle. Nature's way can sometimes sound cruel, how living things can kill each other, but that's life. Usually the beach was pristine and clear with its sparkling white sand, but occasionally a globule of tar would be found sticking to a piece of flotsam or seaweed -- the remnants of a distant oil spill or bilge-cleaning of an ocean-going tanker. The Wesson oil was pretty good for cleaning tar spots on your feet, one nice thing you could say for it.

There were never many people on the beach, so there weren't many restrictive regulations. I don't think there was any prohibition for dogs, and we usually had Tom the hound dog with us. As a puppy, Tom had a twin, Jerry of course, but Jerry died young of distemper while Tom lived on. Hounds may not be water dogs, but Tom loved the ocean, and would swim out and fetch sticks that were kindly thrown for him, as well as for rocks or seashells that were unkindly thrown for him, and of course sank out of sight. Tom once got even though, by picking up a similar shell on the water's edge, bringing it back out, wiggling with pride. Of course he loved chasing the sea gulls too, in vain though it was. I don't remember much about Aunt Claude's dog "Trouvé" at the beach, although he must have been there. Bill usually had a gray cat with him, always called "Tuzzy," known as a "Maltese" because of its gray color. I doubt that the cat's ancestry had anything to do

273

with Malta, but the color gray somehow meant Maltese. I think the cat liked Screven Hills somewhat better than the beach. Tuzzy and Tom always got along fine together, but I don't think either one of them liked Trouvé very much, a testy little fox terrier.

Fort Moultrie

Horses

I didn't know then that Fort Moultrie was famous. It was an active US Army post in the thirties, and they even had horses, a key element in our armed forces in those days. One of our first summers on the island, Dad, who was by then a Major, arranged somehow with the authorities at Fort Moultrie to let the children in his family help out by exercising the horses. Dad was quite a horseman himself, among his many other talents, and sometimes used to speak of the favorite horse he ever owned, "Sis," but that was before I came along and I never saw Sis except in photographs. We dressed up for riding; what I particularly remember was having to wrap our legs from knees to ankles with strips of OD wool cloth like Ace bandages, to prevent chafing of our tender skin. The standard exercise routine meant mostly walking around the ring or paddock. If you trotted around once you had to then walk around three times, and if you cantered around once the formula required you to walk it five times. How frustrating, I thought.

Jumping

They did let us jump a little, though. At first it was just walking over a bar. Then the bar was raised to one foot. When it got to two and a half feet, the horse began to jump a little -- maybe actually got all four feet off the ground. Well, the first time I jumped two and a half feet I took off beautifully balanced, but on landing I was too far forward, and over his head I went, doing a flip I guess, for I remember landing sitting down, perfectly happy with my exploit. The horse kindly avoided stepping on me. Later on, the big kids were allowed limited riding of the horses on the beach itself. That really looked like fun, but alas, was just a little kid. The horses arrangement only lasted one or two years.

Coast Artillery Practice

It was always fun to watch the ships coming in and out of Charleston Harbor. We were around the corner of the island, so could not see the main harbor or Fort Sumter from our beach, but we had a splendid view of the entrance channel. Dad had left us some old field glasses that were idea for boat watching.

Fort Moultrie was active, as I said, and they had guns. Once or twice a summer they would close off the entrance to Charleston Harbor to all shipping traffic and have gunnery practice, shooting their cannons or howitzers out into the ocean to targets several miles distant. Maybe five-inchers or 105 mm. We couldn't see the targets, but from the beach in front we could see the splash, which looked like a great feathery spume of water and foam spouting up out of the horizon like Old Faithful at Yellowstone, shooting up a hundred or two hundred feet. You could hear the sound of the shot and then four or five seconds later see the splash.

In those days there were two branches of Artillery: Field Artillery and Coast Artillery. The Coast Artillery had fixed gun emplacements that were high tech and redoubtable, but in the case ofa real war they would have been sitting ducks. During the War the Germans put their Big Bertha 18-inch coastal cannon on a railroad so the enemy could not zero in on it in a fixed position. But the beautiful, well-oiled gun emplacements around Charleston did give a sense of security and preparedness, in the days before WWII.

The Taylor Cottage

The first two or three summers that I remember at the beach, we stayed at different cottages, gradually getting closer to the ocean itself, much to my delight. Then we found the best house of all, known as the Taylor Cottage, a bit west of where we had been before, nearer the Charleston end of the island. Practically on the beach, a short walk to the ocean itself. It must have been a roomy house; I don't remember ever being crowded. It had running water, and there was a john on the left just as you came in the front door, in case you needed to get there in a hurry.

The Rain

Perhaps it was our second summer in the Taylor Cottage that the rains came. Day and night for forty days it seemed, although maybe only four or five days really. Then it came again the following week. We would go out and jump around in the rain and pretend it was fun, but it wasn't really, and you couldn't go in the ocean even if you wanted to because there might be lightning, and that would be bad (as I personally confirmed many years later). Well, with all that rain the front lawn of the house, the street side, away from the ocean, filled up with water three to six inches deep. The kids didn't mind it much if it was a warm day and you could wear your bathing suit, but of course the adults didn't like it. They had to engage the services of a local carpenter or handyman to build a little bridge or elevated wooden walkway to get out to the street where the car was parked. The water was so bad that the first bridge washed away and a second one had be built to replace it, like the Bridge Over The River Kwai.

The Frogs

By the beginning of the second week, the water had not gone down because the ground was saturated; it was in fact still rising with new rain. That's when the frogs came out. I don't know where the frogs or frog seeds or frog eggs had been up to then, but now they were with us in force. You see, frogs love fresh water. Although their ancestors may have crawled out of the ocean, frogs don't like salt water, but with this new lake in front of our cottage, they had a joyful heyday. They shared their joy with us and the rest of the world by singing most of the day and all night long. I admit that at first it was rather annoying, and some uncaring people, mainly adults, didn't like it at all, but after two or three days their croaking didn't sound so bad. It began to seem natural and a matter of course, and after two and a half weeks of this, when the water finally went down and the frogs disappeared, some of us sort of missed them.

Oh, but we ate. Whether it was raining or not, or whether it was crabs or shrimp or fish or fried chicken, we ate well. Ruth had a unique way of preparing hard-shell crabs. I don't know whether Miss Jule had taught her, or Bonnie had taught her, or her own family, but were they good! No one believes this, but they were fried in a big skillet in deep butter or bacon grease. The spices and flavorings, whatever they were, were of course outside the shell, but you got it on your fingers. You can't eat crabs without your fingers. The only other place I ever ate crabs that way was years later at a roadside restaurant on St. Helena Island, near Beaufort, SC, called "Weezies." Weezie advertised crabs "Maryland style."   I had never heard of Maryland style, and I had never had them that way in Maryland. But they were fried in deep oil, in their shell. Weezie went out of business later because the food inspectors found her kitchen "unsanitary."   I suppose because of all those crab shells piling up. They should be promptly recycled back into the ocean.

Going to Town

Once a week or so we would go to town, which meant driving over the rickety little bridge from Sullivans Island to the mainland, to the store in Mount Pleasant. The big kids, namely Lyman and Bubber, got to ride on the luggage rack over the rear bumper, looking backward, with their feet dangling six or eight inches above the road surface. I never got to ride on the luggage rack -- I was a little kid. We picked up mail that was being held at the post office, always amusing the clerk and ourselves by reciting the list of names of those of us hoping for mail. "Any mail for the Simpson-Daniels-Bond-Willcox-Steel family please?" We

278

all laughed, even those like me who never got any mail. I guess we got most of our groceries at Mt. Pleasant, but what I remember is getting the ice. We got a big, maybe 25 or 50-pound block of ice that rode home on the rear luggage carrier, which meant Lyman and Bubber had to pile in on top of us for the return trip. I was a little kid so I usually got to sit on top of someone. Lucky me!

Oceola's Dungeon

Somewhere nearby, I think also on the island, there was a spooky cavernous underground historic place of some sort, called Oceola's dungeon. It was horrible looking, but we had to look at it because it had a certain local fame. Oceola apparently was an Indian chieftain who had been imprisoned because he was naughty and didn't do what he was told, and of course the big kids had me terrified by saying they would put me in a dungeon like that if I ever misbehaved or didn't do what I was told. It was only much later that I learned we don't put people in dungeons like that anymore, or at least we are not supposed to.

In later years, when we were getting to be teenagers, we went to Pawleys Island once or twice, briefly, during the War. There was talk of House Parties, and Cotillion Dances, and girls and boys, and dates, and things like that. I was still a little kid, therefore much of that passed me by or went over my head. But I do remember Julie inviting her friend Cookie Van Ven Thuysen for the weekend or something. Cookie was very attractive and caught my eye and interest immediately. I have never forgotten her pretty image in her bathing suit there on the beach. I was immediately hoping I might be with her at the dance that evening, but alas, she had a date. With someone else. A big boy, older. She wasn't interested in me. I would dance with Julie. She was my friend. She was the one I really loved in spite of Cookie's radiant charms.

END OF SULLIVANS ISLAND

Screven Hills

SCREVEN HILLS, NORTH CAROLINA

The Place

Screven Hills was fourteen acres of forests and streams with a fairly large, loosely built, two-storey wooden house in a clearing atop one of the two major hills on the property. It was located near the South Carolina State Line, a mile off the Dana Road, at Upwards Crossroads, just east of East Flat Rock, North Carolina, which is 24 miles south of Asheville. The place was purchased in the early nineteen-twenties by the Screven family, which had three children, namely Jule Screven, T. Forman Screven, and May Bond Screven. The house had probably been built around 1900, possibly even earlier. I don't remember ever seeing "Uncle Forman" or his family there. Dad loved the land although he wasn't there much. He bought thirteen adjacent acres on the next hill over to the east.

The People --The Regulars

For most of the six weeks or so we spent there on many successive summers, the regulars were three adults and six children.

The Children

The six children were already mentioned in the Sullivans Island section of this piece, namely: the three Simpsons, -- Mary, Bubber, and Julie, and the Daniels family -- Lyman Willcox, Bill, and Danny.

281

Screven Hills

The Adults

The regular adults there were Miss Jule, Aunt Claude, and Ruth Steel.

Other People

Other people I remember who came to Screven Hills occasionally or lived around there included
(Family): Dad, Bonnie, Daddy Billy.
(Friends): Elizabeth Ravenel, Charlotte Stoney, Donald Black.
(Locals): The Joneses (Miss Lizzy Jones and Mr. Bunion Jones), the Ellick Coxes, The Josh Coxes, Mr. Hoadley, and the Volmers,

Early Memories

I still carry in my mind a clear picture of the layout of the house and the property. You turned off the Dana Road at Upwards Crossroads and went south one mile, then left into the drive for Screven Hills. On the left was a high red clay bank and on the right a tall pine tree. Immediately you crossed a tiny bridge over the little stream, up the hill between double rows of beautiful young long-leaf white pines, bending to the right and another hundred yards up to the house. No garage, of course. Then you came to the house on top, with a commanding view to the south and west, over the valley and the road up the other hills on the far side. A wide porch spread across that side of the house, where you could sit and admire the view, especially if you were a grown-up. Sitting on the porch you could hear a car starting up the drive as it went over the little bridge at the bottom of the hill. The bridge creaked, rattled, and groaned so that you could hear it that far away. But if you were a kid, there were usually too many other things to do instead of sitting on the porch, unless it was raining and you were seeking shelter. The chairs were typical Southern white wicker -- about half of them rocking chairs. At night they were pulled up to lean against the house, to keep from being blown away, I guess.

Getting There

Sometimes we drove up from Sullivans Island; some summers we drove straight to Screven Hills, avoiding Sullivans Island, for fear of the polio in the late 1930's. I remember leaving Philadelphia once, telling my friends we were going to North Carolina. When we got to Hickory NC, I think it was, the nice lady at the tourist home asked me where we were going. I told her North Carolina, much to the amusement of my older brothers. North Carolina to me meant Screven Hills. "We're already in North Carolina, you nincompoop," they jeered at me. But the old lady thought I was cute. We moved to El Paso in 1938 and the next two summers drove a long way to Screven Hills. Bill, the geographer, pointed out with great interest that half of our trip was in Texas (almost 900 miles). That was the first time I saw the Mississippi River. It was Vicksburg. 1940 must have been the last of our regular summers at Screven Hills.

The Woods

The woods in Screven Hills were what the beach was at Sullivans Island. The woods were everything . A most beautiful path through the woods down the northwest side of the hill took you to the Spring where we got our drinking water in little buckets. There was always a dipper there for any passerby who wanted a drink, or you could just bend down and drink like a camel. The spring was well known throughout that part of the county for having delicious water and never going dry. The spring emptied into the stream that, lower down, ran under the little bridge at the driveway entrance. The bridge was just a couple of big pine logs with cross planks on them; it was pretty rickety and had to be repaired or replaced every few years. The pathway to the spring went through an area known as "the grove." I wasn't sure what "grove" meant, but it was a lot of trees with a high canopy -- a mixture of hardwoods and pines. I don't think we had many hemlocks there. Maybe some spruce. There were a lot of different kinds of oaks and various maples. Also gums and beech and willow and maybe some kind of birch, but not the white ones. Sumac and rhododendron and many other shrubs were all around. Also wild vines growing up high that sometimes you could swing on. You could wade in the stream and look for crawfish and salamanders or newts and turtles, and even little minnows. But mainly the stream was good for floating our little boats, made out of shingles with a stick and a leaf for a sail. They always sailed pretty well, downstream especially.

Tom, the Hound

We usually had our hound dog with us, Tom. Another cousin of mine, Jane Hoyt, who never came to Screven Hills, would never let me refer to a hound as a "dog." You see, Jane was a horsewoman. Tom loved the woods

284

probably more than any human being ever could, and when he got out in the morning he spent the day romping over the hills all about, yelping and howling to let the world know when he had picked up the trail of a rabbit or squirrel or something. He would come dragging back in, exhausted, sometimes at five o'clock, and lie down flat out by his water bowl, too tired to pick up his head to drink.

The Tent

One summer when Dad was with us he bought a 10' by 10' tent and built, with some help from the kids, two double bunks out of pine logs and chicken wire. What a treat it was for a kid to sleep out in the woods in a tent! The wonderful sounds of the out-of-doors, the crickets, the whip-poor-wills, owls, frogs, and countless other vibrators adding their own parts to the symphony. It was definitely a guy thing. I don't think the girls ever got to sleep in the tent, and don't know that they ever wanted to. There were some mosquitoes, of course, but I don't remember them. The annoying bugs were always the chiggers. They left a bite that continued to itch for several days. Bubber learned that iodine was the best solution for the itch, and had dots of brown all over him, as indeed most of us did. We must have looked like leopards or Dalmatians sometimes.

The late evening occupation, when we were supposed to be going to sleep in the tent, was to tell ghost stories. This was the opportunity for the big kids to try and scare the little kids with tales of frightening wild creepy things coming out of the woods at night. One of their favorites was the report of the habits of the sylvan vampires that came out at midnight every night, and went ove r the countryside, boring through all obstacles, maintaining a height of exactly three and a half feet above the ground wherever they went. The vampires particularly liked to bore in and suck the blood of small boys in tent bunks made out of pine logs. Bill and I, being the smallest and the lightest, had been assigned the upper bunks that happened to be exactly three and a half feet above ground level. If our fear was real, so much the better. I am glad somebody enjoyed it.

There was one naughty little trick the big kids, who had the lower bunks, would play on the little kids, who had the uppers. When it rained, if you touched the tent roof with your finger and rubbed it a little, it would start a leak, a slow drip where the canvas fibers had been softened. Sometimes there were drips caused by original folds in the canvas; sometimes the drips were caused by pranksters from down below, who of course denied any involvement. You could tell which were which, though, for it was evident that the drip that came in right over your forehead had been carefully calculated by a human mind, or maybe a sub-human mind. Later, Dad got a fly for the tent, which is a second roof above the tent. The fly solved the drips from whatever cause.

Donald

One of Bubber's best friends from Columbia was Donald Black. He is the only friend I remember who ever came to Screven Hills to spend the night or a few days. One time he came when we had been sleeping out in the tent because the weather was so good. Of course Donald had to be given a berth in the tent. Of course I was the youngest and the smallest. Of course I was the one who got kicked out to make room for Donald. Of course I remember hoping that the vampires would get him.

One thing about Donald was his big feet. He had the biggest feet you ever saw. I could wear his shoes right over my shoes, and I walked around the house that way, and he didn't like it at all, said it was breaking down the arches, and made me quit. But it served him right, the bed snatcher.

Flowers

There were rhododendrons in thick profusion around the house, but I never saw them in bloom because we always arrived too late in the summer. I heard tales of how beautiful they were, purple and lavender when in bloom. Miss Jule loved flowers, and planted iris and azaleas as well as annuals like pansies, marigold, and zinnias around the house, hoping to see them prosper in the few weeks we would be there. She did the same in every house we ever lived in, even though they were rental houses where we might live for only a couple of years. That was Miss Jule. She didn't mind sticking her hands in the dirt, although she had the most aristocratic, delicate-looking hands you ever saw. Her bones were small, her fingers slim and pointed. Never would one have suspected they had ever touched soil or been digging in dirt. Mary has hands like that, and Julie too. In spite of her delicate fingers, Miss Jule ruled with an iron hand, ruled the children, only one of which was her own by birth. A mother hen. Ruled the kitchen too. Miss Jule was proud of looking good, and if her children looked good it redounded to her own self-image as well.

287

The most beautiful flora on the place, to me, was the row of five young silver maples across the far edge of the south lawn. They had been planted some twelve or fifteen years before I ever saw them, thoughtfully spaced about ten or twelve feet apart, perfect distance for swinging a hammock, which is exactly what we did. To get into a hammock with a book on a pleasant afternoon was a great treat that all of us often enjoyed.

Bumble Bees

There was also a fine stand of altheas or hollyhocks standing five or six feet tall outside the kitchen window that you saw as you came up the drive. I am not sure which they were; I thought it was two names for the same thing. They had various colored blossoms, similar to an hibiscus flower, trumpet shaped often white with inner red and a yellow pistil at the center. And the bumble bees loved them. One exciting, if rather risky, game was to sneak up to a bee inside the blossom, and with thumb and forefinger starting at the base, smartly gather the blossom over the startled bee, who was then entrapped inside the flower of his own choosing. The bee didn't like this very much, and let you knew it by violent buzzing inside the flower. But besides having a great device to scare the girls with, it was like having a tiger by the tail. When the game was over, it took some care to dispose of the threatened retaliation by flinging the flower and its contents into the bushes and then standing immobile with a "who, me?" expression on your face, while the bee went on off to lick his wounds and nurse his (or her!) wounded pride.

Books

Books

About once a week we went to town -- to Hendersonville. One objective was the county library, but the big grocery market too, no doubt. I think the limit allowed was two books, but one book generally sufficed me for a week. Miss Jule loved Dickens and Sir Walter Scott, and many a rainy evening she gathered the entourage together and read aloud from Ivanhoe or, especially, Pickwick Papers, her favorite. Or maybe The Wind in the Willows. I never cared much for books about talking animals and fairy tales though; I wanted to know what was real. When Peter Pan flew out of the window, I wanted to do it too. It is a wonder I didn't get up there and break my neck, like Icarus the Greek.

My favorite was a big green book called Camping Out and Woodcraft, by Frank Cheley. It was a wonderful book, filled with details about all sorts of plants and animals, and ecological relationships, as well as survival techniques, making shelters, selecting wild plants for food, and much more. I recently looked it up on Amazon to see if it had ever been reprinted. It had not, but used copies were available for prices ranging from $70 to $95 per copy. I enjoyed reading all the Tom Sawyer books, Booth Tarkington's Penrod books, and I even put aside my dislike for fairy tales long enough to read most of the Oz books by L. Frank Baum, with sequels by a relative, maybe his son.

Mary was deep into Blackmore's Lorna Doone. I asked her about it, and her only comment I remember is that it "was rather lengthy." There was a pretty picture of Lorna in the frontispiece, presumably from a painting. It might have been before photographs were common.

289

Lyman and Bubber were into Two Little Savages, a wonderful book by Ernest Thompson Seton, about two white boys who pretended they were Indians. They lived in the Georgia woods, built a teepee, learned to follow animal racks, made fire without matches, and ate wild roots and berries. Later on I read most of it myself; it is rich with wildlife and nature, but surprisingly scholarly and erudite, with many facts and details. I am sure Lyman and Bubber pictured themselves in the rôle.

I remember Julie reading a library book by John Habberton called Helen's Babies. I have to wonder how she got on to it, for the Helen in the book was the mother of two little boys, as was my own mother, Helen Hoyt Daniels. Innocent, crafty, angelic, impish, witching, and repulsive, they were. Julie read a humorous line to me about the older boy correcting the younger boy's speech, but making another error himself in so doing. "'E.G. is a funny little boy,' he said, 'he always says "brep-sup" when he means "brep-bust".'" I guess the moral was that you should be sure of yourself before you correct another person. By the same token, if a person offers to correct you, he is probably right, even if not in the case cited. Philosophy out of children's books: hooray! There was also a copy of "Black Beauty" around the house; maybe Julie read that too; I did not.

Bill was probably reading history books and geography books, and Time Magazine, which he regularly devoured in its entirety at a very early age. (When we were in high school, all the students and the faculty alike were asked to take the annual Time Current Affairs Test. Bill got the second highest grade in the whole school, a 92 I think.

Dad was never there for very long, but one of his ideas of fun was to explain the Binomial Theorem and show us Pascal's Triangle, as well as other little tricks of algebra. I thought it was pretty cute, and even today I can reproduce a Pascal's Triangle in a minute.

Games

There were outdoor games when the weather was good, and indoor games when it was raining or had gotten too dark.

Outdoor Life and Games
The Spears

Romping about the woods was usually enough, but we added to it. There was spear-throwing. We had some big bushes of some kind of saw-grass, that we called broom straw. A shaft could be three or four feet long, with a bushy tail, an ideal spear. Lymbub discovered or invented the game, but we others enjoyed it too. The enemies were "The Box" and "The Bush." One would gallop past an enemy at full speed and heave the spear into the enemy's heart. "The Bush, the Bush," another would cry out, and the new enemy had to be courageously attacked.

Horseshoes

Horseshoes was a favorite game. Once when Dad was with us he stopped the car on the road coming back from East Flat Rock, for he saw a blacksmith's sign. (Dad was fascinated by blacksmithing -- he once made a nice pair of fireplace tongs that he forged himself somewhere, before I was born. We used them for many years.) He took us in to the blacksmith, who showed us his fascinating forge and the red-hot iron rod he was hammering into a horseshoe. For a few cents, Dad bought four little old, worn out, horseshoes from the man, and thus began our game of pitching horseshoes. Dad's instructions were to toss them "high and flat," with a little horizontal twist. This was good advice, for if they landed on edge they could often roll down the hill, and they would go a mile, being practically circular in shape. Real pitching horseshoes you buy in a store have square corners so they don't roll, but you could never get one on a horse. We took turns, alternating, tossing to the stake. You got five points for a ringer, three points for a leaner, and one point for each horseshoe closer than the opponent.

Croquet

Croquet was another. The court was far from regulation, being partly grass and partly the path that went out to the north end by the Delco house. And of course it was on the crown of the hill, which sloped off on both sides where the number 3, 5, 10, and 12 wickets were. If you could hit another's ball, you either got two shots or you could "send" him out of the way by hitting your ball up against his. Of course you tried to send him down the hill. We had to have a ground rule that he could bring his ball back above the crest of the hill where the ball was able to rest without rolling. On starting we each called out the color we wanted. I can remember Lyman, the best player, always saying, "Blacks, last." It was usually an advantage to go last, because then you had more opportunities to pick up two free shots here and there by hitting other balls. We got wise to that, and subsequently agreed to shoot to the stake for the privilege of going last, which went to the man (or woman) with the closest ball.

Badminton

We tried badminton, which was another of Dad's favorite games. He played in sort of a league in the winter and was awfully good. Tennis too. The little kids and maybe the girls were frequently chastised for hitting the shuttlecock on its feathers. They were real feathers then, not plastic ones like they have today. There was also the remains of an old tennis court by the drive coming up to the house. I do not know whether it had ever been in playable condition; I never saw it in use, always full of weeds and ruts from the rain.

Gymnastics

Over by the far corner of the house there was an apple tree, or maybe it was a crab apple tree, that we used to climb, to Aunt Claude's great chagrin, and whose fruit we used to eat in spite of the standard prohibitions. The apples were tiny and worm-eaten, but oh so sweet. Of course the forbidden fruit is the sweetest. That's where the clothes line was where we hung our bathing suits out to dry. Lyman and Bubber had a game where they would wrap themselves in just their towels and perform sort of a fan dance, to the great glee of Mary and Julie, and, perhaps especially, Ruth. Of course Aunt Claude and Miss Jule didn't know anything about such goings on.

There was also a horizontal bar under a sort of porte cochère there, that we used to swing on. You would take turns to hang by your knees and then "skin the cat." In later years I have taught a few kids to skin the cat, surprised that so few have any idea about it. Some of them today would rather watch television. We had no TV of course, but listened to radio serials like Jack Armstrong, The Lone Ranger, The Shadow, and Little Orphan Annie. Like TV parents today, Dad thought we were getting too much radio, and felt we should be limited to 45 minutes a day to avoid getting "radio-itis."

Spud in the Evening

Spud was a game that kids these days never heard of. All you needed was a few kids, a tennis ball, and a little lingering twilight after supper. Each kid would have a number, preferably a number between one and ten, so. "Ninehundredtwentythreethosandfourhundredseven wasn't such allowed. One kid would be "it"; all would gather round as he threw the ball straight up, calling out a number while the ball was still rising. All but one would scamper off as far as they could go while the one with that number ran back and tried to catch the ball, or entrap it as soon as possible, calling out "Spud," whereupon all had to freeze in their tracks. If he had caught the ball he threw it back straight up calling another number. Otherwise he would try to throw the ball to hit someone who would then become "it." If he missed, he had to go on being "it." Playing spud on the hilltop had the disadvantage of frequently having to chase the ball rolling downhill when it missed its target. Sometimes, however, one of the dogs might chase it down the hill for you, but there was always the chance that he wanted it for his own plaything. Man vs Dog, with a ball in the middle, was a constant struggle, the aristocracy against the proletariat, you might say.

Somehow it seemed that Spud was an evening game, after supper, in the back yard. That was the time the bats and swallows came out, and used to dart crisscross back and forth, catching mosquitoes presumably, and maybe other bugs. Bats therefore had to be "good" things. And that's when the owls and Whip-poor-wills started talking to each other. It was a delightful time of day, that Longfellow called "The Children's Hour" in one of his poems.

And fireflies. Later in the evening the hill was sometimes covered with fireflies that we would catch and put in a jar with a suitably ventilated top having holes punched by an icepick. I was always dismayed by the inability of a jar of lightning bugs to give off any real light to replace my bedroom candle. So we let them go. Sometimes we would catch June Bugs, which were like giant Japanese Beetles. You would tie a thread to a hind leg and you had a kite that would fly overhead even when there was no wind at all. I think Lyman developed that technique.

Gliders and Kites

I always loved kites, and planes too. I was born in the month of March, which was supposed to be good for kites, as it was the Windy Month. Kites didn't do too well in Screven Hills though, as there were too many trees around, and not much open space. The tissue paper kites would get torn up when they hit the trees. Dad built us a heavier kite made out of cloth, which could manage the trees all right but couldn't manage to climb up very high, because it was too heavy and there was not enough room for a kid with a string to run and get the kite up. So after that we forgot about kites.

We made paper gliders, but the fun of that wore off soon also, Lyman had a balsa-wood glider that came from the store. If it was a still day he could launch it to his left at a forty-five degree bank angle and it would make a big circle and come back to him, maybe like a boomerang, although it never had to get very high off the ground. Lyman loved planes of all sorts all his life, and of course became an Air Force Pilot after he graduated from West Point. As a kid in the winter he would make flying models of airplanes out of balsa wood, tissue paper, and Duco cement, and got me to do it too. I don't remember whether he ever made airplanes at Screven Hills; maybe not.

The Stars

The stars were often brilliant and clear, for there were no lights in the vicinity. No electricity. The only lights in the house were candles and a few kerosene lamps. Everyone had his own candle to guide his or her way to bed. Dad loved the stars and the constellations, and pointed them out to us: Scorpio and Sagittarius in the south, visible right from the porch, Cassiopeia overhead. Of course there was no horizon, with all the trees around, but what was overhead made up for it. And you could look at the moon as well as Jupiter and Venus with Dad's old WWI field glasses. With the field glasses, the moon almost blinded you.

Boats

Boats were a great plaything, if not exactly a game. I don't think anybody ever had a store-bought boat. The first boats were just sticks or leaves, then shingles, then shingles that we had sharpened to a point, then shingles with a notch on the rear end where you could put in a paddle wheel. A paddle wheel was two flat sticks, notched to fit together in a cross, and strung between the prongs of the rear notch by a rubber band or two. The paddle wheel could be wound up, and then let go in the water, and it made the boat move right along pretty well. Later we learned, or at least I did, to put some center holes in the shingle, with one or two more paddle wheels in tandem to make it really go. Actually, three paddle wheels didn't make it go much faster than one. Maybe we had boat races, I'm not sure, but I think I was the one most interested in boats. I always have been

.The Duck Pond

I think we had a white Muscovy duck for a pet one summer, probably also called Donald. Dad built us a "duck pond" with cement lining, near the southeast corner of the house, a little beyond the end of the row of maple trees. It was a hollow in the dirt, more or less oval in shape, about ten inches deep and ten feet long, with little "harbors" at each end. Then we got better in the boat-making business, and with Dad's help I made a boat with a screw propeller and a rubber-band motor that ran from the prop on the stern to a hook under the prow. It was three times as fast as our old paddle-wheelers. I can see why the real side-wheelers and stern-wheelers plying the lakes and rivers of America

297

in the 19th century were replaced by ships with screw propellers. I think the steamship GREAT EASTERN that laid the Atlantic Cable, around 1870, was one of the last of the side-wheelers. You can look it up.

The idea for the boat propeller came from building model airplanes at home during the winter months. Lyman was the star airplane builder, and I copied him enough to make a couple of flying models too. One was a Taylor Cub, and later a Savoia Marchetti. The propeller mechanism and rubber-band power was what we then used on the boat, with much greater efficiency than the old paddlewheels. I don't know whether Lyman ever made any model airplanes at Screven Hills; maybe he did, but I didn't. Boats were my thing there.

Lake Summit

Occasionally there was another treat for us: Lake Summit. It was a great big lake, although you could see across it. A nice wide white beach, as I remember, and great swimming. It was fed by mountain streams, of course, and was probably pretty cold, but I don't remember that. That is not something a kid would remember. I just remember swimming there, even swimming out over my head, to shrieks of warning and dismay from Aunt Claude or Miss Jule, and even though it was a big lake, really vast, almost like the ocean to me, there were certainly no tides or anything to be afraid of that I could see. There were often a few other people there on the beach and in swimming, although the beach was a lot smaller than the ocean beach was, and had trees coming down to the water at both ends of it. (Years later I drove by Lake Summit and found it enclosed by private housing developments, with no public beach or access. It was hardly one tenth the size that I had remembered, now no bigger that a Texas cow pond.) Of course, as you get older and look back, everything is smaller. The world is getting smaller. People also used to talk about Lake Lure; it was not until many years later that I ever got there. It is indeed a sizeable and beautiful lake, twisting in and out with its many branches and bays among the hills and mountains east of Asheville.

Apple Cider

One time, coming back from Lake Summit, we went by a roadside stand selling apple cider. As Mary later said, "the man there thought his day had come" when he saw this car with eight people pulling up. What he got was fifteen cents for three cups of cider, which six kids had to split, two to a cup. I did manage to get a taste, but the cups were tapered, and I got the small end. In those days a Coca Cola cost five cents, and you could also get a 12-ounce Pepsi Cola or a popsicle for five cents. Popsicles were often separable into two halves, each with its own stick. I guess the makers or the marketers knew that a lot of people during the Depression could not afford five cents per person for popsicles. Most of them were orange, but the best were the banana or vanilla ones, and the drip from them didn't show as much. I can remember being told "You're the smallest," to justify the logic in my having the smallest share. Soon thereafter on another occasion, it would be, "Why don't you grow up and act your age?"

Mary had a sense of humor. On a rare occasion when we had something more than half a cup of cider at a store,

299

maybe hamburgers, she asked the waitress for fou fou sauce on hers. The waitress said nothing, perhaps intending to pass the instructions along to the chef, verbatim. On being served, Mary repeated, "Did you put fou fou sauce on mine?" We all thought she was hilarious, but the poor waitress could only say, "What?"

Claude Pond

Dad was quite an imaginative and inventive person. It may have been on his first trip to Screven Hills that he realized the need for a swimming place -- and the possibilities for such a thing on the premises. With some exploration and consideration, he chose the right place on the easterly stream, designed a dam across the narrows about fifteen feet long, and showed what excavation was needed before he had to go back to work in Washington. The result was Claude Pond, fifteen feet wide, forty or fifty feet long, and eight feet deep in the very center, just deep enough to allow shallow diving. Muddy and cold. Named for Aunt Claude, perhaps to encourage her to dive in or at least be there, as an adult was probably supposed to be there to supervise any activity and report any drownings.

The dam was just dirt, held in place by facing planks, and of course it washed out periodically, even after being reinforced by a six-inch-thick cement core the next year. So what if it had to be rebuilt or repaired every year. We had our own swimming hole -- cold spring-fed water, opaque and muddy from the digging, but a delight.

Bubber brought in or invented the game of Abba-Dabba, which was sort of like a water-borne Spud. One kid would dive in with a tennis ball or a piece of stick, release it under water, and the first one to see it surface would call out "Abba-Dabba." That allowed him (or her) to do something -- I have forgotten exactly what -- maybe to have a head start in diving in to retrieve the ball, if the hound dog didn't dive in and get it first. Tom wasn't supposed to be a water dog like a Spaniel or a Retriever, but he loved the water and children's games. Trouvé spent most of the time in the house on the sofa or in Aunt Claude's lap.

In the pond, I learned from Bubber how to "surface dive." (A few years later, at summer camp on Lake Champlain, I won points by being the best "surface diver" in my group.) A secondary use of the pond was cold storage for the watermelon. Whenever we bought a watermelon it went into the pond to be chilled. That worked pretty well; watermelons float, fortunately. Maybe the water temperature was in the low sixties, about like Casco Bay in Maine. Not ice cold, but it was cold enough. Not too many frogs or snakes in there. Maybe too cold for them. The few snakes you saw were tiny wrigglers, but they could really scoot across the pond just by wriggling. Amazing little things.

In the summer of 1940, which, unbeknownst to us at the time turned out to be the last year of our regular family visits to Screven Hills, I decided to leave my legacy in the form of a row of white pine trees along the path to Claude Pond. I loved the pines on the driveway and my work would imitate them. I found eight or ten seedlings in the woods, dug holes eight feet apart, and planted them carefully. I have always wondered how they prospered, or whether they even lived at all.

301

Screven Hills

One Blue Jay

In the minds of us kids, animals and maybe other things were classified into groups: "good," and "bad." Lizards were good because they ate flies and mosquitoes that were bad. Pine trees and maples were good, because they gave shade and you could climb them; poison ivy and sumac were bad, and even honeysuckle could be "bad," because during the months we were away from Screven Hills it took over the flowerbeds and a lot more, and we had to get Mr. Bunion Jones and his scythe to come and cut it way back. Wrens and mockingbirds were good, because they had nice voices, but blue jays were bad because they had ugly voices and chased other birds away. So that was a come-on for Lyman, who set out to do Justice and have fun in so doing.

Lyman had a .22 rifle, single shot, bolt action, the envy of us all. He didn't really shoot it a lot, maybe because of the cost of ammunition. But he did shoot a bad blue jay, whose wing he saved and, ignoring the smell, he mounted on a suitable little board, painted orange. Using the big reading glass that was simply known as The Magnifying Glass, he took the board out into the sun and burned the following inscription into the wood:

ONE BLUE JAY

-- SHOT BY

LYMAN WILLCOX.

302

That was before Screven was part of his name. The trophy stayed there in the house for many years; I have to wonder what eventually became of it. We also used the magnifying glass to burn ants on the edge of the porch, because ants were "bad," and besides because it was fun and a challenge. Later on, Lyman was on the rifle team at NMMI Military Institute and won some shooting awards before he went to West Point. He was steady and had patience. Besides making model airplanes, he also liked to tinker. One year he got a crystal radio set and spent hours tuning it up, seeking the most favorable spot on the crystal to place the spring needle point. Sometimes you could actually hear faint music or talk beneath the static.

Trees

God did not make trees just for the shade they give, nor for the hammocks you can hang between them, nor for their acorns or chestnuts. Trees were also made for climbing. My favorite was the great black pine tree at the entrance to the drive by the little bridge. It must have been over a hundred feet tall, and you could climb up there and really see a long way, all around. The only problem would be Aunt Claude. If she came looking for you and found that you were up the tree, she would order you to come down immediately before you fell down and broke your neck... I think she would have shaken the tree to expedite your descent if she had been able. Adults don't like kids doing anything they can't do. If an adult can't do it, it's dangerous or immoral, so kids shouldn't do it either. The sticky remnants of pine sap would stick to your hands and maybe your clothes for several days, gradually turning black, with dirt of course, and were a reminder of that adventure.

The Bank

The bank was a steep slope or clay wall on the side of the road, just outside the entrance of the drive. It was a great place to play with tootsie toy cars, for with an old table knife borrowed from Ruth's kitchen you could carve the neatest mountain roads and gas stations right in front of you, chest high. Little trestles and tunnels were possible too, as the road wound its way up to a castle on top. Even Mary participated at least once. Her contribution or invention was her "Kissing Booths" along the highway, where tired motorists could stop for a few minutes respite. Mary must have been a teen-ager by then, to have been so creative. I loved The Bank, although we must have unknowingly contributed greatly to the erosion. It would be a no--no today.

Green River

Green River was a place, a day, a game, an Eden, all in one. A couple of times a summer we would go to Green River. It must have been about a three- or four-mile walk. We would go for the day, maybe taking a picnic. The river was wide and shallow, rocky and sandy, with babbling waters not deep enough to swim in, but great for lying down in and rolling around in and splashing around in and even trying to skip stones in. When it rained, there was an overhanging cliff, almost a cave, where we could huddle up to stay dry. Maybe it was late in the afternoon by then, and getting cooler, otherwise why would you want to stay dry if you were going to back into the river the first chance you got? I always thought it was fun to be in a river or swimming when it was raining. No good, though, if there were threat of a thunderstorm and lightning, as I was to learn many years later.

On the walk along the road there were blackberries to be picked and black-eyed susans and queen anne's lace and shasta daisies to be admired and perhaps picked too. Of course you can't pick roadside flowers with aplomb nowadays, but in those days there were a lot of wildflowers and not many people. The population of the United States is now three times what it was when I was born, and the rest of the world's population has grow even more rapidly.

Berries

Blackberries on the Green River Road were not the only berries around Screven Hills. There were also huckleberries. They are like little blueberries, small but very sweet and tasty. Now, the rule was that kids were not allowed to eat anything that Miss Jule had not given to them or at least specifically approved of. But when one was out playing in the woods, the huckleberries looked very inviting, and it would be inefficient to go all the way back to the house to get permission and then go back to where you had been with the berries. It certainly can't hurt anything to eat a few huckleberries, and maybe because they were forbidden they were a little sweeter than usual. When you got back home with blue berry juice all over your lips and chin, one of the questions you got asked was, "Have you been eating huckleberries?"

Thoughts run through your mind. She is asking you whether you have been eating berries. That must mean she doesn't know. That puts you in a quandary. You know you will get chastised for eating berries if she finds out, and if you admit it she will know, but if you deny it and she finds out, that will be even worse for you. But if she doesn't know, why should I tell her?

"Huckleberries? Me? No way. Why would I eat huckleberries?" So then you are told that you will be sick because you ate huckleberries without permission. So now you have to have a spanking and a big dose of castor oil to keep from being sick. So then you are sick from all that castor oil. Because you ate huckleberries. Miss Jule cannot be crossed. Her power must be absolute. Why can't you learn that? Why can't you learn to behave? And then if you really were sick, you got an enema, the standard treatment. Not just a four-ounce Fleet enema, but a one-quart enema bag filled with Ivory soap suds, ninety-nine and forty-four hundredths percent pure. It could bust a gut, but of course Miss Jule had to do things right -- all the way -- her way, no questions asked. She enjoyed being in control and relished the image and admiration she got from friends and acquaintances for her unstinting devotion to management of a ten-person household with many who were only relatives by marriage.

Miss Jule

Two of Miss Jule's friends that I heard about were Elizabeth Ravenel and Miss Charlotte Stoney. I think Elizabeth Ravenel was a "Miss" too. Miss Jule once went for a drive with her, and described it as hair-raising, as she drove with one hand on the radio and one hand on the cigarette lighter, careening around the turns of the mountain roads at break-neck speeds. Miss Jule could paint a vivid picture. She was not given to understatement.

She referred to these ladies as her "most intimate friends." Miss Jule's friends were either her "intimate friends" or her "most intimate friends." There is only one other person I know who used such terms, and that was Varina Davis, the widow of Jefferson Davis, former Secretary of War under President Franklin Pierce, in the biography of her husband. (A good book, incidentally.) Varina spoke of intimate friends. I guess intimacy means something else nowadays, or else I would have said that Julie and I were intimate friends. Of course, if I said that, I would be misunderstood today

Indoor Life and Games

Monopoly

Monopoly was the dominating indoor game for several summers. At first I think everybody played it, at least most did. Lyman and Bubber perhaps less than the others. Julie and I were always ready to play. If the others got bored with it after a time, we went on, in head to head competition, just the two of us. Julie seemed to like playing Monopoly with me; I don't know whether her liking me made her like Monopoly more, or whether her liking Monopoly made her like me more, because I was always willing to play. I will have to ask Julie that sometime.

Screven Hills

To make the game more exciting, we made extra large bills of money; five-hundred dollar bills were not enough for these materialistic kids. We made thousand-dollar bills, and maybe even more. Perhaps the main reason was that we didn't want the game ever to end, and with enough money you could just play on, MacDuff. Games went on this way for two or three days sometimes. The sociability was the important thing, in spite of a few arguments about how many houses I still had on New York Avenue after I came back from the bathroom. Julie may tell another story -- her way.

Jacks

Julie could boss me around, you know, because she was seven months older than I, and because she was a girl. But that was all right. She was my playmate. I had something there in the summer that I never had in the winter, a real live girl to play with. One of her favorite games was jacks, or jackstones as they were sometimes called. You bounced a little red rubber ball, then adroitly picked up a certain number of tiny six-armed crosses called jacks and then caught the ball in the same hand, if you could. There were many stages of increasing difficulty, some involving catching the stones on the back of your hand, and some involving swinging your left leg under the bouncing ball before it came down. Julie would try new variations until she found those she was best at, where I could not keep up with her. But I was learning -- oh, was I learning. I learned you should always trust a woman, if you know what's good for you. Especially if you want the game to go on, and have her still speak to you. I trusted Julie. Most of the time.

Cards

    We played cards, of course. We even got Aunt Claude in on some of our games; her perennial comment was, "Oh dear, how can you possibly manage to play with these sticky cards?" I fact, I think we liked the sticky, used cards. New ones were always too slippery and hard to hold.

    The first mindless game for little kids was of course War, where the high card won. Maybe it could teach the dummies to count to ten or thirteen, but by the time we were four we were way past that point. The second mindless game, where five or six people could play, was called Michigan, and you merely had to follow suit with the next higher card after the one just played. If by chance you hit a "pay-card" you won some money. Pay-cards were the Jack of clubs, the Queen of diamonds, the King of hearts, and the Ace of spades. But when the chips on the pay-cards built up, it got very exciting. Miss Jule was never really into cards. She didn't play bridge, although Aunt Claude did, at least she talked about having played it with some of her friends. Miss Jule did tolerate Michigan though, and some of the other games. Such games were interesting to us, and briefly quieted us down, and got us off of Miss Jule's back.

    Poker was next on the list. Dad had taught us all the values of the hands, "in case we ever got caught in a game." I thought poker was great fun; I don't know why we didn't play more poker than we did. Of course no money was ever involved, but we did have red, white, and blue chips. The blue ones were the best. We had little concept of winning money from a friend at a card table.

Our table was the big dining table in the great room that served for everything; cards, Monopoly, dining, living, playing, lounging. Petting the dog.

Checkers and Chess

Checkers and chess were less popular, why I don't know. I liked both, especially chess, but it was hard ever to get anybody else to play, except Dad occasionally, the few times he was there. I think Bubber might have been the only one to ever play checkers with me. Maybe Julie once or twice. Later on I played chess with my son Danny, more than with anyone else. In 1956, some sixteen years after our last summer as kids at Screven Hills and Danny was four years old, I took him by to see the place. The old house was gone, but the view and most of the woods were still there.

Duties

Part of the routine dictated by Miss Jule was the assignment of duties. I and maybe Julie had the task of going around the house picking up all the bits of paper or other trash. Bill's job was to take out the garbage or trash from the house. Lyman and Bubber had the best part -- they had to burn the trash in the wire incinerator up the path near the Delco house. That consisted mostly of standing around, admiring the flames. I would go up there too, after my part was done, and watch them watching. I thought then how great it would be when I got to be a big kid too. We all were supposed to make up our own beds. I wasn't very good at that; maybe Julie helped me a little to keep me out of trouble. Julie and Mary's job was to go around outside the house to pick flowers and then help Miss Jule and Aunt Claude arrange them in vases or bowls inside. Also maybe sweep out and tidy up around the house.

And you had to be responsible for your own cup and your own straw hat. The tin cups had names on them, and were hung in a row over the drinking-water bucket in the kitchen. The hats were hung on the other side. Someone mistakenly got Bill's hat once, to his great and vociferous dismay, whereupon Miss Jule took his hat and a can of red paint and, with a good touch of irritation, boldly splashed the letters B-I-L-L across the brim, to Bill's great embarrassment and everybody else's amusement. Miss Jule liked red. Red cheeks and lipstick, red ribbons, red hat, red kitchen chairs and tables. There was usually an open can of red paint around, sometimes with paint still in it.

Snacks

It seemed that there was always a jar of peanut butter in the kitchen, and a box of Saltine crackers that we kids had free access to, without even having to ask specific permission each time -- as long as it wasn't too soon before meals, because we might "spoil our appetites." (What's the difference?" I thought, "between crackers now or potatoes later.") But there it was. Bill, however, preferred plain bread, so much so that Ruth started nicknaming him "Bread." That lasted until the hat episode, after which Ruth changed his sobriquet to "Red." Bill didn't like that very much, and would get mad as a bull, to everybody else's amusement. People can be cruel, even in little ways.

311

Screven Hills

The Plum House

In those days, indoor plumbing was not yet general, and did not exist at Screven Hills. All-purpose water was carried from the spring to the great jug in the kitchen. The streams could be used for washing or bathing. But the real business had to be done in the Plumb House, a euphemistically named two-seater outhouse just off the main pathway below Claude Pond, downstream, of course. Miss Jule's dainty expression for going to the bathroom was "going to pick a plum." That subsequently became the standard term for doing it.

The Plum House door was hung on an angle, and, if not latched or held closed with a brick, it naturally swung halfway open. I was in there one day doing my business and minding my business when Mary started down the path, apparently with some similar business in mind. The upshot was that for the rest of the afternoon and half the next day, Mary announced, and loudly repeated, "I saw Danny sitting on the hole! I saw Danny sitting on the hole!" I don't know why Mary was so excited about it or why I should have been so embarrassed, but I was, much to Mary's amusement, as she had intended. The plum house got its name from the stand of wild plums at the turn of the pathway leading in. Mr. Bunion Jones was hired once a week to come and clean out the pile beneath the Plum House and refill the lime box that served as perfume substitute.

Mr. Bunion and the Yellow Jackets

Mr. Bunion Jones was a local who did odd jobs and came around once or twice a week to do yard work or work on the house. Maybe he was in his forties, but he seemed old as Methuselah and was almost as hard to understand. I dare say he was proud to be considered a hillbilly, although in those days the term definitely had a derogatory connotation, and we would use it only in songs. Other jobs of his I remember were cutting out the overgrown underbrush with a scythe or sickle, and working on the roof of the house, or perhaps doing some heavy digging in a new flower bed. He got ten cents an hour, which was good wages in the Depression years. Mr. Bunion was old and tough, because he spent a lot of time in the sun and only bathed once a week, if that. From the aroma you could always estimate, within two or three days, how long it had been since his last contact with water.

One day Mr. Bunion was clearing out some underbrush by a yellow jackets nest. "Look out, Mr. Bunion, there are yellow jackets in there," we cautioned as they started buzzing around, annoyed at being disturbed.

I was surprised that Mr. Bunion, who had lived his entire life there in the country, was able to respond, "Oh, them things caint hurt me -- my skin's too tough." So he went on about his work. Two minutes later he changed his tune, as he pulled off his shirt and started swatting and waving his arms about madly. Now it was, "Them little things shore cain sting, caint they?"

313

Screven Hills

Well, I guess I know too. A couple of years later I hit a nest of yellow jackets there and was stung eight or ten times. I didn't feel good about that, but had no bad reaction or anything. My reaction came a year later, when a hornet stung me back in Washington, and, having been "sensitized" by the yellow jackets the previous year, I had a violent reaction to the hornet. I broke out in hives, my lips swelled up, and my throat closed down. Fortunately Dad was home and had the presence of mind to call a retired doctor friend from the next block to come quickly. He did come and gave me a shot of adrenaline, which saved my life. Ten more minutes and I would have been gone. Just too hard to breathe. Very simple. So: watch out for yellow jackets. And hornets.

One year in Philadelphia I had my left thumb mashed under a piece of dirty concrete, and had to have anti-tetanus shots as a precaution against lock-jaw, whatever that is. I had a horrible reaction to the shots, which were made from "horse serum." At Screven Hills one time, Bill shrieked that he had stepped on a rusty nail, and images of lock-jaw returned, but he survived with minor medical attention, iodine or mercurochrome. We were lucky those years that there were not more bones broken.

Tincture of iodine was also Bubber's emolument of choice to assuage the nasty itching left in the epidermis by chigger bites. I don't know whether he was more sensitive than most of us to the mites, or whether he spent more time out in the woods exposing himself. After a session with the iodine bottle he would look like some sort of African leopard, with more spots on him that Aunt Claude had on her favorite blue and white polka-dot dress. But I used it

314

sometimes too, and I do admit it eased the itching somewhat, for a time. Maybe it was just the alcohol. Anyway, I don't like chiggers, and don't know what good they are anyway, or why God put them here. There are enough adversities for God-fearing human beings to overcome already, without having chiggers too. Mosquitoes, for instance.

The Roof

As I recall, the roof of the house was a constant problem. Originally it was cheaply made with tarpaper, and it had been cheaply repaired with tar many times over the years. There were always leaks, and when it rained we had to run around the house putting tin cans and dishes under the drips that came down everywhere. Mary used to quip that there was more rain on the inside than on the outside. It didn't bother me, though; I thought it was rather fun, unless it got the monopoly set wet so we would have to pick it up and move it to a drier location, messing up all the houses and giving Julie an opportunity to snitch some of my monopoly money that had slipped off. Or was it the other way around.

Thunderstorms

But those sudden summer thunderstorms were great, I thought. Mary claimed that one time after a lightning flash she saw a ball of fire in the kitchen. I would really have liked to see that, but she said it was frightening. I tried to get her to describe it to me in greater detail, without much success. Balls of fire sounded like fun to me, maybe like Jerry Lee Lewis in years to come.

315

One year we had a goat, Billy. Billy had become a pet. He was tethered out in the back yard when one of the sudden afternoon rainstorms broke with a crash of thunder. He was frightened, broke his tether, and came romping into the house, butting right through the closed screen door, and clomping into the middle of the living room where all his family were gathered with their cans and buckets, ready to give Billy solace and comfort and receive the same in return.

Billy the Goat

It must have been the summer of 1937 or 1938 that we got the goat, a white curly Angora. I had recently been in the hospital with something they called rheumatic fever, although the doctors were never absolutely sure what it was. Anyway, I was supposed to take it easy, and someone in the family got the bright idea that I should have a goat cart. The idea was that if I rode in a goat cart I could accompany the group on its walks to Green River or Upwards Crossroads. It was a great idea but turned out to be a fiasco. The goat would never pull, and wouldn't go anywhere at all unless unhitched and led like a dog on a leash. It was far more work for the driver (me) to try to make the animal pull the cart than it was to get out and walk myself. I guess he became the family's pet, perhaps mostly Bill's, or Julie's, I'm not sure. Not mine. I didn't like the idea or its results, and do not have happy memories of Billy, except for the day he broke in through the screen door during the thunderstorm. Besides, I think he ate someone's straw hat one day, or part of it at least, and perhaps some other things he shouldn't have eaten.

To add to my displeasure and the amusement of others that summer, Mary found out that I had taken a liking to a girl in the same neighborhood that winter named Sally Rice. "He met Sally and got romantic fever," was the taunt, which now sounds laughable but then cut deeply into the heart of a nine-year-old. Sally's tale appears in one of my stories, called, "The Yellow School Bus."

Mr. Hoadley

Anyway, we seemed to have men working on the roof every summer; maybe Mr. Bunion and then Mr. Hoadley and others. After we got to know Mr. Hoadley, we made an arrangement with him: he could live on our property and build a cabin to live in, up the path a couple hundred yards away, in turn for keeping an eye on things during the winter. Even in that remote country, break-ins were, unfortunately, not unknown. That seemed to work out all right, no cash involved. I think Mr. Hoadley may have had a Cherokee Indian wife, but if he did, he kept her hidden, for I don't remember ever seeing her. Mr Hoadley smoked a pipe, like Dad had done. Putting on a nostalgic air, Miss Jule later said it had so reminded her of Dad that she had sometimes followed Mr. Hoadley around the place to enjoy the smoky aroma. I have to wonder about that one though.

Church

Religion did not play a large rôle in our family. Miss Jule was probably the one most religious, and was a good Episcopalian, and I think the Simpsons may have been too. I can't remember any serious discussions about religion. Episcopalians have some rule about the need to attend

317

church at least three times a year in order to maintain your social standing or something. I don't think there was an Episcopal church nearby, so that let us off the hook at Screven Hills. However, there was a cute little fundamentalist church of some sort near the corner by Upwards Crossroads that had evening services we attended occasionally. It was a nice walk after supper, and when the congregation praised the Lord and clapped their hands, you could feel the great uplifting force. And everybody could sing; you didn't have to be a regular member of the church to sing, and I thought that was great fun. They would tell me not to sing so loud, telling me my voice was too loud, which was probably true. It was because around our household I had to talk loud or else no one would pay any attention to me, except Julie maybe, but she was only a little kid too. The preacher would get very excited, and would talk directly to God, and then he would tell us what God had to say. God generally wanted us to love each other and to quit sinning so much. That was all right with me. I think I loved my family, and I didn't think I had been sinning much and felt I could handle that too. I rather liked the church service in the evening; up to then I had only been to church in the morning, when you would rather be doing something else. But in the evening, if you weren't in church, Miss Jule would probably be telling you to go brush your teeth or go to bed. Yes, going to church meant we had the chance to stay up a little longer, and it was dark when we walked back.

The Treasure Drawer

There was a big sideboard, a piece of heavy Victorian furniture in the living room by the door to Aunt Claude's room. It had eight curved drawers, two stacks of four each. Each kid was assigned one drawer to keep things in. One or two of the older kids must have gotten two drawers. I guess it was presumed that, being older, they would have more treasures or bigger treasures than the little kids. Our little drawers held odds and ends, pencils maybe, pocket knife if you were lucky enough to have one, a couple of sea shells that came up from Sullivans Island. You could have kept a naughty book there too, if you had one, or even knew what one was. I had the second drawer on the right. I kept a photograph or two, maybe some extra rubber bands that I could use for boat motors, my sling shot, a rabbit's foot, a few coins and some marbles, maybe an extra deck of cards and a couple of $500 Monopoly bills that I might need in a tight game, and my Little Orphan Annie ring with the secret code -- I didn't wear it all the time but kept it for emergencies, like the Monopoly money.

The Cox's and the Jones's

Local lore had its own Martins and Coys, only this time they were the Coxes and the Joneses. There were two family branches of the Coxes that I had heard about: the Josh Coxes and the Ellick Coxes. I don't know why the distinction was made, or whether the Coxes had an internecine feud of their own, but there it was. The feud with the Joneses had been going on for generations, according to local gossip. At the corner of Upwards Crossroads there were two stores -- general stores with a gas pump out front. One was Amoco and the other was, I am not sure, maybe Pure or Cities Service. Now one store, the Amoco, was owned by the Joneses, and the other belonged to the Coxes. For reasons unknown to me, the store we usually patronized was the Jones's. Maybe it was because we didn't have to cross the Dana highway to get there. Ruth used to walk the mile to buy groceries, often accompanied by some of the kids. A kid could carry one small bag of groceries, but usually it was more fun to carry nothing, but just run along, on the road, or beside it, in and out, throwing stones or looking for arrowheads, and leave the carrying to Ruth. She could tote four big bags of groceries if she could just wrap her arms around them. She was a tough gal. You could buy four big bags of groceries for five dollars.

The Cox's and the Jones's had to maintain their pride and keep the feud going by burning down one of the stores every few years. They pretty much took turns, so it was about even. It was almost a tradition, but it meant that both of the stores were always fairly new, even if built as inexpensively as possible.

There was a giant oak tree in front of the Jones's store. I heard old man Jones once say that he "wouldn't take a hundred dollars for that tree." Saying a hundred dollars was like saying a million; no one had that kind of money in those days. But I had trouble thinking of the value of a tree in monetary terms, and his comment sounded strange to me. I was always inclined to take things literally, and that one didn't make sense. How do you sell a tree and its shade, even for a hundred dollars?

On the adjacent property north of us were a local family, Coxes I believe. It was quite a way through the woods to the decrepit rusty wire fence on the property line, but even from there you couldn't see much. They did have some kids, but we were not allowed to play with them, whether there was fear of our catching diseases or because they were beneath us socially. Miss Jule's laws, of course. She ran things, although I have the idea that Bubber somehow got to know one or two of the Coxes kids, and may have even seen them in later years.

Food

One thing we did well was eat. We kids usually ate in the kitchen. The table was an old door that had been hung horizontally, on the side wall, where it could be swung out for meals. There was a bench long enough for four of us (I got the end on the right) and two kegs, one at each end for Lyman and Bubber to sit on. There was a red checkered table cloth made out of "oil cloth," something that I don't think exists anymore. We ate well. I remember the corn and the chicken, and the corn bread, and the tomatoes and lima beans and grits and greens, collards probably, although I prefer chard by far. The corn was known as silver queen, country gentleman, or golden bantam. It was all delicious, whatever it was, but there was also okra. Miss Jule liked her okra unadulterated, in whole slimy pods, boiled like string beans without even any seasoning. Yuck. I will admit that it was good in the soup though. Miss Jule did make good soup, and got Ruth making it too. I remember Bubber saying he liked a tough piece of corn, so I said I wanted a tough piece too. It was never very tough though. The food was all local produce. Our chicken usually came from a local farm that had chickens running around the yard. The procedure was to pick out the chicken you wanted and then try to catch it, with the help of all the kids, of course. Great fun. Ruth had the task of wringing its neck and picking its feathers, which she did like the trooper that she was.

Screven Hills

Milk

Miss Jule saw milk as the magic elixir of life. If you drank enough milk, nothing bad could happen to you. We each drank about a quart a day, except for Mary. Mary had shot up in her middle teen years, and was very slim. Miss Jule took upon herself the task of fattening Mary up, and made her drink a gallon of milk a day. Maybe that is why Mary was in such a hurry to get to the Plum House that time when I was in there. I never noticed that all Mary's milk ever had the desired effect. Mary was still slim, but had long arms. If you were naughty she could slap your face from across the room, where she was too far away for you to get back at her.

Miss Lizzy Jones

We got milk from Miss Lizzy Jones, an ancient, timeless woman, at least in her late forties but looking ninety, who lived a quarter of a mile up the Howard Gap Road. The kids would take the milk pails to her at milking time, and bring back two or three gallons of milk that was, well, fresh. All foamy on top and still warm when it hit the supper table. When we went back to Philadelphia or somewhere after the summer was over, the milk tasted different, pasteurized as it was, even if it was before the days of homogenization. We once took Miss Lizzy somewhere in the car, I don't remember where. Along the way coming back we stopped for ice cream cones. Miss Lizzy, in her forties or more, had never had an ice cream cone before, and didn't know how she should eat it. We thought that was pretty funny, but nobody laughed.

The Volmers

Later on we also got milk from the Volmers, who lived over the hill to the south, a mile or more away. They had running water in their house, brought in from their creek below by a device called a ram. With no source of power but the water itself, the ram could pump a small steady supply of water up to the house, while it dropped off a larger amount lower downstream. A clever and intriguing device. The Volmers were Seventh Day Adventists; I didn't know what that meant; they looked pretty much like ordinary people as far as I could tell.

Ruth

Besides Miss Jule, the most important and binding force in the household was Ruth Steel. The story I later got was that Bonnie had found Ruth when she was perhaps in her late teens. Ruth was at the railroad station or somewhere, running away from an abusive household, and Bonnie engaged her initially as a baby sitter to watch the children. The arrangement stuck, and Bonnie loaned Ruth to Miss Jule and all of us children for the summer. Bonnie never came very often; after Daddy Billy died she had to work in a dress shop in Columbia.

Ruth had the little room at the end of the hall, across from the kitchen, not much bigger than a closet. Whether or not with Miss Jule's knowledge, we kids loved to visit Ruth in her little room, especially when she was doing her hair. This was a most fascinating process. She had a curved shaped iron rod with teeth like a comb, which she would heat up in a candle and then run through her hair. It was slow going, for she had to reheat the iron frequently, but it made her hair sizzle like frying bacon being overcooked. Steam and fumes would issue forth with fascinating aromas, as she twisted the iron and drew it on through, ostensibly straightening her hair. It looked like great fun, but Ruth took it seriously. She was all business. I have to wonder where she got that straightening iron – I started to say curling-iron. I have never seen another like it. Mary and Julie also spent a lot to time combing their hair, whether we were going anywhere or not, but there was nothing so exciting as watching Ruth comb her hair. Even watching Julie.

Taffy

One of Miss Jule's great rainy-day ideas was to have a "taffy pull." I have to wonder whether it was an old Southern tradition, or a unique abberation. It started with sugar and some butter I guess, that Ruth cooked down slowly until it was all brown and sticky. Then it was stirred and allowed to cool a little, and, when deemed ready, was brought out and kneaded and then passed around in great globs into waiting hands which then kept passing it around, back and forth. Setting up in pairs, the pullers would pull and fold, and double the strings of the taffy, fold it up and pull again. With enough of this, the brown glop eventually turned into a golden cream color. With more pulling, the taffy -- for now it could be called taffy – got stiffer and stiffer. Ultimately the pulling stopped, and the taffy was allowed to cool further. Finally it could be cut or broken into pieces or chunks suitable for licking and sucking and chewing and ultimately swallowing. It was good stuff. I wonder whether anyone ever does that anymore.

Street Dance

On rare occasions, maybe once a summer, we would go to Hendersonville for the evening. On a Saturday night sometimes they had the main street closed off for a country band and a street dance. We had been living in El Paso, Texas, so were familiar with square dances, which of course were very popular out there. At Hendersonville they also had simple square dances, where anybody could join in, kids too. Some of the big country women would almost pick you up and swing you around. Great fun for all. Maybe if Miss Jule was feeling generous we could all split some popsicles before going home.

Ivanhoe

One summer, by letting Mary borrow some of her favorite perfume or something, Miss Jule persuaded Mary to help her with her idea of having us all put on a play. It was to be a scene from Ivanhoe, one of Miss Jule's favorites. (I read in later years that Sir Walter Scott was the most popular writer among the Southern Gentry, Before The War, as his books were laced with nobility and gentry, with lots of class status and stratification.)

The production was never intended to go on the road; it was strictly for internal consumption, and for some photographs that Miss Jule would take with her ubiquitous black box Kodak. Most of the production consisted of finding and assigning pieces of costume and equipment to the various actors. The boys were men and the girls were ladies. Most of them. Mary was to be the Queen of Love and Beauty. Others were knights, pages, grooms. And, of course, ladies in distress, most of whom were named Marion. It took some creativity and imagination. Bill was a knight errant; his steed was Tom the Hound, whom he carefully straddled, but he kept his feet on the ground, to Tom's great pleasure. His shield was the garbage can top, with its handle in the right place. It served as both a defensive weapon and an offensive weapon. Defensive with its strong rim, and offensive with its strong odor. Few dared challenge him. Bubber had to make do with a broom or something for a steed, and might have looked more like a witch than Brian du Bois Gilbert. Lyman was the most elegant of all, and with his long-sleeve jacket, and an inverted traveling bag for a helmet, he was a paragon. All he needed was an appropriate shield. Back into the house he went in his quest for something suitable. He was successful. He came bursting back out to he cheers of all present. He had found the most beautiful shield of all. It was ideal. It was the bedpan. If there was a costume prize, Lyman won it. Miss Jule loved all the proceedings, and laughed heartily with us -- or at us -- I wasn't always sure which.

Music

Singing

Miss Jule liked music and liked getting everybody to sing. We used to sing walking down the road to Green River or the other way to the Joneses' store at Upward Crossroads, things like "Swing Low Sweet Chariot," and "Little David Play on Your Harp," and "I Got Shoes."

Music was a big part of our life, especially among the girls, and especially when it was raining too hard to go outside and play. All the Simpsons were hep to the popular new songs that now, as I write this, are called "oldies." But then we didn't know they were oldies. I remember, later on, my high school English teacher reminding us that "The ancient Greeks didn't know they were ancients." I think of that sometimes and wonder what our generation will look like when viewed two thousand years from now.

The music came from a wooden radio with a round top, but also from a Victrola console 78-rpm with mechanical wind-up crank. No electricity. The vibrating diaphragm was in the playing head, over the needle. Needles had to be changed periodically, for when the tip was worn flat it didn't fit in the groove, and the sound got to be terrible. Records cost 25 cents for a ten-inch, about three minutes playing time, and 35 cents for a twelve-inch. Most were Victor and Decca.

Miss Jule and Aunt Claude detested the crooning of Frank Sinatra and the sliding trombone of Tommy Dorsey about as much as some older people today (including me) dislike hard rock and heavy metal. When Sinatra sang Without a Song, Miss Jule would frown and mock him and say woo woo. She hated Sinatra and didn't like Crosby much better. But we thought they were swell. Here are some of the songs I remember best.

327

Screven Hills

Songs

Without a Song, Dorsey with Sinatra
   -- Bubber's favorite
Frenesi, Artie Shaw
   -- Lyman especially
Copper Colored Gal (Bob Howard)
   -- Mary especially
Stardust
   -- everybody but Miss Jule and Aunt Claude
I'll Never Smile Again, Dorsey, I think
   -- Bubber's favorite
Three Little Fishes
   -- Julie
Flat Foot Floogie (Floozie)
Mairzy Doats
   -- I think Julie liked this.
The Merry-go-Round Broke Down
I'll Be Seeing You
   -- I liked this but Julie didn't.
A Tisket, a Tasket (maybe Ella Fitzgerald)
   -- This might have been Julie's favorite. I liked
     it too. We all sang it ;   I could sing it now,
     if I were urged a little.
Bei Mir Bist du Schoen.
   -- I think a song called "It's Delovely" was on
     the other side.

Miss Jule was able to go along with:

   Shortnin' Bread
   Put Your Little Foot (the Schottische)
   The Lambeth Walk
   Over There
   Schubert Symphony Number 8

Dancing

Mary and Julie loved to dance, and tried to do what they could to get the rest of us into the swing of it. They taught us "The Big Apple," and that was fun. It always made me wonder what the little apple would have been like. I never found out. The beat and rhythm of "The Charleston" was still in the air, and that became the basis of jitterbug and other new steps that were coming along, even the Mambo a few years later. Julie, maybe with a little help from Mary, invented her own little dance, called the "Rocking Step." The rhythm was sort of a slow Charleston. Rock-rock, one-two-three, rock-rock, one-two-three, etc. This was way before rock and roll ever came on to the scene. We were our own inventive bunch, including the girls. I wonder whether Julie even remembers that. If she wanted me to rock-rock, one-two-three, I would rock-rock, one-two-three just as hard as I could, in spite of her admonitions to "relax." Oh my, I was far too excited to relax at a time like that.

Farewell

At the end of the summer, in September, the Daniels family usually left Screven Hills before the Simpsons did. We had a longer drive back home, and maybe our schools started earlier than theirs did. But Miss Jule was a product of her emotions and her feelings, and after we had packed up the car, loaded in all the kids and the dog and cat and had gone back to get the wet bathing suits off the line, and were finally ready to start off down the hill, she started us singing.

329

The song that she always had us sing on leaving went like this:

"I do, I do con friends,
 I do, I do, I do…...
I can no longer stay with you,
 stay with you..."

And then there was another part:

"Feather well, for
 I'm a sleathy,
do not let the
 pardon greethy."

Later I learned it was called The Tavern in the Town. Strange song.

THE END OF "SUMMER FUN"

Addendum

Miss Jule

Miss Jule was always concerned for "her boys," but she was concerned for appearances too. I was twelve years old before I was allowed to wear long pants. In the winter in Philadelphia when it was too cold for shorts, the attire was "knickers" (knickerbockers), over the knee, and long woolen socks. I was not allowed to have a pair of black shoes, even later when I was in high school, because "little boys should wear brown," and that was that. Bill entered Harvard in January, 1943; and that summer we went to

Pawleys Island for a short while. Miss Jule was incensed when Bill arrived wearing a suit -- a suit that he had bought at college. It was "too old for him." Suits were "not proper for boys." And to make it worse, it was a blue suit. It was dark blue, although it was light weight, what we would later call wash-and-wear. Suits, especially blue suits, were "for old men or undertakers."

During the War, a lot of things got hurried up. When Bill was 19, he had already graduated from College, was married, and had a commission in the US Navy Reserve. Miss Jule hated to see her little boy grow up, but was most distressed that he had married "an older woman." (Alice was six months older than he.) It was quite improper, in her view, for an older woman to lead a nice young boy like this astray. (Alice was a Radcliffe graduate and they were married for almost 65 years until Bill died in 2010.) Age and propriety were sensitive matters with Miss Jule. She never let anyone know her own birthday or, God forbid, what year she was born. I don't think Dad ever knew. On her grave marker is inscribed the date of her death in 1959, but no mention of age or date of birth. It was only many years later that I learned she was born in 1892 and hence was almost three years older than Dad, . That explained a lot.

So, Miss Jule had her quirks and ways, but there were a lot of wonderful things about her. I am sure Bill and I were lucky that Dad found her after our real mother, Helen Hoyt, died before I was two years old. It would have been a lot harder growing up from that age without any mother at all.

Addendum

Miss Jule helped arrange for us to get into good schools, that is to say, upper-class schools, and I loved her for that. I am sure she felt it was socially a genteel and proper thing, as much as good education. In the Old South the number of respectable professions was limited. They included the Law, the Military, the Ministry, and perhaps Medicine. Miss Jule hated doctors and anything to do with them; why, I am not sure. She would say that whenever anyone in the family got sick she would "have to fight with the doctors." I was sick on a few occasions, which must have provided several arenas for such fights, I am sorry to say. I naturally got the feeling that doctors were horrible people. When I was in high school and mentioned my possible interest in medicine, it got zero support at home. Miss Jule had no confidence in our ability to make a decision for ourselves. None of the girls that I ever liked in high school was good enough, even if I met them at a socially proper debutante party, like Joan Exnicios (Dad wrinkled up his nose when he heard the name.) I was never encouraged to bring one home to the house, and none was ever invited in for a meal. The only ones Miss Jule ever wanted me to see were the children of her friends or the daughters of other Army officers they knew were "all right," like Ann Clark and Sue Gruver.

The Second World War started when we were in our teens, and the Military looked increasingly likely as a temporary diversion or even as a career. Lyman was in military school 1939-1941 when we lived in El Paso, and entered West Point in the spring of 1942 in time to graduate just as the war was ending in 1945. He was 23 that summer. Bubber graduated from West Point the next year. I finished high school the summer of 1944 when I was 16 and wanted to join up and drive an ambulance, but Miss Jule would hear none of it. When Bill and I broached the possibility of enlisting to do a hitch, her response, in no uncertain terms, was, "It's all right for my boys to go into the military, but if they do they are going in as officers." Those were her words. I had visited Lyman when he was a Cadet at West Point and knew I didn't want to go there, so I opted for the Naval Academy instead, which turned out to be but little different. I went in as a Plebe in the spring of 1945, only a few months before the war ended, but it officially made me a World War II Veteran, being in uniform before the end.

Miss Jule made clear social distinctions between officers and non-coms, even to the point of commenting on the type of undershirt they wore. Non-coms wore singlets, with thin shoulder straps. Officers wore full undershirts, like T-shirts with shoulders, or none at all. It was with some pride that she accomplished her two goals of keeping her boys out of the enlisted ranks, and also of keeping them safely out of any fighting. Most of her family, I mean her ancestors, who went off to war were killed, although she wasn't there. That was the Civil War, and the institutional memory lived on vividly in her mind. She was born only 27 years after the end of that war, and its violent picture of death and devastation stayed etched in her mind throughout her lifetime. You can imagine what deep inner emotional conflicts she must have had when she married a Yankee, even as fine a man as my father was, not that he didn't have a few prejudices himself.

END OF ADDENDUM TO SUMMER FUN

THE FINAL END